LOST GIRLS

A NOVEL

J. Michael Stewart

For my grandmothers,
Faye and Nina

LOST
GIRLS

1

All eyes are on me.

They always are.

It's become as much a part of my life as breathing. It's what I've become. What I've always wanted. What I'm *meant* to be.

A celebrity.

Usually, I'm performing in front of a throng of screaming teenagers and young adults. People who are still living a carefree existence, whose daily schedules haven't yet been contorted into the predictable, miserable routine that comes along with the responsibilities of a mortgage payment, kids, and a boring job.

But tonight's crowd is small and exclusive, their reactions to my performance muted by expensive champagne and stiff personalities. And no one is screaming uncontrollably for me, because I'm not the center of this celebration.

I don't like that.

But doing occasional favors like this for influential people within the industry comes with the territory. I loathe the whole idea of such a thing, of course, but it's expected of me, no matter how fervently I protest.

I'm Lauren Miller—why should I have to do a favor for anyone?

From my elevated position onstage, I scan the large grassy area that stretches out in front of me. It's a sea of white tablecloths and expensive floral centerpieces. A waiter, dressed in a crisp tuxedo, is moving among the multitude of affluent guests, offering them glasses of champagne from atop an ornate silver tray. Flickering candlelight emanates from the paper luminaries that have been scattered throughout the backyard.

The mid-June air is still warm and humid, though the sun set an hour ago. To my left, a large tent has been erected to provide shelter for the food and catering staff. The scent of braised beef and garlic mix with that of the freshly cut lawn, creating a sickly sweet aroma that wafts across my face.

The truth is, I don't want to be in front of this stuffy horde of gawkers at all. And that's how I view them—stuffy. They're dull and boring. I don't relate to these people. I'm young and vibrant, just like my fans. I don't worry about mundane things like starting a family or paying bills. Why should I? One, I have no desire to shackle myself to the responsibilities of being a wife and mother. And two, I have people who pay my bills.

Across the yard, the bride and groom, both looking like they just stepped out of the pages of *Modern Bride* magazine, sit at the center of a long table with their family members flanking them on either side. I try to read their expressions. They seem happy, smiling at me and sharing laughs between themselves. The bride moves her shoulders back and forth in rhythm with the music and mouths the lyrics as she turns her head and smiles at her new husband.

Ugh.

It's sickening. No one is truly that happy. I know better. It's impossible. One of them is hiding something. I'm sure of it.

Several possibilities run through my mind before I settle on one.

I imagine the groom is having an affair with one of the bridesmaids, and his new wife will only learn the truth after they return from the honeymoon. Okay, maybe it's not the most likely scenario, but it is the most entertaining, and I have to do something to amuse myself while I get through this last set.

Though I know it's wrong of me, I giggle to myself at the thought of such a thing happening.

This whole production, with its fancy dresses and sharp tuxedos, its expensive champagne and handsome waiters, seems so fake to me. As if the bride and groom are perpetrating one big fraud on all of us.

The perfect family, the perfect life—it doesn't exist. Maybe it does in books and movies, but certainly not in the real world. At least, not that I've ever seen.

This is just a giant smoke screen. Yes, that's it. A smoke screen. Their giddy faces and exaggerated smiles are simply a façade to convince all of us of their true happiness.

I'm not buying it.

Because they're doing the same thing I am—just putting on a show.

I'm pretending I'm excited to be singing at their stupid wedding, but do they really think I want to be here? That I enjoy being forced to do yet another favor when I could be at home, alone, with a glass of wine and no one to bother me? They're probably so naïve that they do actually believe that.

The real world is going to eat these two alive.

Perhaps I shouldn't judge them so harshly, though. I suppose my cynical attitude has a lot to do with the bitterness I feel about being here in the first place. My free time is precious, and it infuriates me that I've been forced to give it up in order to sing for a couple of hundred people in the backyard of this summer home in the North Georgia mountains. The worst part is, I'm doing this for practically free.

That bugs me.

Not that I need the cash, because I don't. But if I'm going to relinquish my free time, I'd prefer to be playing a sold-out arena, where I'd at least be making real money.

Throwing my head back, I raise the microphone to my mouth and belt out the last note of the song. In just a few hours I'll be back home, drinking that glass of wine and sleeping in my own bed.

Alone and away from all these ridiculously happy, counterfeit faces that are staring at me now.

I finish the song with an overly dramatic flair of my head and arms, a stage move I've perfected during the last few years. I open my eyes and take a few seconds to catch my breath as the applause rains. I take a small bow and wave at the audience. "Thank you. Thank you," I say, pretending to be embarrassed by all the clapping.

But I'm not embarrassed—not even a little bit.

I smile widely and wave at the bride and groom. Then I manufacture a humble and grateful tilt of my lips and widening of my eyes. I've perfected this move too. "It's been an honor to be here on your special day, Doug and Charlotte, and I hope you have a wonderful life together."

The two of them smile and wave back at me. The bride even blows me a kiss.

I want to gag.

But I keep smiling, just as I always do in public. I have to—it's my job.

"I'm going to do one more song for you," I say, speaking directly to the newly wedded couple. "It's one of my favorites." It's really not. "So I want everyone to get up, grab your special someone, and have a dance on me." I turn and, with a nod of my head, cue the band. As the music starts, I begin to sing softly.

Doug and Charlotte are the first to rise from their seats and make their way to the center of the yard, where a parquet hardwood floor has been installed over the grass. Charlotte wraps her arms around Doug's neck, her white wedding gown elegantly flowing behind her. They start to dance, and I watch as she whispers something into his ear.

My guess is that they are as anxious to leave this party as I am. I laugh to myself again.

Just wait until you find out about Doug's affair after the honeymoon, Charlotte. You won't be whispering into his ear then.

Closing my eyes for dramatic effect, I continue to sing the love song. I've performed this particular song so many times that the words spring from my mouth automatically, which is a good thing, because my mind is already elsewhere.

Maybe I'll be able to catch a quick nap on the flight back to Nashville. Once I get home, I'll take a hot shower, then find a movie on Netflix and watch it until I drift off in my warm bed. I have an early day tomorrow, and the longer I stay at this wedding, the less sleep I'll get.

Why did I even agree to do this asinine event in the first place?

But all I have to do is finish this last song, shake a few hands, sign some autographs, maybe pose for a few quick pictures as I leave, and then I'll be on my way.

It seems to take an eternity to reach the end of the song. I sing the final words in my silky smooth voice, smile another fake smile, and wave wildly at the crowd. "Thank you again! It's been a pleasure to be with you tonight! Let's give Doug and Charlotte another hand." The crowd joins me in applauding the couple. "I wish you two the best life has to offer and a long and happy marriage." I wave to the crowd one last time as I quickly exit the stage.

A small flight of metal stairs leads from the stage, and Kelsey, my personal assistant, is waiting for me at the bottom of them. I quickly take three large gulps of cold water from the open bottle she hands me and then give it back to her.

My heels sink into the soft earth of the backyard and I'm about to curse, but I spot a young girl approaching me for an autograph and manage to hold my tongue.

I'm being filmed every minute I'm out in public, or at least, I have to assume that's the case. Everyone has a video recorder in the palm of their hand nowadays.

Turning to Kelsey, I roll my eyes and take the Sharpie from her hand that she always has at the ready. I snatch the photograph from the girl's hand, sign it, and give it back to her.

"Can I get a quick picture of you two together?" a woman asks, holding a cellphone in her hand. I assume she is the girl's mother.

An autograph isn't enough . . . her daughter wants a picture too. Of *course* she does.

Some days, I hate my job.

"Sure," I reply and pat the girl on the shoulder. What else can I say, really? It's not as though I can turn the little girl away, unless I want my actions splashed across a multitude of social media platforms before I even get back home. I really have no choice in the matter.

I quickly lean over and place my smiling face right next to hers while the girl's mother snaps a photo on her cellphone. As I stand up, the girl starts to say something to me, but the glazed-over look in her eyes tells me she's so starstruck that she's lost her train of thought. I'm not in the mood for a long conversation, so I don't wait for her to gather herself. "It was nice meeting you, sweetie," I say and nudge her gently back toward her mother.

As the mother leads the little girl away, I turn and begin to follow Kelsey down the driveway, toward the van that is waiting to take us back to the airport. But before I can make my escape, the bride and groom rush toward me, forcing me to stop a second time.

"Thank you so much for coming, Lauren. It means so much to both of us," Charlotte says, her face beaming. She looks at her new husband, who quickly nods in agreement. Doug doesn't seem the typical country music fan to me. He seems more the clean-cut, Wall Street type, and I doubt that, before tonight, he's even listened to one of my songs.

He hasn't even been married twenty-four hours yet and he's already agreeing to whatever his wife says, regardless of what he really thinks.

It's pathetic.

"You're more than welcome." I flash a smile and start to walk away.

"We couldn't believe it when Daddy told us you were coming to the wedding," Charlotte adds, interrupting my exit.

I turn back to face them. "Well, your father has done so much for me, it was the least I could do." The statement is true. Larry has done a lot for my career, but I've done a lot for his too. Without me, he would still be working with musicians whose only gigs were dive bars and dilapidated honky-tonks. He certainly wouldn't be able to afford this palatial mountain home he uses whenever he wants to escape Nashville. I made him who he is, not the other way around.

"Oh, that's so sweet of you to say." Charlotte's pouting face looks like she is encouraging a toddler to eat her vegetables.

I'm still smiling on the outside, but inside I want to scream.

"Do you mind if we get a picture?" she asks.

"Oh, of course not," I say through gritted teeth. A nod of my head signals Kelsey, who steps forward and takes the cellphone from Charlotte's outstretched hand. I position myself between the bride and groom and smile for the camera as Kelsey snaps the picture.

I remember the first time someone asked me for a photograph. It was inside a run-down bar outside of Knoxville. The request was so unexpected I stammered out a weak, "Yes . . . yes, of course." Back then, I had no assistant, so the bartender took the woman's phone and snapped the picture. I think I was more excited than she was, ecstatic that someone actually wanted a picture with me.

But now, I've done the same routine—place arm around fan's shoulders, slight tilt of my head, and smile—so many times that I find it boring and, more important, a complete waste of my time.

But I still have to do it because, like so many other things, it's expected of me.

"Okay, well, I have to get going," I say in an attempt to extricate myself from the couple. "Congratulations again."

Charlotte looks shocked that I want to leave her reception so soon. "Oh . . . of course. Have a safe trip back to Nashville, Lauren."

I don't care if she expects me to mingle with her friends and family after the concert. I've met my obligation by showing up and performing. I don't plan on doing any more than that.

The pampered bride will just have to get over it.

I start walking toward the van again. As I pick up my pace, desperate to get away, another fan rushes up to me and shoves a CD case in my face. I quickly scribble my signature across the plastic with the Sharpie that's still in my hand. I don't slow down or even acknowledge her. "Th-thanks," the girl says softly. I keep walking.

The driver is waiting for us as Kelsey and I approach the black van. He looks the part of a professional bodyguard: big, burly, and dressed in a black suit and tie. But he doesn't work for me. He's just an employee from a local transportation company, hired to ferry me to and from the wedding.

He slides open the side door and I hop inside. I scoot to the far side of the bench seat, as Kelsey climbs aboard and settles beside me. The door slams shut, and I wait impatiently as the driver walks around the vehicle and climbs inside. He puts the van in gear.

I want to get out of here as soon as possible.

If I were attending an awards show or similar high-profile event, I would be riding in a limousine with all the bells and whistles. But I've discovered through experience that whenever my picture isn't going to end up on the cover of a magazine, it's better to travel in a nondescript van. They still provide the room I need, but draw less attention at airports and other locations than a limo would, which means I'm subjected to fewer interactions with fans.

And that's a good thing.

I glance over my shoulder and out the window as the van pulls away from the wedding party. The glass is deeply tinted, another must-have of any vehicle I use. It keeps the gawkers at bay. But even through the dark glass, I can see that some of the other guests are following my lead and beginning to disperse, ready to call it a night.

Charlotte can't be happy that her time in the spotlight is almost over. Or maybe she is. I don't know and don't really care.

"You know, you could've stayed a little longer," Kelsey says. "And you should've spoken to Larry again before we left."

I growl under my breath.

Kelsey has worked for me for almost three years now. We both speak our minds to one another, unfiltered. I view everyone else around me with deep suspicion. Most of them just want to be close to me so they can advance their own careers or motives, but I know Kelsey is different, though I sometimes ignore this fact when I'm angry.

"I'm just saying, it would've been a kind gesture. He *is* your record producer and the bride's father," she adds.

"He'll get over it. I showed up to his daughter's wedding. That's more than enough in my book."

She sighs. "Whatever."

"What does it matter to you anyway?" I snap.

She turns her head from me. "I guess it doesn't."

My skin is wet from the heat of the stage lights and the Georgia humidity. I wipe my forehead with the back of my hand, smearing my makeup. "I'm going to get cleaned up before we get to the airport."

I hop over the seat and into the rear storage compartment, where my suitcase is. I unzip the carry-on bag I packed for this quick trip and begin to clean my face with a makeup remover cloth. There will be no fans or paparazzi to photograph me on the plane, so I'd rather be as comfortable as possible during the flight.

My private jet and my home are the only places I find any semblance of solitude anymore.

"I shouldn't have been forced to do this in the first place," I say angrily. "You're supposed to run interference for me, Kelsey. That's *your* job. You know I hate doing this type of thing." I kick off my heels.

"But you *did* agree to do it," Kelsey replies matter-of-factly, without turning around to face me.

"Only after *you* told Larry you thought I'd be happy to do it for him. *You* put *me* in an impossible situation . . . and it wasn't your decision to make."

"You'll survive."

I want to scream at her, but let out another low growl instead, just so she understands how frustrated I am. I shimmy out of the sequin dress I'm wearing, wad it up, and toss it into the suitcase. "How much did I make for flying down here to the middle of nowhere and wasting one of my few days off? A couple of grand? I could've made that at a hole-in-the-wall club back in Nashville."

Kelsey keeps staring out the side window of the van, refusing to look at me or answer my question.

"Well?" I persist, determined to make her tell me.

"He paid your travel expenses. That's it."

"You've *got* to be kidding me."

"No, I'm not kidding." She pauses, and I can tell by the tone of her voice that she's angry now too. "Why do you even care? It's not as though you need the money," she adds.

"That's not the point."

"Well, if it's not about the money, then why are you so upset?"

I huff. "I *hate* doing these things. That's all. I don't get much downtime." I pause and grab a pair of jeans from the suitcase. "I'm busy all the time, either in the studio or touring, so when I do get a rare day off, I sure don't want to be gallivanting across the country to perform at some rich girl's wedding, even if her father is my record producer. You should know that by now." I lie down and wiggle on the floor as I struggle to get the jeans over my hips inside the confined space of the van.

"You're impossible. You know that, Lauren? No wonder—" She stops midsentence.

I know what she was about to say. "No wonder, what, Kelsey? Go ahead . . . finish what you were going to say."

She doesn't respond.

I button the jeans and sit back up. "Go ahead," I prod her. "Tell me."

She huffs, but still doesn't look at me. "I was going to say, 'No wonder no one in Nashville wants to work with you anymore.' "

That's exactly what I thought she was going to say to me. "Yeah, well, they sure aren't complaining when they cash their paychecks, are they?" I snap.

She sighs. "Like I said . . . you're impossible."

I scoff. "Oh, really?"

"Yes, you are. Take tonight for instance. You had an opportunity to do something nice for someone, but all you've done since we left Nashville is complain about it. You should've been happy to do this for Larry . . . and to do it for free. He's been a big part of your success. The least you could do is show him a little appreciation."

Her comment enrages me, and I feel the heat rise in my chest. "Please! He owes me more than I'll ever owe him. He was a nobody in the music industry before he signed me."

I rummage through the contents of the carry-on, tossing items back and forth as I search for a top. Even though it's still warm outside, the air-conditioned cabin of the airplane will be downright nippy, so I pull out a gray cotton sweatshirt that has *Nashville* emblazoned across the chest in bright pink lettering.

"*I* made Larry what he is today," I say as I slip the sweatshirt over my head. "Do you really think he could afford that mountain mansion if it weren't for me?" I grab an elastic band and pull my blonde hair into a ponytail. "I don't think so," I add forcefully when Kelsey doesn't respond. I gather my heels from the floor of the van, exchange them for a pair of tennis shoes, and close the carry-on with a violent zip.

Confident that I've won the argument, I climb back over the seat, tennis shoes in hand, and plant myself next to Kelsey. I slip the shoes onto my feet. They'll be much more comfortable during the ride home than the heels I wore onstage.

"What happened to you?" she asks. "You weren't like this when I first met you."

I can feel her glaring at me as I tie my shoelaces, waiting for a response, but I don't give her one. Instead, I ignore her and gaze out the window. The van is passing through a section of forest, and even though it's dark outside, I can see the trees whizzing by in the periphery of the van's headlights.

Kelsey's question is offensive. It insinuates there's something wrong with me, that I'm just some ill-tempered narcissist who cares only for herself. I don't see myself that way at all.

I'm just a realist.

She knows very well how many people earn a living from my success. *How dare she?* The more I think about it, the angrier I become, until, finally, I can't hold it in any longer. "I became famous . . . *that's* what happened to me," I say.

"What?" she asks.

She's apparently been taken aback by my response, but she shouldn't have been. She, of all people, should know what I'm talking about. But if I must, I'll spell it out for her plainly. I turn my head and face her. "You have to understand something, Kelsey. People will take advantage of someone like me. That's just a fact, and it's something I've been trying to get you to see, but you obviously still don't get it." I punctuate my speech with firm hand gestures to drive home my point. "That's why I don't like doing these *favors*, why I don't let people get close to me. You do the simplest thing for someone, and before you know it, others are coming out of the woodwork wanting you to do the same for them."

She mumbles something under her breath that I don't comprehend.

"What?" I ask.

She clears her throat. "Is that what you think of me too? That I'm just here to take advantage of you?"

I return to staring out the window, watching the tree trunks and asphalt rush by, not wanting to respond to her question. Even though she infuriates me at times and we often fight, I trust her. Unlike most everyone else, she isn't in this to get something from me. I know that. I sigh heavily. "No, of course not."

"Good. I sure hope that's not how you feel about me because I would *never* do anything to intentionally damage you or your career." She pauses and lets out an exasperated sigh of her own. "But you need to know something else. Everyone you meet isn't out to just use you, Lauren. I'm sure that some are, but not everyone. And I don't think Larry is like that at all." She reaches across the bench seat and places her hand on my forearm. "It was one night. You did something nice for him . . . and it didn't kill you. Stop being such a diva."

A diva? Really?

I let the snide comment slide and don't respond. Instead, I hold my fire and continue to look out the window, my head pinned against the cool glass. I'm exhausted from a long day, and I'm through talking about the subject. She doesn't say anything else either, which I'm thankful for.

We ride on in silence.

Several minutes pass, and I'm anxious to get aboard my plane, where I can rest. "How much longer until we reach the airport?" I ask.

"About five more minutes, I believe."

"And what time do I have to be at the studio in the morning?"

Kelsey scrolls through her smartphone. "Nine o'clock."

"And what time is it now?"

"It's ten fifteen."

"Great . . . just *great*." A frustrated moan emanates from my throat as I slump in my seat.

"It'll be fine," Kelsey says. "Don't be so dramatic."

"Easy for you to say. By the time our plane lands in Nashville and I make it back home, I'll be lucky to get three hours of sleep."

"I have to be there in the morning too."

That comment gets my juices flowing again. I fire another shot across Kelsey's bow. "Yes, but only *I* have to perform." I shake my head in disgust. "This is all *your* fault."

She grumbles. "Fine, it's my fault. It's *all* my fault, Lauren! Is that what you want to hear? How dare I think you might actually be willing to do something nice for someone? I'm sorry, okay? Can we just drop it?"

"Fine." Normally, I wouldn't cede the argument so easily, but right now, all I want to do is get on my jet and go to sleep.

The sound of Kelsey's cellphone ringing breaks the tense silence in the van. I listen as she answers, and it's quickly apparent by the tone of the conversation that something is wrong. She ends the call, and I lift my head from the side window. "Who was that?"

She sighs, obviously not wanting to reveal the bad news.

"Who was that, Kelsey?" I ask again, this time in a firm, demanding tone that reinforces the employer-employee hierarchical relationship. It doesn't hurt to remind her, every so often, that I'm her boss.

She takes a deep breath and says, "That was Steve. There's something wrong with the plane."

I sit straight up in my seat and scoff. "What do you mean there's something wrong with the plane?"

"He said there's a problem with the radio. It's not transmitting correctly or something, and a replacement won't arrive until tomorrow."

"What about another plane?" I fire back.

"I asked. There isn't one available."

"No . . . no . . . no!" I slam my head against the back of the seat in frustration. "This isn't happening. I *have* to be at the studio in the morning."

"We'll be at the airport in a couple of minutes. We'll talk to Steve and figure something out."

I'm fuming. "*We* aren't going to do anything. *You* are going to figure this out, understand?" I don't pause for a response. "I have to be back in Nashville tonight, and I don't care *how* you do it, but I'd better be on a plane headed that way soon." I shake my head and huff. "I swear, Kelsey, sometimes you . . . *disappoint* me. If I hadn't come here to play at this stupid wedding to begin with, I wouldn't be in this situation."

Even inside the dimly lit van, I notice her wipe a tear from her cheek. I'm not sure if it's a tear of anger or one of fear—it doesn't really matter either way. I pay her a lot of money to handle these issues, and her feelings on the situation aren't really any concern of mine. It's simply her job to make sure it gets fixed, and fixed fast.

The van slows, makes a sharp right turn, and stops in front of an iron security gate. The driver rolls down his window and enters a code into the keypad. I collapse back into my seat as the gate slides open. My mind races, focused on the problem at hand. If I don't get back to Nashville tonight, my entire schedule will be screwed up. I'm so frustrated I have to bite my lower lip to keep from lashing out at Kelsey again.

The van quickly glides across the tarmac of the small airport and pulls alongside my private jet. The driver exits, walks around the back of the van, and opens the door for us.

Kelsey jumps out without saying a word and immediately starts walking toward the plane. I scoot across the bench seat, jump out the open door, and make my way quickly toward Steve, who is already talking with Kelsey next to the front steps of the plane.

The lights are on inside the aircraft's cabin, and an electrical generator hums near the nose, filling the air with diesel fumes.

Despite the bad news I received on the ride over, I'm still hopeful that whatever problem there is with the plane isn't as serious as first thought. Hopefully, there's a workable solution that will allow us to fly back tonight.

"What's going on with the plane, Steve?" I ask my pilot as I draw next to him, my hands on my hips.

He looks frustrated and runs his hand through his salt-and-pepper hair that has begun to thin. He's also carrying some extra weight around his midsection that's common for middle-aged men. "The radio isn't working correctly, and without it, we can't communicate with air traffic control," he says. "I checked with the only mechanic on duty here at the airport, and he doesn't have a replacement available. I had him order one through his supplier, but he says it won't get here until around noon tomorrow."

"You're sure we can't just fly back to Nashville and have it fixed there?" I ask, but as soon as the question leaves my lips, I know it's a stupid one.

"Uh . . . no, Lauren, we can't." He looks at me as if I'm an idiot.

I feel like an idiot too, but at this point, I'm desperate for any good news.

The van driver sets our suitcases down next to Kelsey. I nod my head and she pulls a twenty out of her wallet and tips him. "Thanks!" he says and hurries back to his van. Kelsey pulls her cellphone from her purse and begins to feverishly tap the screen with her fingers as the van drives away.

I turn my attention back to Steve. "So what are our options?"

He stifles a laugh and shakes his head. "Our option is to wait until tomorrow, replace the faulty radio, then fly back home." I must have an incredulous look on my face because his eyes widen and he adds, "That's it, Lauren. That's our only option. Sorry."

"No, no . . . no! You don't understand. I *have* to be in the recording studio in the morning. I have a very important session for my new album."

He shrugs his shoulders. "Sorry. I don't know what to tell you. This plane"—he points his thumb over his shoulder—"isn't going anywhere until the radio is working . . . and that's final. There's nothing I can do about it. I wish I could, but I'm afraid we're stuck here until tomorrow."

"Isn't there another flight we can take or something?"

He waves his arm across the tarmac. "Take a look around. This isn't a sprawling commercial airport. It's a small operation. Only private planes come in and out of here. There are no commercial flights." He seems offended, as if I'm questioning his competence or something.

I look around and spot several small, propeller-driven aircraft lined up along the edge of the tarmac. My jet is the largest aircraft in sight, and, undoubtedly, the nicest one this rinky-dink airport has seen in years. Frustrated, angry, and tired of trying to convince myself the situation isn't as dire as it truly is, I acquiesce and nod at Steve. "Okay. Thanks."

He places his foot on the bottom step of the plane and starts to walk up, but pauses and turns back to face me. "Look, we'll get the radio fixed as quickly as possible tomorrow. I have a few things to finish up here with the copilot tonight, then we're headed to a motel just down the road to try to get some sleep. I called a cab to come pick us up, and it should be here in about half an hour. Do you want to ride back with us and see if they have an extra room available?"

I glance over at Kelsey, who is still working on her smartphone. "Maybe. I think Kelsey is trying to find another option for us. Maybe we can catch a ride with someone driving back tonight. I'll let you know."

"Okay," he says. "We'll get back out here first thing in the morning. Maybe the part will show up early and we can be on our way. We'll just have to wait and see. I'm sorry this happened, but when you're dealing with aircraft, sometimes things just break."

I place my hands in the back pockets of my jeans and nod. "Of course." Steve turns and bounds up the stairs and into the aircraft cabin. Kelsey is still looking at her phone. "Well, have you found us a way out of here yet?" I ask her.

She lowers the phone and shakes her head. "Sorry. The last flight from Atlanta to Nashville leaves at midnight, and it's at least a two-hour drive from here to the airport, so that's not an option. I've checked Asheville and Spartanburg too. Neither of them has additional flights tonight."

I stomp past her and let out a prolonged, frustrated groan. "I can't believe this," I say.

I'm still furious about the whole situation. Of all nights for something like this to happen, it has to happen now. If I don't make it back in time for my studio session tomorrow, my entire schedule for the next week will have to be rearranged. I stop and turn back around. "What if we rent a car? You could drive and I could try to get some sleep on the way. How many hours is it back to Nashville from here? Four? Five? That might just work if—"

"No," she says, interrupting me.

"What? Why not?"

"Look." Kelsey motions with her hand over my shoulder. I turn and see a small neon sign that reads Car Rentals on the front of one of the buildings near the airport exit. The inside of the office, however, is completely dark.

"They're closed," Kelsey says. "I already checked. They won't open until seven tomorrow morning."

"Unbelievable." I turn back around to face her. "Can this night possibly get any worse?"

"I did think of one option . . . but it's not a good one."

"Well, right now, it seems we have no options at all, so let's hear it."

"We could have the band swing by here and pick us up on their way back, but it will probably take them another hour to get packed up at the wedding and headed our way, then an additional four or five hours on the bus to make it home. I know it's not a great option, but it's the only one we have left."

I shake my head in disbelief. The thought of having to ride back on the bus makes my stomach turn. It's been years since I've had to do that. I've done my time in the back of cramped vans and hot, stuffy buses, traveling thousands of miles all over the country. That was back when I was still struggling to break into the top-tier level of country artists. I did make that jump and, since then, I fly in my private jet almost everywhere I go. I certainly don't miss the days of endless hours on the road, and I have no intention of ever going back to them.

But tonight, I'm out of choices. Taking the bus back to Nashville is the only realistic shot I have to make it to the studio by tomorrow morning, and I *have* to make it to the session on time. "Okay, fine. Have you called them yet?"

"No, not yet. I was waiting to see what you wanted to do." Kelsey looks at her phone's screen again and starts to dial, but stops and snaps her head up. She stares over my shoulder.

"What is it?" I ask.

She nods. "Over there."

I turn around to see what she's looking at. A car pulls up and stops beside another plane about thirty yards behind mine. A well-dressed man, woman, and small child exit the vehicle, and remove several pieces of luggage from the trunk. The headlights from the car bathe us in bright light for a second as the driver turns and leaves.

"I think I recognize that family from the wedding," Kelsey says.

"Really?"

"Yes." She places her hand on her forehead as if in deep thought. "I've got an idea. Stay here for a minute." She rushes past me and runs toward the other aircraft.

"Wait, you idiot! Don't just leave me here!" I scream, but she doesn't slow down. She's dragging her suitcase quickly across the tarmac, the plastic wheels bouncing violently on the concrete. I pick up my carry-on bag and hurry after her.

I should already be airborne, inside an air-conditioned cabin instead of running through the Georgia humidity, and the sweatshirt I chose to wear is already making me sweat. Kelsey beats me to the other plane by at least ten seconds, and by the time I arrive, I'm breathing heavily.

"Excuse me, sir?" Kelsey says.

The man tosses the last piece of the family's luggage into the aircraft cabin through the side doors that are open aft of the wing. "Yes?" he says and turns to face us.

I'm still trying to catch my breath, so I let Kelsey do the talking. She smiles at the gentleman and lets out a long, exaggerated sigh. "We are in a little bit of a mess here, and I was hoping that you might be able to help us out."

Nice . . . the old damsel-in-distress routine. Appeal to his sense of chivalry.

I play along by transforming my face into that of a worried, helpless female: a furrowed brow, sad eyes, and a nervous smile. I even pretend to be biting my fingernails for extra impact. It's completely beneath me, of course, and normally I wouldn't even consider doing such a thing—playing the part of a helpless woman, because I'm far from that—but I'm so desperate to get back to Nashville tonight that I'm willing to compromise my standards.

The man starts to answer, but Kelsey cuts him off before he has the opportunity to say no to her request for help. "Do I know you? Have we met before?"

Good, establish a rapport with him. Make him feel comfortable, I silently encourage Kelsey.

The man hesitates at first, as if he's sizing us up and trying to determine if he's going to continue the conversation or, instead, hop in the plane with his family and leave us stranded here on the tarmac. Finally, he says, "I . . . I'm not sure."

"Yes!" Kelsey says, pointing at him and smiling wide. "I *knew* you looked familiar." She turns to me. "Didn't I tell you he looked familiar?"

I nod and smile. "Yes, you sure did." I'm still playing along, even though I can tell the man doesn't recognize either of us.

But I also know Kelsey isn't done with him yet. As angry as I am about being in this situation in the first place, I have to admit she is good at this part of her job. One of the best. She can smooth talk almost anyone, especially men, into doing whatever she wants them to do—and that is a very valuable skill to have if you work as a personal assistant to a celebrity. It doesn't hurt that she is gorgeous too, with flowing auburn hair and bright green eyes.

Kelsey snaps her fingers at the man and points her index finger at his chest. "The wedding!" she exclaims, as if the thought has just popped into her mind this very second. "Weren't you just at the wedding at Larry Sinclair's house? Yes, that's where I know you from."

The man lets go of a tense breath he's been holding in, and his shoulders droop to express his embarrassment. He laughs softly. "Yes, of course . . . the wedding." He squints, pretending to study both of us closely in the dim glow of the overhead tarmac lights. He nods. "I think I recognize you too."

I can tell he's lying, but it doesn't matter. Kelsey has established the connection and convinced him it's okay to let his guard down. He's comfortable with us now, and he's more apt to agree to the request I know Kelsey is about to make.

"Like I said, we are in a bit of a mess here. Our plane"—she motions with her arm back toward my jet—"has broken down and won't be fixed until tomorrow. And we *really* need to get back to Nashville tonight. We were hoping that since you were friends with Larry, you might be heading that way."

The man stares toward my private jet. "That's *your* plane?" he asks her.

"Yes. Well, actually, it's hers." Kelsey points at me.

"Wow," he says, shifting his eyes my way. "That's some plane. A lot larger than this one." He taps the side of his aircraft. "What is it, a Citation III?"

The plane isn't actually *mine* per se. It belongs to my record label, but why clear up an innocent misconception that seems to have really impressed him? And I really have no idea what model it is either, but I smile and say, "Sure is," just to bolster his ego. "You certainly know your aircraft."

He smiles at my comment, obviously proud of his discerning eye. He nods. "That's sure a great plane."

Kelsey lets out a friendly chuckle. "Well, maybe so, but right now it's broken, and it sure isn't going to get us home tonight. Did you say if you were heading to Nashville?" she asks, gently reminding the man of her previous question.

"Well, as a matter of fact, I am," he replies.

I feel a glint of hope spring up within me.

The woman turns her attention from the young child and steps forward, joining the man at his side. She looks directly at me for a second, studying my face intently. In a flash, her eyes go wide with recognition. "Aren't you Lauren Miller?"

I take advantage of the opening. It's what I've been waiting for. "Yes! I sure am." I extend my hand to her. "It's so nice to meet you."

An enthusiastic smile paints her face. She's obviously thrilled to be meeting a real-life superstar, but I'm used to this type of reaction. When I first became famous, I loved seeing this expression on fans' faces, but I've long since grown tired of it. I don't particularly care for close interactions with people. But on occasions such as this, my celebrity status is a very valuable asset, and I certainly know how to turn on the charm in order to get what I want.

The woman shakes my hand with excitement. The smile on her face tells me I have her right where I want her. "It's a pleasure to meet you too, Ms. Miller. I'm . . . I'm a big . . . well, huge really, fan of yours," she says, struggling to get her words out. She's older than most of my fans, mid to late thirties, I think. Maybe even early forties, it's hard to tell in the dim light. The man, who I assume is her husband, seems to be a few years older than her, but there isn't such an age difference that it's awkward.

I lock my blue eyes on her, letting my face convey a false sense of enthusiasm at meeting such a *huge* fan, as if it's my first time. "Please, just call me Lauren."

"Okay . . . Lauren," she says and releases my hand. "It took me a second to recognize you. You look diff—" The woman stops abruptly and blinks her eyes, obviously afraid she has said something offensive to her idol.

I laugh, trying to put her mind at ease. "You mean I look different than I did onstage at the wedding?"

She nods sheepishly.

I allow a wide, friendly smile to light up my face. "Well, yes. I took off all of my war paint on the ride over here and changed into something a bit more comfortable for the flight back." I chuckle, pretending to not be offended in the least. I am, though. I'm not ugly without my makeup. Far from it. But I let her ill-timed comment slide in order to achieve my greater objective.

"Of course," the woman responds. "I'm sorry—"

"Nonsense, don't worry about it," I say, cutting off her apology and waving my hand dismissively. "What's your name?"

"Oh, my gosh! I can't believe I haven't introduced myself." She's obviously embarrassed by the oversight. "My name is Juliette Crenshaw . . . and this is our daughter, Macy." She pats the little girl standing next to her on the top of the head. The child's eyes are sleepy and keep drifting closed. "And this is my husband, Adam. He works for an investment firm in Nashville," she adds, pointing toward the man.

I extend my hand to him. "Pleasure to meet you, Adam." He smiles and shakes my hand, now clearly comfortable with the situation he finds himself in. After all, it's not every day that someone has a celebrity approach them asking for a favor.

Although I'm almost certain this thing is a done deal, I bend over to talk to the daughter, just to firm up my connection with the family. "Hi, Macy, I'm Lauren. It's nice to meet you." I offer my hand, but the little girl has a death grip on her mother's leg and buries her face in Juliette's blue dress. "Your hair is beautiful," I say, in an attempt to win her over. "It's blonde, just like mine. How old are you?" She doesn't move or acknowledge me at all.

"I'm sorry," Juliette says. "Macy's very shy."

You little brat.

I straighten up. "Oh, that's okay. It can be scary meeting strangers at her age. I was the same way when I was a kid." I wasn't at all. I have wanted to be the center of attention for as long as I can remember. But I let the little girl be and don't push any further. I turn and motion with my hand toward Kelsey. "Everyone, this is Kelsey. She's my assistant."

Kelsey shakes hands with Adam and Juliette. "I know this is a lot to ask, but is there any way we can catch a ride back to Nashville with you folks?" she says, finally getting to the direct point.

I interject before either of them can answer, on the off chance they're not as excited to do me a favor as I think. "I have a very important studio session in the morning for my upcoming album. If you could help us out, it would be a *lifesaver*. I'll be happy to pay the fuel bill, and I'll also make sure you all get VIP passes to my next concert . . . if you would like to come see a show." The offer of free concert tickets and VIP passes always works. It makes people feel important—a dangling carrot they can't refuse.

Human character is so predictable.

The fact is, I've discovered most people are more than willing to help me whenever I ask, no matter how much it inconveniences them. They just want to be able to go home and tell their family and friends they met the great Lauren Miller, and that they were even asked to assist me in some way.

I'm more than willing to use my fame for my own advantage when it's called for.

Adam looks at his wife, and I know he's waiting to receive her nonverbal agreement. She nods to him, and he turns back to me. "We would be happy to help you out."

I clap my hands together and smile widely, exaggerating my gratitude. "Oh, thank you so much. I don't know what I would do if it weren't for you nice folks. Thank you. Thank you. Thank you!"

He waves his hand dismissively. "Not to worry. We're glad to be able to help. Just give me a few minutes while I get the plane ready, and we'll be on our way."

"That sounds great," I say and breathe a sigh of relief. I know it's all going to work out now, thanks to my skills of manipulation. Kelsey laid the groundwork, but I was the one who sealed the deal.

Adam and Juliette have no idea they've just been played. Yes, I'll have to spend some time backstage at my next show, pretending these people are long-lost friends, but it's a sacrifice I'm willing to make, because, in the end, I'm getting what I want.

Now, I'll make it back home tonight and maybe even get a few hours of sleep before I have to be at the studio in the morning.

"Let me grab your bags and get them strapped in," Adam says.

Kelsey and I push our carry-ons forward. He picks them up and places them into the cargo area behind the last row of cabin seats, and on top of his family's bags.

"How long will the flight back to Nashville be?" I ask.

He laughs. "Well, a lot slower than it would be on your jet, that's for sure. This is a Piper Saratoga II." He pats the fuselage again, obviously proud of his aircraft. "It's a good, reliable plane, but the cruising speed is much slower than your jet. So it will take us around an hour and a half, maybe a little bit longer, depending on the weather."

That's slightly longer than I was expecting, but I don't let my expression betray my disappointment. "That's fine. Thank you again."

"You said something about the weather," Kelsey says. "Is it bad tonight?"

"Oh, not really," he replies. "There are a few storms moving through the northern portions of Tennessee and North Carolina right now, but we should be able to make it back before they cross our flight path."

"I see," she replies, with just a hint of anxiety peppering her voice. "Well, that sounds like good news."

Kelsey is a nervous flyer, always has been, and I can see from the disquieted look on her face that the wheels inside her mind are already turning. Any mention of bad weather or potential problems makes her uncomfortable. But she has been forced to get over that phobia, even if it does occasionally resurface, working as my assistant. She travels everywhere I do, which means she's forced to fly often.

Suddenly, she grabs my arm and pulls me aside, out of earshot of the family. Adam is completing his pre-flight inspection of the aircraft, and Juliette and Macy have already climbed inside the cabin.

"I'm not so sure about this now," Kelsey says to me with deep concern in her eyes. "It seemed like a good idea at first, but now I'm—" She pauses and rubs her forehead. "You know I hate flying in these smaller planes. Adam said there were some storms in the area."

I roll my eyes. "No, he said there were some storms far away from here, but that we will be back to Nashville before they even come near our flight path."

She wraps her arms around her midsection. She doesn't look convinced. "You're sure we can't just wait until tomorrow and fly back then? Steve said the radio might be fixed early. If that happens, we could be back in time for you to still get some studio work in."

"No! Absolutely not." I'm in no mood to argue about this. We finally have a solution to our predicament—a predicament, by the way, that Kelsey caused in the first place by hooking me into the wedding gig—and now she's getting cold feet.

It's infuriating.

"Look, I *have* to be at the studio tomorrow morning," I say through gritted teeth. "That's a fact. And I have to get on this cramped plane, and fly home with people I don't even know. And do you want to know why, Kelsey? Because *you* put me in this situation to begin with by telling Larry I'd be happy to sing at his daughter's wedding. Do you think I'm happy about it? No, I'm not. Not at all! But do you know what? I'm going to suck it up and suffer through this because it's what I have to do. It's my job, and I'm going to do my job . . . I suggest you do yours too."

Kelsey nods her head in defeat, unwilling to continue the argument any longer. "Okay," she says softly.

"Good. That's what I wanted to hear." Even though I know I probably should, I feel no sympathy for her. This whole thing is her fault, and the way I see it, she should suffer right along with me. Maybe she'll be more careful the next time someone asks for a favor.

I turn and storm off, back toward the plane.

Adam pulls a large strap tight across the pile of suitcases behind the seats. He works the ratchet mechanism three times to secure the load for flight and climbs from the plane, his feet landing on the tarmac with a thud. "You two ready?" he asks.

"Yes, we are." I take his outstretched hand, and he helps me climb inside the passenger cabin. I turn around and notice that Kelsey is hesitating outside, her face pale and worried. "Well, are you coming or not?" I ask.

She looks at me with fearful, angry eyes but doesn't speak. Finally, she draws in a deep breath and nods.

She takes a step forward, and climbs aboard.

2

I press my head against the small window as the plane begins to taxi away from its parking space. The glass is cool against my warm skin and feels refreshing. White lights in the wings illuminate the tarmac, while a red strobe light flashes from the tail of the aircraft, shattering the darkness with bursts of crimson. The plane's single engine spins the prop at the nose of the aircraft, creating a thundering purr and sending a penetrating vibration through my seat and into my body.

I turn from the window. The cabin is dim, the bright overhead lights having been extinguished by Adam a couple of minutes ago in preparation for takeoff, but I can still see from the soft glow of a reading lamp above my head. At the front of the plane, Adam occupies the left seat, and Juliette is seated next to him in the copilot's position. Both have headsets on, and they appear to be talking to one another, but I can't hear them over the roar of the engine.

I wonder if Juliette is also a pilot, or if she just travels next to her husband to keep him company. He flips some switches on the instrument panel and moves the yoke back and forth.

While the plane is a definite departure from the business jet I'm accustomed to traveling on, I'm thankful to finally be heading home, even if it does mean I have to spend an hour and a half inside this cramped cabin.

Behind the pilot and copilot positions there are four seats for passengers, two seats per row, with the rows opposing one another. I occupy the right, rear seat, while Kelsey sits in the seat to my left. Macy, the young blonde-haired girl who snubbed me earlier, sits opposite me in the aft-facing right seat, our knees almost touching due to the confined space of the cabin.

She's clutching a stuffed bear and staring out the window. She seems unaware that she is flying with a celebrity, but even if she does know it, she obviously doesn't care.

As Adam turns the plane off the taxiway and onto the runway, I look over at Kelsey. Her face is pale and she is squeezing her hands together in a tight ball across her lap. She doesn't turn her head to acknowledge my gaze, although I know she must see me in her peripheral vision. Instead, she keeps her eyes laser-focused on the empty seat in front of her.

I look away and tug on my seat belt to make sure it is snug. The engine rumbles louder as Adam applies more pressure to the throttle. The plane lurches forward, as if it's being shot from a cannon, and propels us down the runway.

I glance out the window again and watch as the asphalt, illuminated by the aircraft's lights, speeds past me. The plane moves faster. I feel the power of the sudden acceleration in my chest, the forward momentum pushing me back against the seat. I glance over at Kelsey again, who now has her eyes closed. She has also removed her hands from her lap, but her right one is still visible—it's gripping the side of her seat with such force that her knuckles have turned white.

The nose of the plane tilts skyward, and I feel the familiar weightless sensation in the pit of my stomach as the aircraft leaves the earth.

It continues on, barreling into the vacuity of the black night.

3

Five minutes into the flight, my wish for rest eludes me. I don't feel like sleeping at all; I'm still too amped up from the near scheduling disaster I just avoided. I wish I had a book to read, a magazine, anything to pass the time. My jet has movies on demand, a vast music selection, and even video games to keep passengers occupied. This plane has none of those things.

Kelsey's eyes are still closed, but the terrified look from earlier has vanished. She's now quiescent, and I wonder if she is asleep.

Macy sits relaxed, her small head resting halfway up the seat back. She's probably flown numerous times with her parents, confident in her father's ability to safely pilot the plane. She continues to ignore me. Her tiny eyelids fight to keep themselves open against the pull of sleep.

I'm glad the two of them aren't bothering me. After the night I've had, I'm not in any mood to talk. All I can think about is getting home, taking a shower, and crawling into my own bed. I'll make it back to my place later than originally scheduled, but at least I'm headed there now, instead of being stuck in Georgia.

I recalculate what time I will arrive, hoping I can get at least a few hours of sleep before I have to leave for the studio tomorrow morning.

Under normal conditions, it's only a twenty-minute drive from the airport to my house. I don't actually live *in* Nashville. My home is in Brentwood, an upscale suburb on the south side of the city. Even though it's already late in the evening, this is Saturday night, so the traffic will be worse on I-440 and I-65 than on a weeknight. It could take me thirty minutes tonight.

But I realize that Kelsey didn't call the car service to apprise them we would be arriving on a different aircraft and later than expected. Our change in plans was made at the last minute, and I know she didn't have time to make the necessary arrangements. She'll have to call once we land, and that will cost me even more time, maybe an additional twenty minutes. I'm so far behind schedule at this point, the Netflix movie will definitely have to wait until another night.

My schedule has me in the studio for the next three days working on the new album, then I have one day off before hitting the road again for the tour. I think my next show is in Dallas, but I'm not completely sure I'm right about that. Kelsey, along with my manager and booking agent, handle all those details for me.

I just show up and sing.

That's the reason I'm so protective of my downtime—because there's so little of it.

Being a modern-day country superstar is more than just having a great voice. I'm also the head of a business empire, and that comes with its own set of stressors. I have to market myself, stay in good physical shape, and I always have to be looking over my shoulder to make sure the next rising young star doesn't have her eyes set on me. There's always someone new clawing to make a name for themselves and knock me off my throne.

And those are just a few of the things I worry about.

There are others. Lots of them. And, at times, it can be a downright cutthroat business. I have to be willing to fight for what I want and to keep what I've worked so hard for. That part doesn't bother me, though—I know how to fight dirty when I have to.

Maybe Kelsey doesn't understand my anger at this entire trip, but neither she, nor any of the other people who work for me, are the ones paying the bills. Whether they want to admit it or not, each and every one of them is dependent on *me* to do *my* job, and to do it well. Without my efforts, they would all be out on the street looking for work, and I don't get why that is so hard for them to understand.

I'm the one who does the really hard work.

I'm the one who travels from city to city, often not remembering where I was the night before or knowing where I'm going the following day. *I'm* the one who has to go countless nights with little sleep, contend with constant jet lag, then go out and perform in front of thousands of screaming fans who couldn't care less if I'm not feeling my best. They pay good money to see me, and they expect a flawless show. No excuses.

In the end, the success and failure of everything I've worked for comes down to just one person.

Me.

I know that, and if the others don't recognize that fact and start appreciating me for all I've done for them, I will find people who will. It's just that simple.

I lean my head against the window again and fight to clear my mind of everything. I close my eyes and try for a second time to sleep. Any rest I can bank during the flight home will be a bonus. I take slow, deep breaths, in an attempt to force myself asleep.

The perpetual hum of the aircraft's engine, its vibrations traveling through the metal fuselage and into my body, has a calming effect. I allow the lulling sensations to clear everything else away, all my thoughts and worries, and take me completely. I feel myself drift toward the precipice of sleep.

I'm jolted from my semiconscious state by a sudden, violent tremor that reverberates through the aircraft. Startled, I sit up, and my eyes snap open. But the shaking disappears as quickly as it came, leaving behind only the monotonous sound of the plane's engine droning on.

Just a little turbulence.

I fall back in my seat. Just as my eyes close, another sharp rumble sweeps through me. This one is not as severe as the first, though, so I don't even flinch, hoping that the sleep I so desperately need will finally come.

I lie there for several minutes, trying to relax, but keep being interrupted by the intermittent shaking of the aircraft. Over the past few years, I've grown accustomed to flying through all sorts of situations. I've seen it all: ice, snow, severe turbulence, thunderstorms, and even an emergency landing one time in Tulsa after an engine on my jet had to be shut down.

So a little bump here and there doesn't even raise my heart rate.

Kelsey is a different story. Although she has been through all the same experiences with me, she has never been able to completely overcome her anxieties about flying. I glance over at her and see that she is, once again, gripping the sides of her seat. Her eyes are still closed, but I can tell by the tension on her face that she is now fully awake.

A streak of lightning illuminates the world outside and bathes the cabin in a brilliant flash of light. I jump slightly in my seat.

Another flash.

The plane is rocked by a subsequent blast of turbulence, this one more violent than the others.

Kelsey's death grip on the seat cushion has only intensified, her face taut and full of fear. She finally opens her eyes and looks over at me. She is terrified, her brow furrowed with deep lines of stress and her eyes as wide as fifty-cent pieces.

I smile, hoping to calm her—the last thing I need at this moment is for her to freak out on me—but it doesn't work. She snaps her head forward and squeezes her eyes closed again.

The plane flies on, but the rapid-fire turbulence from the storm outside continues to batter us. The flashes of lightning become more frequent, until the sky and the interior of the aircraft are in a state of almost constant illumination. Sharp reports of thunder crash around us, temporarily drowning out the noise from the plane's engine. Rain floods the outside of my window so heavily that it seems as if we are flying through a waterfall.

My stomach lurches into my chest as the aircraft suddenly plummets. It falls, and falls some more, so far that I begin to wonder if it will ever end. I'm weightless, my seat belt the only thing keeping me from floating up to the ceiling. A sharp, violent thud throws me hard against the seat as the plane reaches the bottom of the air pocket.

We must've fallen several hundred feet.

I look forward and see Adam moving the control yoke back and forth, fighting to regain control of the aircraft. Kelsey screams. I yell at her. "It's okay, Kelsey! It's just a thunderstorm." She answers with only a muffled sob.

The plane starts to climb again, but continues to be tossed back and forth by the wind outside, its wingtips dipping violently up and down with each gust. Adam is still working the controls, and I find myself wishing he would turn around for just one second so that I can measure his level of concern, but he keeps his gaze firmly planted on the instrument panel in front of him.

Macy starts to cry. I don't know what to do about that. I've never been good with kids, but I know I should do something. I reach out and start to touch the little girl's knee in an effort to comfort her, but pull back when Juliette turns her head from the copilot's seat. "It's okay, Macy! Momma's here!" she yells over the cacophony of engine noise and thunder. "Just hang on, baby! Okay?"

Macy tries to turn around in order to gain a comforting look from her mother, but she's restrained by her seat belt, and the back of the seat is too tall for her to see over. She twists back and forth, struggling to catch a glimpse of Juliette.

Tears begin to roll freely down the little girl's rosy cheeks. I reach out again and, this time, actually place my hand on Macy's knee. "It's okay," I say, my voice barely audible over the crashes of thunder outside. I fight to keep myself upright in the seat, but the storm combats my every move. "Everything's going to be all right. Just hang on!"

I can tell she heard me this time, because her teary eyes focus on me as if saying, *I'm scared. Please help me!* But I don't know what else to do. What can I do, trapped in my own seat? I'm not about to unbuckle my belt just to give her a hug.

Adam finally turns his head and looks at me. I'm not immediately sure why he does this, but his face shows me what I feared it might.

Worry. More than just worry—genuine fear. Drawn on his face is the kind of look I imagine a death row inmate might have as he's walked to the execution chamber. His brow is sweating profusely, his lips drawn and thin.

Even though I've been desperately trying to convince myself everything will be fine, seeing Adam's fear makes me finally face the truth. If he is this concerned about our situation, then we're in real trouble.

I've always made it through troublesome flights before, but this time seems different.

It feels as if we've flown straight into the heart of a massive storm.

Adam removes the headset off his right ear. "Sorry, but we're going to have to turn around and go back," he yells at me. "The storms have moved in faster than they were forecast to, and there isn't a way around them . . . at least not that I can find."

Another round of turbulence pulverizes my insides. Although I've been insistent on getting back to Nashville as soon as possible, right now, I'm just hoping to make it safely back to solid ground, no matter where that happens to be. I nod at him and yell, "Okay!" but I'm unsure if he can hear me over all the noise.

He must have, because he motions with his head toward both Kelsey and Macy. "Try to keep everyone calm . . . no matter what happens . . . you understand?"

I give another affirmative nod, but don't speak this time.

He offers me a brief smile, but I know it's forced, and I find no comfort in it whatsoever. He places the headset back over his exposed ear and turns around. He says something to his wife that I can't make out. I can only see the left side of Juliette's face as she turns to respond, but that's all I need to see to know how scared she is.

The plane makes a sweeping turn to the right, all the while continuing to be pounded by a torrent of rain and constant turbulence. The realization that we may not make it back to the small airport we departed just fifteen minutes ago begins to sink in, and I feel my whole body tense with the new understanding.

But as the plane completes the right-hand turn, the turbulence slowly begins to subside and the flashes of lightning become less frequent. I let out a deep sigh of relief. My stomach is still in a torturous knot, and my heart continues to pound inside my chest as if it were a giant bass drum, but I'm now convinced that we are going to be okay. The crisis has passed.

I fall back into my seat, emotionally drained from the tension of the past few minutes. I take four deep, calming breaths, holding the oxygen inside my lungs for a few seconds with each one before exhaling, in an attempt to slow my heart rate. It works, and I feel the anxiety melt away and my mind return to a calm state.

The same can't be said of Kelsey.

I glance over at my assistant. She continues to grip her seat, and her eyes are closed with such force that the skin on her forehead and the side of her face is stretched tight and void of color.

"Kelsey?" I say, trying to snap her out of her panic. She doesn't respond. "It's going to be okay. Adam turned the plane back toward the airport. We should be on the ground in a few minutes."

But she doesn't acknowledge my words at all—she's still trapped in her own world of unadulterated terror.

There's nothing else I can do for her at the moment, so I turn my attention back to Macy, who is still clutching her stuffed bear. Even though her tears have dried, it's obvious that she's still frightened. I can't blame her. I lean forward and pat her on the leg. "Just hang on, okay? We'll be back on the ground in no time." But just as Kelsey did, Macy ignores me. Her eyes are trained out the small window, her lower lip trembling and moving in and out with each breath.

Confident I've helped both of them as much as possible considering the circumstances, I slump back into the aircraft seat and try to focus on the fact that we will be landing soon. I close my eyes so I won't be forced to keep looking at the lingering fear on Macy's face, nor the near hysteria on Kelsey's.

I just need to block all of it out.

Now that it's clear this attempt to hitchhike back to Nashville with Adam and his family has turned into a disaster, I realize I should've gone with Kelsey's suggestion of riding back on the bus with my band. Even though I hadn't seen it as a good solution earlier, now I find myself wishing I'd opted for the bus, no matter how unpleasant the experience. At least I would be heading home. But that's an option that is no longer available to me. I'm sure the band has already packed and left the wedding, and is currently headed back to Nashville. I'm stuck now, with no alternative other than to wait for my own plane to be fixed tomorrow, and that ruins my chance of making the studio session.

And where am I going to sleep tonight?

Maybe Steve will still be at the airport when we arrive and Kelsey and I can hop a ride with him back to the motel he mentioned earlier. I doubt that, though. He's probably already gone, and finding another room in the boondocks of Northern Georgia at midnight won't be easy. I'm not sure what I'll do.

But that's the reality of my current situation.

And I decide it sucks.

The studio session will have to be pushed one day, which means that the backup singers and the audio engineer will have to be rescheduled. All the band members have already finished their parts, but I still need to lay down the vocals on a few more tracks to complete the new album. It was hard enough getting everyone to agree to work on the weekend, but I'm the one in charge, so they really didn't have much say-so in the matter anyway.

I just let them think they did.

I'll have Kelsey get up early tomorrow morning and make the appropriate calls. I imagine none of them will be disappointed they get to stay home on a Sunday. I'm really the only one who has been inconvenienced in this whole ordeal, as usual.

The worst part about the session being delayed is not the re-shuffling that will have to occur, it's the fact that I will lose the one day off I had built into my schedule following my work in the studio, a down day to relax before I return to the concert tour. I've been looking so forward to finally having a little time off, if only a single day, and now that's gone too.

And that *really* sucks.

As angry as I am about it, there's nothing else I can do. There's no way I'm getting back home tonight.

In an instant, my breath is snatched from my lungs and my stomach shoots into my throat as the plane falls again, this time even faster and farther than before.

It stops with a tremendous bang, rattling my teeth and throwing me forward in the seat with such force that the shoulder belt digs into my chest, and it feels as though I'm about to be cut in two and my eyeballs are going to pop out of their sockets.

I scream, my cry melding with those of Kelsey and Macy.

The plane shoots up again, recovering some of the altitude it had lost to the pocket of turbulence. This quick, violent shift in momentum throws me rearward and causes my head to snap against the back of the seat. I'm tossed to the left and, just as hard, back to the right.

Lightning strikes the right wingtip of the plane and sends a thunderous roar through the cabin. The engine struggles, moans, against the storm. I manage to lift my head and see Adam wrestling with the yoke again. Even in the dim light of the cabin, I notice that the muscles in his right forearm are taut as he fiercely grips the controls. I catch the grimace on his face as he turns his head quickly and screams something to Juliette.

I've been wrong—very wrong. Everything isn't going to be okay.

Because somehow . . . we've flown straight into the middle of another storm.

4

My head slams against the window.

I'm flung back to the left in an equally violent response to the plane's uncontrollable movements.

Thrust forward.

Knocked backward.

Over and over again, I'm tossed in every direction. My head spins, and I lose my spatial orientation, unsure of which way is up or down, left or right.

Brilliant streaks of lightning flash repeatedly outside the window. The sharp cracking of thunder assaults my eardrums and reverberates in my chest.

I attempt to steal a glance at Kelsey, but I'm so dizzy, my center of gravity so off-kilter, my eyes refuse to focus.

The plane enters another steep dive, slams to a stop, and rockets skyward just as quickly. My insides are doing somersaults.

A torrent of rain continues to pelt the outside of the aircraft and obscures the windows. I feel as though we've all just been thrown into a giant washing machine on the heavy-duty cycle.

Screams of fear and panic radiate throughout the cabin, mixing with the noise of the thunder, wind, and rain into a dreadful symphony of terror. I can no longer distinguish one voice from the other—even my own screams are gobbled up by the others and become indistinguishable in the litany of sounds.

The plane loses more altitude, and though Adam continues his fight to regain control of the aircraft, recovers only a little. I can't imagine the battle he's enduring right now, just struggling to keep the plane in the air.

How high are we above the ground? The thought terrifies me because I know there's only one endgame if we keep losing more altitude than we are able to regain.

I shake my head and blink repeatedly and forcefully, struggling to make my eyes refocus. Slowly, my vision clears enough that I can again see the inside of the cabin clearly.

The sudden sound of a thousand hammers banging against the thin skin of the aircraft pummels my ears. This new, foreign noise is so deafening it drowns out all the others: the thunder, the engine . . . our screams. Every other sound is overpowered by this new, chilling one—a great rumbling assault that only grows more intense.

I have no idea what could be causing this new sound. I glance around and my eyes settle forward just as the windshield in front of Adam shatters in a spider-web pattern. It's instantly clear to me what caused it.

Hail.

I'm still being rocked left and right, up and down, but now it's as if someone has tossed a handful of large rocks into the giant washing machine I find myself in.

This isn't good.

The window to my right is struck by a large hailstone, and the sharp report of the glass cracking causes me to instinctively snap my head away and hide my face in the crook of my left arm. Macy's window is the next to go. I raise my head and see her again crying out for Juliette, but the stentorian roar of the hail obliterates her young voice.

The sound of the massive ice chunks blasting the sheet metal causes me to consider the effect the hail is having on the engine propeller. How much more damage can it withstand? There's no doubt it's getting pummeled, and I worry that, very soon, it will be unable to function properly.

Kelsey screams as the window next to her is struck too. I start to say something reassuring to her, even if I won't believe a word of it myself, but she does something before I can speak that stops me cold.

She unbuckles her seat belt.

"What are you doing?" I shout at the top of my lungs, fighting to be heard above the hammering of the hailstones. Kelsey falls out of her seat, landing in a heap on the floor. "Sit back down! Put your seat belt on!" I yell at her.

Even though I know she must've heard me, she doesn't respond.

She gets onto her knees and turns to face the tail of the plane. I yell at her again to get back into her seat, but she still doesn't acknowledge me. The wild look in her eyes tells me that she's in such a deep state of panic that she's detached herself from all reality and isn't hearing anything I say to her. As far as she's concerned, I'm not even here.

She's in her own world.

Kelsey grabs the back of her seat, hurls her upper torso over the top of it, and vomits into the luggage area. A rancid smell immediately saturates the air inside the cabin. Macy retches, and I quickly turn my head toward her. She has become sick also, her white blouse is now soiled with her own yellowish-orange vomit.

I instinctively gag at the repulsive sights and smells and almost lose control of my own stomach, but manage to beat back my natural reaction just in time.

I scream at Kelsey again, trying to warn her. "Sit down now, and buckle your seat belt!" She's still out of it, unaware that I'm just trying to help her.

But it doesn't matter anyway.

My warning comes too late.

Another downdraft hits the plane, hurtling it toward the earth at breakneck speed. Everything inside the cabin that isn't strapped down begins to float—including Kelsey.

My assistant rises to the ceiling as if she's being levitated by a magician. The puddle of vomit that she left behind her seat disperses and splatters on everything and everyone inside the cabin.

The plane makes a sudden bank to the right, and Kelsey crashes against the side of the plane, striking her head hard against the cabin wall. Macy's stuffed bear flies by my head. The plane continues to roll onto its side. I close my eyes, not wanting to see what is about to happen, but as I feel my ponytail fall from my neck and hang below my head, I peek through squinted eyelids to see that the plane is completely inverted—the floor is now the ceiling.

And we are still falling.

Suddenly, the cacophonous noise that has been assaulting my ears loses a very important component—the plane's engine.

I'm honestly surprised that I'm even able to discern the death of a single member of the horrific symphony, but it's as if the *thump! thump!* of the propeller completing its last feeble revolutions overpowers every other sound around me. It's just me and the crippled piece of machinery, alone and together, falling through empty space.

And with its failure, I know my fate has just been sealed.

This is it. I'm not going to make it. This is how I'm going to die.

But instead of my life flashing before my eyes or seeing visions of my family members back in Oklahoma, my focus is on how I'll be remembered.

Who will sing for me when they honor my life and accomplishments at next year's awards show?

They always do something special when a fellow entertainer passes away, especially if the departed was young and the death unexpected, as will be the case with me.

This ritual normally consists of a poignant video tribute, accompanied by a soul-stirring musical performance from one of the artist's friends or contemporaries. The whole production is designed to leave the crowd solemn and watery-eyed. If the tears are heavy enough to produce vivid streaks on the makeup-covered faces, then it's all the better. Of course, the camera always zooms in on the grief-stricken for a significant amount of time, to ensure maximum effect on the audience at home.

Surely they will do the same thing for me. Won't they?

Of course they will.

After all, I'm Lauren Miller—the most recognizable female face in country music. And the reality that I'll have been cut down in the prime of life and at the top of a soaring career will mean my tragic death will garner even more attention.

What will they say about me?

Will other superstars celebrate the great talent I was, reminisce about my beautiful voice, and talk about how they just can't grasp that I am truly gone? Wish they could hear me sing just one more song? Will they lament that they've been robbed of my life and everything I would've accomplished?

But the icing on the proverbial cake will be the fact that I'll have died trying to make it back to Nashville for a scheduled studio session. Yes, they will all talk about how that was just like me . . . how I was always so dedicated to my craft.

So in this moment, falling from the sky to what I hope will be a quick and painless death, I find solace in the truth that if I must die, at least I'm going out in a way people will remember forever.

Someone will probably even write a song about me.

It's not that I want to die. I don't. Not at all. But even dead, I'll still be famous—and with that reality fortified in my mind, I find comfort.

The sound of Adam screaming and grunting as he tries to right the plane snaps me away from my thoughts. The nose tilts over, positioning the aircraft in a steep inverted dive. Another loud groan from him and the plane begins to slowly rotate back to the left, until we are once again right-side up. Kelsey drops to the floor, limp and motionless, as Adam pulls the plane out of the dive and levels it off.

The hail and thunder cease.

An eerie silence descends over the cabin, the only sound the whistling of the wind as it rushes by the cracked windows of our stricken plane.

Adam shatters the calm. "We aren't going to make it!" he screams in a cracking, grunting voice. "I love you, Macy! I love you, Juliette! Here we go!"

"Mommy!" Macy screams.

Juliette yells back to her daughter, "Momma loves you, baby!" She turns and strains against the seat belt, extending her left arm backward in an effort to reach Macy's outstretched hand, but her fingertips only come within a few inches of Macy's.

Adam lets out another loud, straining groan as he pulls back on the yoke and fights to bring the nose up and slow the plane before impact. "Here we go!" he screams again, his words a death knell. "Hang on . . . HANG ON!"

Kelsey isn't moving, still lying frozen on the floor.

Macy is crying and still trying to grasp her mother's hand. I scream to her, "Macy! Do what I do!" Her eyes fix on me, and I don't waste another second. I bring my arms to the side of my face, interlock my fingers behind my head, and bend over until the tips of my elbows touch my knees. I plant my chin firmly against my chest.

My heart races. My breath has been stolen from me.

The wings of the plane smash against treetops, sending a horrendous vibration through the cabin.

I grip my hands tighter behind my head as the shaking intensifies, my whole body straining against the belt that holds me in place.

A ghastly screeching slices through the air.

The piercing sound of the aircraft crashing against the trees grows so intense, so utterly unbearable, that if I were able, I'd pierce my own eardrums just to make it stop. It's unlike anything I've heard before. It's horrible . . . unworldly . . . a terrifying concoction of sheet metal being ripped apart and tree limbs shattering into a thousand tiny pieces.

My teeth knock violently against one another, and I clench my jaw tightly to hold them together.

The sound of Kelsey being slammed repeatedly about the cabin urges me to look up—but I don't dare raise my head even an inch.

I keep my chin down and my elbows pinned to my knees.

And I wait for impact.

This is it.

The end of everything . . .

5

I'm aware of my own consciousness, but nothing more.
I have no idea what time, or even what day, it is. My mind is clouded, as if someone has placed a black veil over my brain, and I can't remember how I came to be lying flat on my back.

All I know is that I'm cold.

And wet.

The back of my head is pounding, shooting rivers of pain around the sides of my face and down my spine. I let out a soft moan—it's all I can manage.

My eyes are closed, but I'm afraid to open them. Although I can't remember specifically what has happened to me, I know whatever it is, it isn't good.

And I'm not at all sure I want to find out.

A bird chirps, drawing me further out of the darkness. Finally, I try to force my eyelids open, but they react the same way as when I'm awakened from a nap too soon, rising in flickering jerks before slamming shut again. Another try meets the same result. On my third attempt, my eyelids open halfway and remain there.

Light beats against my pupils, and I immediately have a strong urge to close my eyes again to shield them from the painful brightness. But I stop myself from doing so, afraid that I might not be able to open them a second time.

I lie on the ground and allow my eyes to adjust. Once they do, I find myself staring up into a thick forest canopy. Blankets of green leaves are being permeated by rays of sunlight that fall to the ground and across my face. My entire body is shivering, my wet clothing drawing heat away from my skin, so I'm grateful for the little warmth the broken rays of sun provide.

I slowly turn my head to the left. It hurts. My neck muscles are so sore that they fight against even this small motion.

Trees stretch endlessly before me, and a blanket of brown leaf litter covers the forest floor.

I move my head back until I'm once again staring at the leafy dome above me and pause to let the muscles in my neck relax. A deep breath causes another sharp pain to radiate through my chest. I resist the urge to turn my head to the right, because if whatever has caused me to be in this position isn't on my left side, then it must be on my right.

And a big part of me doesn't want to know, as if my own denial will spare me from an awful truth. I fight against my mind's curiosity as long as I can but eventually realize I must look.

I exhale slowly and gently tilt my head to the right, again fighting my tense muscles, which seem frozen, but I persist until the landscape on my right side is visible.

A crashed airplane lies across from me. Its nose resembles a crushed aluminum can against the base of a giant oak tree, a twisted mess of sheet metal and wood. The body is covered with large dents, as if someone has repeatedly hit it with a baseball bat. The wing on the right side is completely torn off, and I spot it lying thirty yards down the mountain, mangled and broken. The fuselage is ripped apart where the wing should be attached, creating a gaping hole in the side. I squint, trying to see inside the cabin, but it's obscured by the shadows of the surrounding large trees, denying me a clear view.

I remember Kelsey being on the plane with me, but for some reason, I can't determine exactly *why* we were on this particular aircraft in the first place. It's not the jet I normally use. This plane is much smaller.

I recall being at a concert as well, but beyond that, my mind is a blank sheet. I struggle to recollect exactly what happened, what caused the plane in front of me to crash, but my memories are fuzzy, indistinct, as if someone has sprayed my brain with Silly String, and I simply can't remember.

Is Kelsey somewhere nearby?

If so, I need her help. I try to speak, attempt to yell toward the plane and summon her, but my voice fails me. I can only manage a disappointing, soft whimper. I try again with the same result. It's no use. I'm unable to call loudly enough for anyone to hear me, so I stop even trying. My body is simply too exhausted.

How did I even manage to get out of the plane?

I'm not sure of the answer to that question either. But I must've somehow crawled through the hole that was created in the side of the fuselage during the crash. That's the only logical explanation as to why I'm lying on the ground several yards away.

My throat is dry and scratchy. I swallow, but it doesn't help. I desperately need a drink of water, but there's none here.

Turning my head away from the plane and staring again at the dense tree canopy above me, I close my eyes and drift off into the black world where I was before.

6

I want to stay in the darkness—it's comforting . . . safe.

But something keeps drawing me away from it—a shrill, annoying sound that I just wish would stop. Trying to ignore it doesn't work, because every time I'm about to drift off again, the strange noise returns and snatches me away from sleep. It's a fierce tug-of-war between the sound outside, which seems to be fighting for my attention, and my brain, which simply wants rest.

I struggle to push it away, refusing to open my eyes, hoping that the darkness will take me again.

But the sound won't be quelled.

It keeps coming, again and again. In both intermittent, rapid bursts and slow, mournful sobs, it persists.

What is that? Just shut up already!

But the sound doesn't heed my pleas; instead, it keeps fighting for my attention like an annoying bee buzzing incessantly around my head.

My eyes finally flutter open, and I find myself looking straight above me, into the green umbrella. The sun is directly overhead now, and the air is much warmer than before. Flat on my back, a breeze blows across my cheek.

The sound rings in my ears again. It's coming from my right side.

I turn my head toward the plane. Seeing the crashed aircraft for a second time draws forth snippets of terrorizing memories.

The turbulence.

The lightning.

The hail.

And falling.

I squeeze my eyes closed to block the sight of the wreckage and hopefully banish the flashbacks too.

Suddenly, the penetrating sound echoes through the forest again, as if it's jealous I'm fixated on the memories of the crash instead of focused on it.

And it works.

Now fully alert, I recognize the sound immediately.

Someone is crying.

My eyes fly open, but nothing seems different than before. The same gaping hole in the side of the fuselage dominates my view. I gaze intently into it, but there's nothing discernible inside, only darkness. No movement that might indicate a person is inside.

Nothing.

The cry comes again, and this time, there's no doubt that it's originating from inside the plane.

The realization that someone else is alive sends my spirits soaring. It sounds like Kelsey. Hopefully, she's in better shape than I am and can help me.

"Kel—Kelsey," I mumble, but my throat is so dry now that my voice is barely audible. I try again. "Kelsey!" My second effort proves much stronger, and I think she might've actually heard me this time. I listen for a reply, but none comes. I call her name again, but the only response I get is the same irritating cry from inside the plane. Despite my hope, it's obvious that she can't hear me.

I attempt to roll over, but my body immediately screams at me to stop. Every muscle above my waist is on fire. My neck and shoulders feel as if someone's beaten them with a hammer.

I return to my back, and again stare up at the green leaves and the rays of sun that penetrate into the forest through the small openings in the foliage. I take a deep breath, trying to work up the nerve to try again. My mind tells me I have to move, but my body begs me to stay put.

The cry from the plane comes again.

I have to move, even if it's excruciating, and I decide that it's better to just do it quickly and get it over with. Gritting my teeth, I roll off my back and onto my forearms and knees in one swift, agonizing movement. "Aaaggghhhh!"

My head swims and dizziness overtakes me. I remain motionless, too afraid to move any farther, my arms and legs trembling in misery. My heart races as beads of sweat pop out on my brow. I gasp for air and fight through the pain. I know I can't retreat to the ground, back to a more comfortable position, because if I do, I might never find the courage to move again.

I take my time and allow my body to adjust. Gradually, my heart rate slows and the pain-induced vertigo clears from my head.

I'm going to attempt to crawl to the plane. I have to. It's the only option. I don't even want to think about trying to walk right now. If I just take it easy, I'll be able to deal with the discomfort . . . I hope.

I timidly move my right knee forward a small distance. Now my left forearm in the same direction. I repeat the motion with my left leg and right arm. My muscles are so tense and sore that it takes several seconds for me to complete even one simple movement. The pain returns, shooting from my neck to my toes.

I wince, bite my lip, and repeat the motions.

The ground is drenched from last night's storm, and my legs and arms quickly become covered with a gluey mixture of dirt and wet leaves as I move forward. The back of my sweatshirt and my hair are soaked too, thanks to the fact that I've been lying on the forest floor since the crash.

I keep moving, inching closer to the downed aircraft with each forward push of my arms and legs. The air is so humid from the recent rainfall I can almost taste it, and I begin to perspire heavily. A bead of sweat rolls off my forehead and into my left eye, causing a sharp, burning sensation. I blink three times to clear it away and keep going.

Another sound comes from the aircraft's cabin, but this time it's just a muffled sob. I continue moving forward, each foot gained seeming to lessen the stiffness in my muscles and joints.

I draw to within twenty feet of the gaping hole in the side of the plane and stop. The sobs are muted now, barely audible. "Hello?" I say. "Kelsey, are you okay?"

The cries from inside stop.

The potent smell of spilled aircraft fuel burns my nostrils. The ground around where the right wing separated from the fuselage is soaked with it. It's a miracle the whole plane wasn't engulfed in a giant fireball when we crashed.

I inch forward and pause again. A startling thought invades my mind. It occurs to me that I may come across something inside the wreckage I don't want to find.

What if there are dead bodies inside?

I don't want to see that. Besides Kelsey, I can't recall who else was on board the plane, though I know there had to be at least a pilot with us. But what if there are more? What if there are a *bunch* of dead people? I don't know if I'd be able to handle such a thing.

On top of it all, I still have no idea what I was doing on this plane to begin with, even though I'm desperately trying to remember. But I *do* know that someone inside is crying, and that means no matter how hesitant I am to look inside the wreckage, I must.

I slowly crawl until I'm at the edge of the fuselage. The plane is leaning slightly toward me with the floor of the cabin at ground level. "Hello?" I say tentatively into the black void of the cabin. "Kelsey?"

There's no response.

I'm frustrated . . . and a little scared too, I guess. I so wish she would just acknowledge me. Simply hearing her voice would ease the gnawing anxiety in my gut, make me confident I'm not about to find her dead. I call her name again.

Silence is my only reply.

7

I *am* scared now—there's no use in pretending otherwise any longer.

Seeing the wreckage from a distance was one thing, but being this close to it, staring into the blackness of the passenger cabin, not knowing what awaits me inside, is terrifying.

Even though I'm frightened of what I'll find, there's at least one other person inside who's alive, which leaves me no choice.

I ease my head past the torn sheet metal where the tail section has been partially separated from the main fuselage. It's dark inside, and it takes a few seconds for my eyes to adjust.

The interior of the cabin finally comes into focus, and I glance to my right, toward the cockpit. Two bodies occupy the seats at the front of the plane, and it's immediately obvious they are dead. The impact with the large oak tree had caved the nose of the aircraft in completely, driving the engine backward and crushing the two individuals as they sat in their seats. Their bodies are mangled and distorted, their heads twisted back at a gruesome angle. I can tell one is a man and the other a woman, but I don't recognize them.

I quickly avert my eyes from the horrible sight and stare at the floor of the plane for a moment, struggling to compose myself. The only other time I've seen a dead body was at my grandmother's funeral. But this is a completely different situation. This is experiencing death head-on—raw, unfiltered, and without the aid of a skilled mortician.

Then the smell overtakes me. It's a nauseating mixture of blood, urine, and feces. Someone has vomited too. All of it blends into a sickening brew with the warm, humid air. My head spins and I gag. I try to stop my body's reaction to the dreadful odor, but I'm unable to stave off the inevitable. I retch and vomit on the floor.

The sudden contraction of my midsection sends another river of pain through my body. I cry out and try to stop it, but the retching continues until there's nothing left in my stomach.

The agonizing episode causes my breaths to come in short, rapid bursts. My lips quiver as I moan and try to catch my breath. I wipe my mouth on the sleeve of my sweatshirt, leaving residue of my stomach contents on the fabric.

As I lift my head, I notice Kelsey crumpled into a ball against the left side of the plane, her right arm twisted and pinned behind her neck in an unnatural manner. "Kelsey?" I say softly. She doesn't move at all, not even a flinch.

I scramble on my hands and knees toward her. A piece of broken glass punctures my left palm as I slide my hands across the floor of the plane. I wince at the sharp sting, but keep moving.

I crawl beside her and place my hand under her chin. Shaking her face, I try to get her to acknowledge me. "Kelsey! We crashed. Wake up!" But she still doesn't respond. I slap her hard on both cheeks. Nothing. I jostle her again, but notice something odd this time.

Her body is stiff and cold.

As I gaze into her lifeless, pale face, I have another flashback of the flight. My mind plays the scene back for me as if it's a movie—Kelsey taking her seat belt off, then being thrown violently around the cabin just prior to the crash. The memory is sharp and painful, and more tangible than I can bear. I gasp and retreat from her.

I have to get out! Now!

I scurry backwards as fast as I can and scoot out of the plane the same way I came in, through the hole torn in the fuselage. Outside, away from the polluted, stale air of the aircraft, I suck in oxygen, desperate to clear not only my lungs, but also my mind from what I've just seen.

The realization that Kelsey is dead sends a wave of panic through me. I try to slow my breathing and stave off the desire to freak out, but short, intense wheezes is all I can manage.

As I fight to regain control of my own body, it feels as if I'm once again back inside the plane just before the crash, falling helplessly toward the earth. The panic is winning. Part of me *wants* it to win. After all, why shouldn't I panic? I have every reason to. I've just been in a plane crash, and I have no idea where I am. Even worse, I am the only survivor.

I'm alone.

That fact—that I'm truly alone and without help—scares me more than anything else.

Another sob from inside the plane. How is that possible? Everyone inside is dead. But something or someone is still making the same sound that drew me from my sleep and toward the wreckage in the first place. The shock of seeing Kelsey's dead body caused me to temporarily forget about the noise, but it's still here.

I lean closer to the opening I just exited in a terrified rush. "Hello?"

Another soft cry comes from inside.

Sticking my head back through the gaping hole in the fuselage, I again say, "Hello?"

Another sob rings through the darkness of the plane, but this time it's clear that it originated from my right side. I turn my head slowly, glaring into the shadows.

A small, blonde-haired girl is still strapped into a passenger seat.

8

I gasp at the sight of her.

Tears are running down the girl's face, and her lower lip is quivering uncontrollably. It takes a moment for the reality of her presence to sink in. I don't know what to say or do. I'm absolutely frozen.

What *can* I say? It's not as if I've been in this situation before.

I remain speechless, trying to think of something comforting to say to this little girl in front of me, but all I can come up with seems underwhelming. "Hi . . . I'm . . . Lauren," I say in a hesitant voice. "What's your name?"

She looks at me with sad eyes, but doesn't speak.

I scour my foggy memory, trying to recall who the young girl is and what she was doing on the flight with me, but I'm unable to find a reasonable answer. It simply makes no sense that the two of us were traveling together.

A memory of meeting a family at the airport seizes me—Adam and Juliette, wasn't it?

A picture of a little girl flashes in my mind. She's blonde and shy. She's hiding her face in her mother's blue dress.

I again look closely at the girl who's strapped into the aircraft seat in front of me. She's dressed in a white blouse and a red skirt with leggings underneath. Black Mary Janes cover her feet. Although the crash has affected her appearance—her hair is disheveled and out of place—I recognize her as the same girl in my memory, the one I met on the tarmac with her parents.

I was at a wedding? Yes. A wedding. That's right . . . I think. I was singing for a group of people . . . a bride and groom were there. I remember them. Then I was at the airport with Kelsey. An urgent feeling of having to return to Nashville.

As I focus on the little girl's face, the cobwebs clear from my mind.

Closing my eyes, I grimace as the memories of the thunderstorm, the awful turbulence and hail, the lightning, all of it, come back in a surging flood. Kelsey is flying around the cabin, unrestrained, everyone is screaming, the blonde girl is crying.

Her name is? It starts with . . . M? Yes, an M, I'm fairly certain of that. Is it Ma—? Macy? I believe that's right.

I open my eyes to find her still staring at me with fear in hers. "Macy? Isn't your name Macy?"

She nods softly.

I let out a sigh of relief at knowing my mind is still intact. "Good. My name's Lauren," I say, introducing myself for the second time. I extend my hand to her, but she just sits there, her own hands locked in a tight grip across her lap. She eyes me with suspicion, and I lower my hand slowly. "Okay, you're shy. I get that. I don't like people much myself."

She just drops her head and stares at the floor.

"We need to get you out of the plane, okay?" I crawl toward her and try to release the seat belt that still restrains her, but quickly realize that the buckle is jammed against the small center console that separates the two aft-facing seats.

I shove my hand between the seat and console, trying to reach the locking mechanism, but can't. The console was warped during the crash, shifting it toward Macy's seat, and my hand is too large to fit into the tight space. I try again, stretching and wiggling my fingers in an attempt to reach the buckle, but it's no use.

Macy sobs again.

I know she must be terrified, but I don't have time to stop and console her. I have to find a way to free her. I rack my brain, trying to think of something I can use to cut the belt. Surely there's a knife or something else sharp on board . . . but, if there is, I have no idea where to find it.

I keep thinking.

My makeup kit.

"Wait just a minute," I say to Macy. "I have an idea." I turn and crawl across the cabin floor, dodging pieces of torn sheet metal and broken glass.

I'm in good physical shape, and normally, squeezing between the two aircraft seats Kelsey and I occupied during the flight wouldn't be a big deal, but my sore muscles fight against my every move. Taking a few deep breaths to chase away the blinding pain, I place my hands against the back of the seats and try again. This time, I manage to pull myself into the small storage area where Adam strapped down the luggage prior to taking off.

Fortunately, this area of the plane has suffered the least amount of damage, and I quickly release the ratchet strap that runs across the top of the bags, and toss it out of the way. My carry-on is on top. I unzip it and shove my hand inside, searching for the makeup kit. I feel the familiar plastic case against my fingers and withdraw it. Tucking it under my left armpit, I weave my way back between the seats. I crawl back to Macy, but I'm gasping for air and weak, the short trip to the rear of the plane leaving me exhausted.

Opening the makeup kit, I retrieve the nail clippers and the file. I fling the case to the floor, because concealer and eyeshadow will be of no use to me in the middle of the woods.

"I'm going to have to cut your seat belt, okay?" I tell Macy. She nods, but looks dubious of the plan. "It's going to be fine. I promise I'll be careful."

The best place to cut the belt appears to be right above where it disappears between the seat cushion and the console. The belt is taut in this location, and it's clear of Macy's hip, which lessens the chance that I'll slip and cut her.

Grabbing the lap belt with my left hand, I begin to snip and tear at the webbing with the curved blades of the clippers. I pull and pry and cut at it until I've managed to create a small slit at the top of the belt. The work is tedious, the material refusing to tear easily in response to my work with the small pair of nail clippers, but I keep at it until the tear is big enough for the nail file to slip into. I set the clippers down and try to cut through the seat belt with the file, but the webbing is much too tough, as if I'm attempting to saw through an oak stump with a butter knife. I drop the file and begin working with the clippers again.

It takes a long time to cut through the belt, but when it's finally in two pieces, I feel a great sense of accomplishment and shout, "Yes! I did it!"

Macy doesn't react to my victory at all. She's proving to be even more of an introvert than I am. But I guess I can't blame her; I'm sure she's terrified too.

The shoulder belt is independent of the lap belt, but, thankfully, there's enough slack in it that I won't have to cut through it too. I pull against the shoulder belt, gently working it up and over Macy's chest and head. I let out a sigh of relief and say, "Okay, you're free. Let's go."

She finally speaks, but it isn't the response that I'm expecting. Instead of being grateful for my help, she is defiant. "No."

"What?"

"No," she repeats in a soft, broken voice. "I can't leave Mommy and Daddy. When they wake up they won't know where I am."

My heart sinks.

I don't know what to say. I don't want to tell the girl her parents are dead, but I also can't let her stay here. It's not safe. So I decide to try to lure her out. "Why don't you come outside with me? It's much nicer out there. We can play in the woods and sing a song together. Do you like to sing?"

She shakes her head.

My attempt to convince her to come with me sounded completely silly, of course, and I'm sure that if I were in her shoes, it wouldn't work on me either.

But my patience is wearing thin.

I've just spent the last half hour using precious energy I'll need later freeing a girl I barely know, just to have my efforts go unappreciated. I remember thinking the girl was a little brat when I first met her at the airport because she wouldn't talk to me. Maybe I was right.

"Macy, we have to go!" My voice sounds harsh and angry.

She still doesn't budge.

Exasperated and tired of trying to coax her outside, I grab her by the armpits and lift her out of the seat, the strain sending another shooting pain through my chest and shoulders. I collapse to the floor and she falls on top of me, landing right on my sternum. I scream out. Now, I'm really mad. "We are going outside whether you want to or not, do you understand?" I tell her firmly.

Her blue eyes narrow in defiance.

I don't care.

Pushing her off of me, I manage to roll onto my side, which causes another bout of agony. I take a deep breath and bite my lower lip. Without waiting for her to protest further, I grasp her by the hand and start crawling toward the opening in the fuselage.

She whimpers and cries as we move along. "Mommy! Daddy!"

I keep going, dragging her behind me.

I tried to be nice to her, but that didn't work, so now I'm doing things my way. I'm desperate to be out of this metallic coffin once and for all, and if Macy had any sense, she'd want that too.

We break through the opening, leaving the aircraft behind, and crawl out into the forest. I take a deep breath of the clean mountain air, purging my lungs of the stench of death and vomit.

I lead Macy downhill and well away from the crash site before I collapse from exhaustion.

Lying back against the sloped terrain of the mountain, I rest my head in a thick pile of dead, wet leaves. "Lie down," I order her. She obeys and stretches out on the ground an arm's length from me. She's still crying, and I just wish she would shut up.

Doesn't she know this is no picnic for me either?

I try to take my mind off of her. Staring blankly into the trees above, I struggle to clear my head and come to terms with what's happened to me. Before now, my mind was focused on trying to remember the events of last night, getting inside the plane to investigate the cries, and then getting Macy safely out of the wreckage. The reality that I'd been in a plane crash hadn't even fully sunk in.

But now it does.

And it terrifies me.

Surrounding me, there's nothing but dense wilderness, and I feel alone and lost and scared. I'm in pain and utterly exhausted.

I just want to sleep.

It's noticeably darker outside than when I first ventured into the wreckage, and the sunlight is quickly retreating from the forest. There won't be usable light much longer.

The dryness in the back of my throat returns. I guess it's been there the whole time, but I was so focused on getting to the plane and then rescuing Macy, that my mind must've blocked out my body's desperate need of fluids. But now it feels as if my whole mouth is a parched desert. I have to find water soon.

But I have no energy left to search.

A large clump of bright green moss is growing on top of a rock just to my right. I peel off a large section and hold it in my hand. It's wet from last night's rain.

I can't believe I'm about to suck on dirty, nasty moss.

But the desperate and growing need for some form of moisture inside my mouth overpowers my disgust.

I raise the moss to my lips and suck.

My mouth is instantly filled with a stale, earthy flavor that shocks my taste buds. The sensation is so repulsive that I have to fight against the urge to immediately spit it out. But I keep going, pulling from several different spots on the clump and gleaning a few precious drops of moisture from it. It's certainly not as much water as I need, but it's enough to wet my mouth and the back of my throat.

Even as revolting as the act itself was, it's a victory. Perhaps the slight easing of my thirst will allow me to get some rest tonight.

I wipe my teeth clean with the inside of my filthy sweatshirt and tear another piece of moss from the rock and offer it to Macy. "Suck on this," I tell her. "There's water in it."

She wrinkles her nose, obviously appalled by the idea.

"Fine." I toss the moss away, aggravated.

Macy has stopped sobbing, but her eyes are still filled with tears. I figure that if she still has enough water in her body to form tears, then she isn't dangerously dehydrated. I'm not at all sure I'm right about this, but there's nothing more I can do for her now. I'll have to find water tomorrow, though. Sucking on moss just isn't going to cut it—for me or for her.

"I lost Mr. Pebbles," she says in a timid, almost inaudible voice.

"What?"

"I lost Mr. Pebbles."

I have no idea whom she is talking about. I try to recall if there was another passenger on the plane with us, but come up empty. Did I somehow miss another body inside the wreckage? I don't think so. Too tired to think about it anymore, I give up. "Who in the world is Mr. Pebbles?"

"I lost him last night when the plane was shaking really bad."

The memory of a stuffed bear flying past my head during the storm comes to me, and I realize that must be what she is talking about. "Your bear? You lost your stuffed bear?"

"Yeah. His name is Mr. Pebbles. I think he's still inside the plane. He helps me sleep. Can we go get him?"

Her request causes something to register in my brain that, up until now, I haven't considered. Not only am I lost in the wilderness with no idea where I am, no food or water, and no suitable shelter . . . but I'm now also responsible for a little girl who appears to be only six or seven years old.

Great . . . just great.

Why is this happening to me?

I know nothing about caring for kids. The truth is, I really don't like them at all. I didn't even babysit as a teenager to make extra money because I couldn't stand to be around their crying and their tantrums.

"Can we go get Mr. Pebbles?" Macy asks again softly, begging me to do a useless errand I have no energy for. "Please?" she whimpers.

I'm so worn out I can barely move. No way am I trekking back to the plane and searching through that dark, vile-smelling cabin for some stupid stuffed animal. "We'll get him tomorrow."

"But I need him tonight. I can't go to sleep without him," she says flatly.

"No!" I snap. As soon as the word leaves my mouth, Macy looks as if she is about to start crying again, and I definitely don't need that. "I'm sorry," I say in a calmer tone, trying to keep her from bursting into tears. "I'm just too tired to go back tonight. I promise I'll find him for you tomorrow. Just try to relax and go to sleep."

She sighs. "Okay, I guess that will be all right. Besides, I bet when Mommy wakes up, she'll bring Mr. Pebbles to me." She pauses. "Don't you think so?"

"Maybe," I reply.

9

I'm already awake as the first glimmer of daylight scatters through the trees and into the forest. It's Monday morning. I've always hated Mondays, but this one really stinks.

I barely slept at all. I think maybe I dozed off for a few minutes four or five times, but that's about it. I'm even more exhausted than I was last night when I first lay down.

Trying to sleep on the ground sucks—it's cold, wet, and hard. I'd gladly give a small fortune for a good, comfortable mattress right now.

And then there are the bugs. Hundreds of them. They tortured me all night, biting at my flesh and crawling all over my exposed skin. It was a constant battle to keep them at bay—swatting at them wildly with my hands—and it was a battle I lost. My face, neck, and hands are covered with mosquito bites that itch like crazy. I try not to scratch at them, but at times the urge is so great that I'm unable to stop myself from it.

The back of my sweatshirt is soaked through, the cotton fabric frigid against my skin. My hair and face are both damp too, covered with the heavy dew that's coating everything in the forest with a million tiny drops of water.

I wish that during my trip inside the plane wreckage yesterday, I would've thought to search for something that could serve as a moisture barrier between me and the ground, like a blanket, but I was so focused on getting Macy out of the plane that I didn't take time to consider anything else.

Macy has rolled onto her side and is now facing away from me. Her small rib cage moves up and down as she breathes. I wonder if she is really asleep or if she is just as cold and restless as I am.

A shiver runs across the little girl's arms and back. Even though it's June, the air in the woods is still very chilly during the nights and early mornings. Add to the mix humidity so thick you can almost cut it, along with the lack of any suitable shelter, and it's just a downright wretched experience.

I turn my head back toward the brightening sky. A mixture of purple and crimson bursts through the small holes in the leafy roof as the sun begins to rise. It's actually quite beautiful. It's the kind of day that I would normally take advantage of. I would go for an early morning jog or simply relax and enjoy a cup of coffee on the back deck of my house in Brentwood.

But this isn't a normal day. I wish it were, but it's not.

Seeing this sunrise, here in this place and from the perspective of a plane crash survivor, the natural scenery just underscores my feelings of isolation and helplessness.

One thing is for certain: My money and fame mean nothing in the wilderness. The mountains couldn't care less who I am or how rich I've become. Out here, I am a pauper. I have nothing.

I'm scared.

And I'm cold.

My muscles still ache from the crash, my stomach feels as if it's about to eat itself, and my mouth is screaming for a real drink of water rather than just a few drops from dirty moss.

But maybe I won't be stranded much longer. Someone will find me soon. Right?

Of course they will. They have to—I'm Lauren Miller, superstar.

My disappearance is probably already plastered over every cable news channel, and reporters are undoubtedly scratching out stories on the massive search effort that is now underway. This makes me feel better.

But my optimism is fleeting.

I recall the fact that my own plane broke down the night of the wedding and was unable to fly back to Nashville. That's why Kelsey and I ended up on the flight with Adam, Juliette, and Macy.

I also remember having a conversation with Steve, my pilot, on the tarmac. But did I tell him that we were going to fly home in another plane? I rack my brain, trying to glean from my memory the details of our conversation. The answer comes to me, and it makes my heart jolt.

Not only did I not tell Steve about the change in plans, I told no one at all.

I told Steve that Kelsey and I might hitch a ride with someone who was driving back to Nashville and left it at that, then he returned to the inside of the plane to finish up his work. Right after that, Kelsey noticed Adam and his family pulling up to their aircraft. She ran off to talk to them and I followed her. I never saw or spoke to Steve again.

My band won't know anything has happened to me, because they drove back on the tour bus, just as usual, and they expected me to be on my own private aircraft. None of them even knew there was a mechanical problem with the jet, because Kelsey only found out about it as we were en route to the airport.

The realization that no one knew of our last-minute change of plans, leads me to one inescapable conclusion—none of my staff has any idea that I was with Adam and his family aboard the doomed airplane.

I shudder at the revelation.

What if I'm never found?

I can't think like that. I have to stay optimistic.

Maybe the situation isn't completely hopeless. I recall the reason I was in such a rush to get back to Nashville in the first place—the recording session in the studio. The session was scheduled for yesterday morning, and surely, when Kelsey and I didn't show up, someone tried to locate us. They must have.

But what if everyone else at the studio just assumed I overslept after a long night, and instead of being concerned for my safety, they became pissed at me for wasting their time?

The fact that Kelsey also wasn't there wouldn't have raised any eyebrows, because she is always with me. They would've simply thought she was at my house trying to get me to the studio on time.

It wouldn't have been the first time I blew off my schedule without explanation.

Sometimes I just don't feel like going to the studio early in the morning and stay in bed instead. It's a rare occurrence, but it has happened more than once.

Did everyone simply chalk up my absence to me being me?

Over the last couple of years, I have earned a reputation around Nashville of being difficult to work with, so it's definitely possible. As much as I don't want to admit it to myself, it's not unreasonable to believe that no one contacted the authorities or even tried to locate me yesterday.

Even though I fully intended to be on time for this particular studio session, because the pressure on me to complete the upcoming album has been growing for weeks, the others I work with may not have recognized this.

But there were three consecutive days of session work scheduled, the second of which is this morning. That detail brings me a little peace, because I know for a fact that when I don't show up today, someone will try to locate me. I've never missed two sessions in a row, and my absence today will certainly raise red flags.

Of course, the disappearance of *any* plane, even the single-engine one I was flying in with Adam and his family, will cause a search to be initiated, but without the knowledge that a celebrity was on board, it will not garner the media attention and public pressure that it will once that fact comes to light. Once known, the searchers will be forced to provide daily updates to the media concerning the effort to find me, and the added scrutiny will cause them to conduct a more thorough and intense search. At least I hope that's the case.

Any advantage my fame gains me in this situation, is a bonus.

But due to my previous lackadaisical schedule keeping, it's certainly possible, even likely I would say, that the fact I was aboard the now-missing aircraft won't be discovered until sometime later today. It will take a while for my people back in Nashville to connect the dots to the missing plane and my simultaneous disappearance. I want to believe they figured it out yesterday, when I failed to make the first studio session, but I know that's probably just wishful thinking.

And even after they determine what happened to me, it will still take more time for the search to be ramped up.

Time I might not have.

I've already gone well over twenty-four hours without water, except for the trivial amount I gathered from the moss. I know that after three days without water the human body is in serious trouble.

What am I going to do?

I'm not the outdoors type, not at all. I trek through high-end boutiques in Nashville on weekends, not through the middle of the woods.

The *only* time I've ever slept outside was when I was eight years old and my brother, Luke, decided he wanted to give camping a try. After some coaxing, I agreed to give it a shot too, and the two of us set up a tent that belonged to our father behind the house. But after that miserable night in the hot, humid air of Northeastern Oklahoma, I decided it would be best if, in the future, I spent my nights inside an air-conditioned room and on top of a comfortable mattress.

But now I'm in a much more serious situation than just a backyard campout, where the safety of home is just a few yards away. I'm lost in the mountains. Really lost. There's no sign of civilization anywhere. Only trees ... and more trees. No, I'm not at all prepared for something such as this. I can't do it. There's just no way.

My mind runs wild. What if the rescuers don't find me in time? What does it feel like to die from dehydration anyway? What if the lack of food and water causes me to go crazy and I do something stupid that dooms me? Will I even know I'm screwing up before it's too late?

If I'm not found, will I die a slow, painful death or a quick one?

Sudden, penetrating panic seizes my core and races down my extremities. I sit bolt upright, ignoring the shooting pain that the movement causes, and scream at the top of my lungs.

"HELP!" I yell. "I need help! Is anyone out there? Please help me! Someone! Anyone! HELP!" My voice rips through the dense forest, bounces off nearby hillsides, and returns to me in a sickening, empty echo.

I scream again and wait desperately for a response, but, just as before, none comes.

Defeated, I fall back to the wet earth.

Macy, stirred by my outburst, sits up and looks at me with startled and confused eyes. "What's wrong?"

I sigh. "Nothing. Just go back to sleep."

She lies back down and doesn't ask any more questions, which I'm thankful for. I don't want to talk to her right now. I imagine she is full of questions, just like any normal child in this situation would be, but I don't have answers to any of them.

Where are we? When can we go home? When are Mommy and Daddy going to wake up?

I huff. I simply can't believe this is happening to me.

The unenviable task of telling a young girl that her parents aren't just asleep but are, in reality, dead, has fallen on my shoulders. I wonder how long I can hold off the inevitable.

I've never been in a situation like this, and I have no idea how one even goes about delivering such horrible news to a little girl.

If Kelsey were still here, I'd make her do it. But she's not here, and sooner rather than later, the subject will come up and I'll have to tell Macy the truth.

What's the best way to do it?

I have no clue.

Should I do it quickly, like ripping off a Band-Aid, or should I sit her down and gently walk her through what happened?

The truth is . . . there is no *best* way.

And because of this, I decide to simply wait until the difficult question is forced upon me and deal with it then. Go with whatever my gut tells me to do in the moment.

I clear away the thoughts of the grim and awkward task that lies ahead of me, and try to focus on the more important issue.

What am I going to do in order to survive long enough for rescuers to find me?

First, I need to stop focusing on all the obstacles and concentrate on the positive instead. I must reinforce to myself that even though I have no training or supplies, I can survive out here just as long as I keep trying.

What a load of crap.

I sound like some idiot self-help guru.

Okay, so maybe I don't have to lie to myself about my wilderness skills and think that everything's going to work out just peachy, but if I'm to survive this, I do know that I need to look at the situation analytically and try not to let my emotions take over—think with my head, not my heart.

Yeah, right.

Sure, that sounds great in theory, but my bet is that during an experience such as this, emotional detachment will prove virtually impossible.

There is no easy way. None.

I'll just have to take each problem as it arises and deal with it the best that I can . . . and hope that I don't make a stupid decision that ends up costing us our lives. It's all I can do, really.

I need a plan—a list of things to accomplish. I'm good with lists. I can do lists.

But the first thing I need to determine before I can make a solid plan is how long we're going to be stranded here. That will give me a goal—something to shoot for and help keep my mind focused.

Of course, I don't know if I can even come close to making an accurate estimate of how long it will take rescuers to find us, but even if I miscalculate, just creating a mental timeline will give me something to work toward.

So I begin to brainstorm.

Even if the search doesn't get ramped up until later today, I can't imagine it will take a large search party more than two days, three at the most, to find us. That's not so bad. I can make it that long. Sure, it will be miserable and difficult . . . but survivable.

But I feel as though I'm not considering everything I should be, that I'm missing something. I focus intently and try to determine what I could've possibly overlooked. The answer comes to me in a flash and brands my mind with the hot iron of reality.

I haven't heard another aircraft since the crash.

And this fact troubles me for one very important reason.

I don't know a lot about airplanes. My familiarity with them is limited to using them to fly from one location to another, but I've watched enough news coverage of past crashes to know that planes are equipped with an onboard emergency transponder which, in the event of a crash, emits a distress signal so that rescuers can quickly locate the aircraft.

Why didn't I think of this yesterday?

I was too rattled from the crash and wasn't thinking clearly, that's why. But now that the fuzziness has cleared from my brain, I wonder why someone hasn't found us yet. The weather has been good since the night of the crash. From what I could see through the trees, the sky was crystal clear yesterday.

Terrifying thoughts assault my mind.

What if the plane doesn't even have an emergency transponder?

Or what if it does and it has malfunctioned?

Without the aid of a beacon, how will anyone know where we are?

The answer to my last question is obvious—they won't.

The crash was well over twenty-four hours ago. If a beacon had been sending out an emergency signal for searchers to home in on ever since, as it is designed to do, then there's no logical reason someone hasn't already located the crash site, celebrity or no celebrity aboard.

So either the aircraft didn't have an emergency transponder to begin with, or it has malfunctioned. Neither scenario is good news.

There's nothing I can do about it, though. I don't even know what an emergency transponder looks like. I've just heard about them on TV, so there's no way I can try to fix it. I wouldn't even know where to begin.

If there's no beacon, then the searchers will only have the planned flight path of the aircraft to guide them. Did Adam even file a flight plan? I don't know.

Would it even matter if he had?

We flew into a terrible storm, and I remember he turned the aircraft around in an attempt to return to the small airport. But we never made it; instead, we flew into another thunderstorm and crashed. How far were we blown off course?

If I remember correctly, we'd only been in the air approximately fifteen minutes when we first encountered the bad weather, so we couldn't have been far from the airport in North Georgia we departed from. My best guess, based on the timeline of the flight and the landscape surrounding me, is that we crashed somewhere in the rugged mountains of Western North Carolina or East Tennessee.

And I know that's not good.

I've visited the Smoky Mountains several times for short getaways since I moved to Nashville, and much of the area is sparsely populated, with rugged terrain and miles of dense forest.

I glance back toward the aircraft wreckage and the surrounding trees. The plane is pointed uphill and appears to have slid up the mountain on its belly before the nose smashed into the large oak, the sudden impact killing Adam and Juliette instantly.

For them, sitting in the front seats behind the controls, there was never much hope of survival, but his last-minute efforts to right the plane and bring it in at an advantageous angle likely saved my life, and Macy's too.

Still, it's a miracle anyone survived.

The leaves and underbrush behind the tail are obliterated for a hundred yards down the mountain, and the nearby tree trunks show signs of impact with the wings. Chunks of wood and bark litter the forest floor. One of the smaller trees is even broken over completely. But, all things considered, there's not a massive amount of damage to the mountainside.

Although I'm thankful that the plane came in at the optimal angle for Macy and me to survive, there's also another side to that coin: Relatively little evidence of the crash exists in the forest. There's no large crater with everything surrounding it burned away, or even a swath of broken trees. It will be difficult, if not impossible, for aerial searchers to see the downed aircraft through the thick tree canopy.

This realization causes me to sink into a pit of despair, one so deep that it seems as if I may not be able to pull myself out.

I don't know what to do now. I'm completely at a loss. The emergency transponder obviously isn't working, we were off our planned course at the time of the crash, and the dense forest is camouflaging the crash site.

I can develop the best survival plan possible, create a dozen lists of things to accomplish so that I stay focused and optimistic, but the truth is, all of it will mean nothing if no hope of rescue exists.

For the first time, I feel I must honestly consider the fact that we may not be found at all, at least not in time to save us.

And this cold reality isn't the result of irrational panic brought on by a traumatic event. Rather, it's simply facing facts after a well-reasoned examination of our situation.

We might very well die from lack of water, or a host of other possibilities, before anyone finds us. The desire to curl up in a ball and sob at this revelation is overpowering, but I doubt my dehydrated body is still capable of producing tears. Even if it is, crying would just be a waste of energy and moisture.

And then there's the girl.

I glance over at Macy. She is once again facing away from me, her skinny back just feet from my face. Her lungs expand and deflate as she sleeps. I'm glad she is sleeping again, because I really don't want to be forced to talk to her. Part of me resents the fact that she is here at all.

Does that make me a horrible person? Or just a logical one?

I'm not sure.

It's going to be a desperate struggle just to keep myself alive long enough to be rescued. I certainly don't need the extra burden of caring for a small child I barely know. It's simply too much for me to handle.

But what other choice do I have?

I can't just leave her to fend for herself. She would be dead in no time, and then what would everyone think of me in the event that I actually do make it out of here alive? That I selfishly let a little girl—a girl so cute she should be selling cereal on TV—die on my watch while I survived? That certainly wouldn't be good for my public image.

I sigh.

I can't help but wonder, just as I always do whenever something bad happens to me, if this is—

No, it can't be. It's just a coincidence.

As much as I fight to subdue the thought, it won't be quelled, so I finally give in and allow myself to consider the question that haunts me.

Is this whole nightmare punishment for what I did back in Oklahoma?

But there wasn't another option. I was so desperate to escape that small, run-down town that I was willing to do anything to be free of it. I wanted out of there with every fiber of my being. The place was crushing me, pulling me into its ensnaring web of decaying trailer parks and minimum-wage jobs. I simply made the decision I had to.

Sometimes life requires boldness, requires a hard choice. I chose to be bold. I made the hard choice because I wasn't willing to live a life of poverty.

Maybe what I did was wrong. But even if it was, doesn't everyone mess up from time to time?

Of course they do.

But the mistakes of others don't absolve me. I know this.

With Macy lying by my side, I stare into the trees above and wonder if I'm finally going to pay for what I did—for the decision I made.

10

I chase the thoughts of the past from my mind. It's useless to dwell on things that can no longer be changed.

I have to remain focused on staying alive long enough to make it back to my comfortable life in Nashville—and forget about Oklahoma, once and for all.

As bad as our situation is, I know that I must hold on to the hope that we will be rescued, even if it takes longer than I first thought. And if I'm going to survive long enough to make it back to Nashville, I can't remain motionless on the ground any longer. The sun is now well above the horizon, and I'm just wasting time lying here with my thoughts. I must start making decisions and taking action.

I pull in a deep breath and raise myself off the ground with my elbows. The muscles in my back tense as I struggle to a sitting position. My neck, shoulders, and chest are still sore from the crash. It's hard to tell if the pain is worse today than it was yesterday, but it certainly isn't any better.

If I have any hope of rehabilitating my muscles, I have to get up and get moving. Crawling on my hands and knees, as I did yesterday during my trip to the wreckage, isn't going to get the job done.

I rock forward and gingerly place my weight on the balls of my feet. It hurts, but it also feels good to be off the cold, wet ground. I continue taking deep breaths to calm myself. Slowly, I attempt to stand up. My quadriceps shake and jerk as if I'm a toddler just learning to walk. I fight through the pain and awkwardness and continue to rise until I'm standing.

An explosion of pain shoots through my upper body and down my legs, and I almost fall back to the ground. Desperate, I extend my arms and wave them wildly, like some drunken tight-rope walker, and manage to stay upright.

It's the first time I've stood since I boarded the plane at the air-port, and I feel a great sense of accomplishment at completing the mundane task. Under normal circumstances, I certainly wouldn't view standing on my feet as something worthy of celebration, but today, it's a victory.

I examine my arms and legs for injuries. They seem fine. I lift my sweatshirt and check my abdomen. The seat belt has left a red stripe across my chest that's tender and sore, but I see nothing else. I feel my face and run my hands through my hair, inspecting my skull for cuts or other damage. I'm thankful when I find none.

I glance over at the mangled aircraft and again consider myself fortunate.

I'll need to check Macy for injuries too, but she's still sleeping, so I'll do it once she wakes up. Besides, given the way she was struggling with me yesterday as I pulled her from the wreckage, it's pretty obvious she has no major injuries.

I take a small, timid step with my right foot and follow it with another small one with my left. At first, my legs don't want to move, as if they are glued in place, but I fight with them until they have no choice but to obey my brain's commands. I take several clumsy steps around the uneven terrain until I feel my muscles begin to loosen and I can move in a halfway normal fashion.

I walk for at least a half hour, making wide circles around the area where I slept last night, and my body seems to become more agile with each circuit I complete. I stay far enough away from Macy that I don't wake her. I need this time alone to think and consider my next move—I don't need to be distracted by her juvenile questions.

I have no idea how long it will take searchers to find us without the aid of an emergency transponder. A few days? A week? Two?

The idea of attempting to hike out and find help crosses my mind. But the notion of trying such a thing terrifies me. I push it away because I don't even want to contemplate that scenario right now.

Maybe I haven't given the rescuers enough time. Perhaps the transponder is working and, for whatever reason, the searchers have simply been delayed. For all I know, they could be on their way to save us at this very moment.

I have to keep hoping for the best, even if I eventually have to plan for the worst.

I survey the landscape around me. What's left of the plane rests on a fairly steep mountainside. I can't tell how far it is to the top either, because large trees and a thick blanket of underbrush block my view. High ridges extend from the mountain, one on my left and another on my right. Below me, the terrain slopes downward into the same never-ending forest. Perhaps there is a house or a road or something at the bottom of the mountain that can help us, but I have no way of knowing how far it is to the bottom. And all I can see through the gaps in the tree trunks are more mountains spreading out in the distance against the blue sky.

The scary thought I banished from my mind just a minute ago returns with a vengeance.

Staring at the vast wilderness in front of me, I realize that if it comes down to it and we're forced to try to hike out of here, we might walk for days before reaching help—if we're able to find help at all.

Could Macy and I even survive such an attempt?

Yes, our best chance of being rescued is to wait near the crash site. I'm sure of it. Even though the wreckage won't be easily seen from the air through the thick canopy of green leaves, the odds of it being spotted are greater than searchers locating two individuals trudging through the dense forest.

But if we're going to stay here, I must find water soon. My mouth is on fire with thirst, and I know Macy needs water too.

I scan the area for a small stream or even a spring and listen for the sound of running water. There is nothing. I don't see anything that looks even remotely promising, and all I hear is a bird chirping and a hungry squirrel rustling through the leaves searching for something to eat.

Discouraged, I sigh and run my hands down the front of my jeans. I feel something hard in my left pocket, and I recognize the familiar shape immediately. It's my cellphone. How did I not think about it yesterday when I first woke? How stupid of me!

I withdraw the phone from my pocket at once and swipe my finger across the screen. Nothing happens, and I remember that I shut it down prior to takeoff at Adam's request. I press the power button and wait for the phone to boot up.

The screen comes to life, and I stare at the selfie that appears. The picture was taken a year ago, right after my last album dropped and just before I left on the grueling national tour. In it, I'm seated outside of my favorite coffee shop back in Nashville, my smiling face looking happy and satisfied, my designer sunglasses shielding my eyes from the warm rays of the summer sun.

If I took a selfie right now, I know what I would look like. I would appear as I feel inside—tired, dirty, and miserable.

I've become the antithesis of the girl on my phone's screen.

I swipe my thumb across the screen, banishing *Happy Lauren* to cyberspace. I don't want to look at her any longer. My eyes drift to the signal indicator at the top right corner of the screen and my stomach drops. There's no service available. "No, no, no!"

I walk around the mountainside holding the phone skyward for several minutes, trying to acquire even a weak signal, but there isn't one.

I've grown so accustomed to always having my phone at my disposal that it's infuriating not to be able to use it for help when I really need it. But right now, it's nothing more than a useless brick of electronic components that are unable to communicate with the outside world.

To make matters worse, the phone is almost dead; the meter shows only ten percent of battery life remaining. I used it the entire day before arriving at the wedding and forgot to have Kelsey charge it for me while I was onstage. Another stupid mistake.

I growl in frustration and hold down the power button until the screen goes black again. If the worst happens and I'm forced to walk out of here, I may need it.

There's a rustle in the leaves to my right. Startled, I turn my head to see what caused it. It's just Macy, who is finally waking up.

I walk toward her, passing below the crashed plane and across the section of forest floor that was ripped clean of underbrush by the skidding fuselage. Parts of the ground are torn up, exposing clods of earth where the metal dug into the ground. I carefully navigate around the obstacles. While much better than earlier, my leg strength is still nowhere near normal, and I struggle to keep my balance.

"How are you feeling?" I ask Macy as I reach the area where we spent the night together.

She looks up at me with groggy and confused eyes. "O-okay. Are we still in the woods?"

"Yes. And we are probably going to have to stay here for a while longer."

She rubs the sleep from her eyes with the backs of her small hands. "What's your name? I forgot."

"My name's Lauren."

She nods. "Why can't we go home, Miss Lauren?"

How am I supposed to explain this situation to her? I'm not talking to an adult with mature and rational reasoning skills. I really have no idea how to help her understand, but I give it my best shot anyway. "We can't go home. Not yet. We have to stay here a little while longer."

"Why?" she asks.

Of course she's not satisfied with my explanation. What young child is ever content with the first answer they're given?

I don't want to spend a lot of time answering the questions of a young girl who can offer no help. It's a waste of mental energy. But I know she, like every other young person I've dealt with, will have lots of questions. It's just what they do. "We were in a plane crash, and no one has shown up to help us yet. That's why," I say flatly.

"I know. It was scary." Macy hangs her head as if she's ashamed the crash frightened her.

As much as I hate all her questions, I feel sympathy for the girl. She's just lost her parents, even though, so far at least, she seems unaware of that fact. I kneel down and place my hand on her shoulder. "It scared me too." I attempt to offer her a comforting smile, but I'm not great at conveying emotions, so my gesture feels awkward. "Are you hurt?" I ask, desperate to change the subject before she asks about her parents.

"Yes. My whole body hurts."

"That's probably just because you are sore from the crash. I felt the same way until I got on my feet and started moving around. But are you bleeding or anything?"

Macy looks down at her arms, turning them over in the sunlight. After she's satisfied they are okay, she inspects her legs also. I almost laugh at her self-examination, the girl scouring her body and prodding it with her small index finger, as if she were a real doctor. She shakes her head as she finishes. "No, I don't think so."

"That's good," I tell her. "Can you open your mouth for me?"

She complies, revealing a set of baby teeth, two of which along the front section of her lower jaw have already fallen out. There's no sign of bleeding inside her mouth. Her eyes appear clear and responsive. There's also no evidence of blood coming from her ears. I move my hands over her skull. I don't feel any cuts or swollen areas. "Do you mind if I lift your shirt up, just to make sure you're okay?"

"I guess not," she replies.

I lift her blouse up to her shoulders. The garment is crusty and stiff and smells of vomit.

I bite my lower lip and hold my breath to keep from gagging.

I examine her back first and it looks normal. Across her chest, the aircraft seat belt has left the same reddish stripe that I found on my own body. I lay my hand flat against her stomach and gently press in. "Does this hurt?"

"A little, but not too bad."

I continue to move my hand over her abdomen and rib cage, slightly pressing in at several different locations. I feel nothing abnormal, and when Macy doesn't cry out in pain, I am satisfied there are no severe injuries. Of course, I'm no doctor and I've never received formal medical training, but I feel fairly confident that she's not in any immediate danger.

"Thank you," I say and pull her blouse back down. "I think you're going to be fine." I give her lower body a cursory examination and see nothing troubling, so I don't feel it's necessary to ask her to remove her skirt or leggings. Although the femoral artery runs through the pelvic region, if it had been severed, she would've already been dead by the time I found her in the plane yesterday. I've watched enough hospital dramas during late-night TV binges to know that much. All things considered, she's in pretty good shape.

The stench of stale urine burns my nostrils. I look down and realize that Macy has wet herself at some point.

"I had an accident," she says, her face red with embarrassment, "when we were flying down to the ground." She motions with her hand, mimicking the plane falling from the sky. "I'm sorry."

I smile at her softly. "It's okay. I had an accident too." I hope the lie will make her feel better about what has happened. I know it's embarrassing for her, especially having to admit it to a stranger.

"You did?" she asks, her eyes wide with shock at my revelation.

I nod and let out an exaggerated sigh. "I sure did. That was some scary plane ride."

She shakes her head. "It sure was."

I pat her on the back. "You need to get up and walk around. It will help with the soreness in your muscles," I tell her, changing the subject to forestall more questions about the crash.

She nods and, grasping her hand, I help her stand. "Take it easy. It will be hard at first. Just take your time, okay?"

"Okay."

I move behind her and place my hands under her armpits so that I can support her weight until she gains enough strength to walk on her own. "Now, just take a small step forward."

She moves her right leg hesitantly, followed by her left. I stay behind her until she has taken several steps and appears to be in no danger of falling. I remove my hands from under her shoulders and move to her side, holding her hand in mine just to be safe. "Keep walking," I tell her. "I know it's tough at first, but it will get better soon."

"I'm seven years old," Macy says.

"What?" I wonder why she has suddenly offered an answer to a question I didn't ask.

"I'm seven years old," she repeats. "You asked me how old I was before we got on the plane, but I didn't tell you then."

"You remember that?"

"Uh-huh." She takes a few more steps forward. "I'm sorry I didn't answer you the first time. Sometimes I'm shy. I was real tired too. It was past my bedtime."

I chuckle. "That's okay."

The fact that her memory is still intact is another positive sign. If she can recall my mundane question from before the crash, it's unlikely she has suffered any serious head trauma.

We continue to walk together, making large circles below the wreckage just as I had earlier, but I'm careful to avoid getting too close to the plane. I don't want there to be any chance she might catch a glimpse of the destroyed cockpit where her parents' bodies are.

Once Macy seems steady on her feet again, we return to the area where we spent the night. "Did you find Mr. Pebbles yet?" she asks as she takes a seat on the damp ground.

I've forgotten all about Mr. Pebbles. What a stupid name for a teddy bear. "No, I haven't been back to the plane yet."

"When are you going back?"

I sigh. Just as I was beginning to think it might not be so bad having Macy around, her request reminds me why I didn't want the responsibility of caring for a small child in the first place. Doesn't she understand we are in a survival situation? Of course she doesn't. She's only seven. She still thinks her parents are only asleep, and all she is worried about is her stupid stuffed bear.

"I'm thirsty," she declares, as if I can simply summon water from my fingertips.

My temper flares. *I'm thirsty too! Don't you know that? Do you even care how I'm feeling? I'm doing the best I can! All I've done is try to help you. A little appreciation would be nice.* I stop myself from lashing out verbally and manage to keep my feelings private. "I know you're thirsty. I am too. Just be patient, okay? Somebody will come to help us soon." I hope she will take my hint and stop complaining.

As I'm reassuring her that help is on the way, it strikes me that I don't have any real confidence in my own statement. I wish I could be sure someone was coming for us, but I'm not.

Even though Macy's request for something to drink angered me, it is an important one. I have to find water somehow, and soon. If not, neither of us is going to survive very long.

Should I leave her here and search through the forest for a water source? But what if I'm unable to find one? I'll have just wasted needed energy on a fruitless search. And what if I get lost in the dense forest and am unable to find my way back to the crash site? That would be disastrous for both of us.

"Will you go get Mr. Pebbles now? I miss him," she says firmly, interrupting my thoughts.

Aaaggghhhh! I want to scream at her for pestering me about the stupid stuffed animal while I'm trying to figure out a way for both of us to survive this horrendous situation. My patience with her is growing thinner by the minute, and her continued fretting about Mr. Pebbles is about to push me over the edge.

But in the midst of my anger, Macy's trivial request causes an important thought to enter my mind.

I have a habit of watching television late at night after my concerts, sometimes well into the next morning if I become engrossed in a certain program. One show in particular pricks my memory. On it, participants were placed on an island off the Canadian Pacific Coast. Each was stranded in a separate remote location, alone and with only a few essentials for survival. Each person was also given a satellite radio to signal for help or to quit the game whenever they wanted. The last one to remain on the island won $500,000.

What I wouldn't give to have a satellite radio at my disposal that I could use to summon help and extract myself from this situation at once, just like the participants on the show. Even having the few survival items they were allowed to bring along would help my odds considerably.

But this isn't a reality television program, and no production crew is going to swoop in and save me.

This is real life.

Although I don't have at my disposal the same things the people on the show had, such as a magnesium fire starter, a knife, or a satellite radio, I *can* use some of the skills and techniques they did.

I recall that the contestants, in addition to what they were allowed to bring with them into the wilderness, were also permitted to use anything that washed up on the beach. It was amazing to me how the participants put to use objects that others would've just considered garbage. Empty plastic bottles became makeshift showers. Twisted bundles of rope were straightened and fashioned into gill nets for fishing. Plastic bags were made into rain suits. Their ingenuity was truly remarkable.

And while I don't have an ocean nearby that will wash up useful items, there is something I can use as my own personal beach to scavenge.

The crashed airplane.

Yes, Mr. Pebbles is somewhere inside the twisted wreckage, but so are other items I might be able to use to survive.

11

I approach the crash site, ready for my scavenging mission. Macy is waiting a safe distance away.

I develop a mental list of items to search for inside the plane: something to start a fire, string or rope, extra clothes for both Macy and me, an extra cellphone with more battery life left, and some form of liquid to quench our thirst. I desperately hope someone on board shoved a bottle of water or soda into their luggage before the flight—because right now, that could literally be a lifesaver. Food would be nice too, but I'm not getting my hopes up.

And, of course, Mr. Pebbles.

He was at the top of Macy's requests ... which means the stuffed animal is high on my priority list as well. If a bundle of synthetic wadding and fur makes the little girl feel better and less likely to constantly annoy me, then it will be a win for both of us.

I reach the fuselage and place my hand against the sun-warmed sheet metal. I bend down and peer into the cabin through the gaping wound in the aircraft's side. The last time I visited, I was crawling on my hands and knees. Now, I can at least stand, and that's something to be celebrated.

The inside of the fuselage is dark. Depressing.

I hadn't planned on returning to the plane after I rescued Macy from it. It certainly isn't a place I want to be. But venturing back into the cabin one more time is necessary. I have no choice. Hopefully, I won't suffer any more flashbacks of the crash while inside. I don't want to think about what happened ever again.

I simply want to forget it.

But as soon as I stick my head through the opening, I know I'll never be able to forget what happened to me.

Ever.

The putrid, rotting stench of death permeates the air, thick and so heavy I can taste it.

I instantly retreat, pulling my head back outside. The smell is much worse today than yesterday. Ten times worse. I heave. Two, three times my stomach convulses, but only a few strings of thick saliva trail off my lips and fall to the ground.

That's not a good sign either. My dehydration is worsening with each passing minute.

I stand and glance down the mountainside toward Macy, who has also stood up. I lift my hand and wave to let her know I'm okay. She sits down, and I turn my eyes back toward the plane.

Although I would give anything to avoid going back inside that tin can of death—the smell is unlike anything I've ever experienced—I must. I don't have a choice. In order to survive and return to my life in Nashville, back to all the comforts my money can buy, I'll have to force myself to do things that are unpleasant, if not downright disgusting.

I do want to survive. Yesterday, when forced to crawl on my hands and knees to the plane, maybe I wasn't so sure, but now I am. I'm not ready to die. Not yet. I have a lot more living to do. More songs to create. More awards to win.

More money to make.

I'm not finished, not by a long shot.

I take a breath and let it out slowly, preparing my lungs for the onslaught they are about to endure, when a pine tree on my right catches my attention. My habit of watching too much TV gives me an idea. On some crime dramas I've watched, crime-scene technicians and coroners sometimes place a substance on their upper lips, just under their nostrils, to help mask the smell of human decay. Of course, I have no such substance available, but the pine tree I'm staring at may provide me with a suitable substitute.

I walk to it and search the bark until I find a large clump of sap that has oozed out. I peel it off the tree, divide it into two equal pieces, and roll them into tapered plugs. I place one of the plugs in each of my nostrils, the sticky resin adhering to my skin. The strong scent of pine floods my nose. I'm not sure it will keep out the more overpowering smell inside the airplane, but it should, I hope, lessen the effect of it.

Now breathing through my mouth, I move back to the wreckage and get on my knees. I'm afraid that my idea won't work and I'll again be subjected to the putrid smells inside, but I decide to stop worrying about it and just get it over with, so I shove my head inside.

It's still awful.

But it's not quite as bad as it was before. The plugs in my nose block some of the odor.

I crawl across the floor until I reach Kelsey's body on the opposite side of the plane. Surprisingly, I'm now able to study her closely, unlike yesterday. Maybe it's because I knew coming in this time what was waiting for me. Even so, I'm still disturbed by what I see.

Her body looks worse than I remember. It's obvious the decomposition process has begun in the warm summer air; her skin is bloated and slick with moisture. Her eyes are open, milky and glazed over, with the empty, fixed stare that only death brings. A fly crawls across her bottom lip and into her mouth. Her right arm is still twisted behind her neck, just as I remember it, but now I notice something I missed yesterday. Her head is cocked to the side, at an angle that indicates to me that her neck must've been broken during the crash.

But it was probably the panic that actually killed her. If she hadn't made the stupid decision to take her seat belt off just prior to the crash, she might've survived also.

I'm angry. Angry at her for doing such an idiotic thing when we were flying through a thunderstorm. Angry she isn't here to help me. I could sure use her right now, especially with Macy. Kelsey always was better at handling kids than me. She would talk to them and keep them entertained while they waited along a rope line for my autograph.

I'm angry that she's gone.

My hand inches closer to her body at a slow, tentative pace. I place it across her face and feel her warm, slippery skin. It isn't a pleasant experience at all. In fact, it's revolting, and I have to fight the overpowering urge to jerk my hand away. But I feel I must complete this simple act of respect. I owe her that much. I gently force her eyelids closed with my fingertips and hold them in place for several seconds, hoping they will remain closed once I remove my hand.

They don't, but reopen to narrow slits, which is even more un-nerving. I quickly avert my eyes from hers. "Sorry, Kelsey, that's the best I can do."

I slip my hand into the right pocket of her dress pants, desperately hoping that what I'm looking for is there.

It isn't.

The left pocket is pinned between her body and the floor. I don't want to do this. Just the thought of rolling her over makes me want to puke, but as with so many unpleasant things out here, I don't have a choice.

I force my hands under her left hip and gently lift up, praying the pine-sap plugs in my nose don't fail me. With another thrust of my arms, I manage to tilt her body enough so that I'm able to wiggle my hand inside the pocket.

The entire process makes me feel dirty, as if I'm desecrating her . . . but I'm desperate.

I withdraw Kelsey's cellphone and immediately realize all my efforts have been in vain—the phone's plastic case is cracked, its screen shattered into tiny pieces of glass that crumble away and fall to the floor of the cabin. I toss the phone away in anger and defeat.

It's hot in here. Really hot. And humid. I wipe the sweat from my brow with the back of my hand.

I stare at Adam and Juliette at the front of the plane. It's a good thing I didn't dwell on their appearance yesterday, else I may never have come back, no matter how badly I need supplies.

The scene before me is horrendous.

Both their bodies are mangled and contorted in a grotesque fashion, crushed by the instrument panel that was pushed backward when the nose of the plane smashed into the large oak tree. Thick blankets of congealed, black blood coat their clothes and the seats they occupy. Their heads are cranked around, held in place by twisted layers of sheet metal. Their open eyes stare at me with the same milky, lifeless appearance as Kelsey's, haunting me. It's almost as if they are pleading with me to do something for them. To help them in some way. I drop my head and close my eyes, unable to look at them any longer.

Rifling through their pockets for useful items or even getting close enough to close their eyelids isn't an option. I can't. It's all too horrifying. Besides, anything they were carrying has likely either been destroyed in the crash or is now unreachable in the jumbled-up mess that was once the cockpit.

I ponder what their last minutes of life must've been like. Worried for their daughter who was separated from them and in the back of the plane with two strangers? Of course.

Fear? Panic? Terror?

Anguish that their lives were about to end?

Surely, Adam must've known he wasn't going to survive the crash, yet he never gave up. He fought with the plummeting aircraft until the last moment to give his daughter and passengers a chance to survive.

I'm thankful he didn't give up.

I turn and work my way over the back seats and into the area where the luggage is stored. The pungent aroma of Kelsey's vomit, which has now baked in the summer heat for a day and a half, assaults me as I climb to the pile of bags, causing me to gag. I almost send my nose plugs flying across the plane, but with sheer willpower I'm able to control my body and stop that from happening.

I notice the top of a black backpack sticking out from the middle of the pile. I tug on it until it pops free and unzip it. My heart leaps in my chest as I peer into the main compartment.

Inside, there's a change of clothes for Macy, a package of moist towelettes, two bottles of water, and a small container of grape juice. The rush of excitement that floods over me is like nothing I've ever felt before. I'm so relieved that I want to jump up and down, and I would too, if not for the confining aircraft ceiling just above my head. "Yes!" I scream.

Pushing the clothing aside, I search deeper in the bag. At the bottom, I discover one small package of Wheat Thins, a bag of apple slices that have started to turn a brownish color but still appear edible, and a single pack of Teddy Grahams. I let out an excited squeal.

Of course! What mother of a young child doesn't carry a bag full of snacks and drinks when she travels?

Finding these meager rations feels better than when I won the Entertainer of the Year award last year.

It's another victory. And a big one.

My thirst is so extreme that I very much want to twist off the top on one of the bottles of water and down the whole thing at once. I can't do that, though. There's no way to know how much longer we will be out here, and the relatively small amount of water I've just found needs to be rationed. Besides, I find my-self strangely eager to share the excitement of the discovery with Macy. We can take our first drink together.

Thinking of Macy reminds me of Mr. Pebbles. I search the area around the suitcases and finally spot the stuffed bear lying in the rear corner of the compartment, its white-and-purple-mottled fur now stained from the dirt and debris that penetrated the cabin during the crash. I pick it up and clean it off the best that I can.

Yet another victory—Mr. Pebbles has been located.

If things keep going like this, we might just make it out of here alive.

12

I exit the plane for the final time. Although I don't wear a watch, I must've been inside for over an hour this time, scavenging for anything that might help us.

I wince as I pull the pine-sap plugs out of my nose, the sticky resin refusing to turn loose of the tiny hairs inside my nose. I toss them away because I have no intention of ever needing them again.

I'm never returning to the plane.

Dragging my carry-on, Juliette's black backpack, and Macy's small pink Dora the Explorer suitcase behind me, I move away from the plane and down the mountainside.

Macy's suitcase holds more of her clothes and a pair of tennis shoes, which I'm thankful for, since she's still wearing her outfit from the wedding. I know she'll be happy to put on something more comfortable. There are also some toiletries and a hairbrush inside, which will be helpful as well.

I recovered the nail file and clippers I used to cut Macy free, took some of Juliette's clothes for myself since she was roughly the same size as me, and I was ecstatic to discover that Adam enjoyed a smoke from time to time. Inside his suitcase was half a pack of Marlboros and a small plastic lighter. I left the cigarettes, but kept the lighter. I'm going to try to build a fire tonight to keep us warm.

Inside Kelsey's suitcase, I found a pair of sneakers and removed the shoelaces to use as cordage.

Perhaps my best find, besides the food and water, was the first aid kit that's now stuffed inside Juliette's backpack. It was strapped against the interior of the fuselage behind the rear seats, and I was overjoyed when the white plastic container emblazoned with a large red cross caught my eye. A quick inventory revealed some gauze, an assortment of Band-Aids, a small tube of antibiotic ointment, two packages each of Tylenol and Benadryl, a pair of nitrile gloves, and tweezers.

As I move closer to Macy, a smile comes across my face. It's odd that the few meager items I drag behind me evoke such a sense of accomplishment and joy, especially considering that only a few days ago I wouldn't have given any of them a second thought. Right now, however, I couldn't be happier if I were singing to a sold-out coliseum.

For the first time, I feel as if we might actually survive this ordeal, that we're going to be all right.

I'm still lost in an unfamiliar landscape, far away from help, but that doesn't matter at the moment. The only thing that matters is that Macy and I have enough food and water to last a couple of days—three if we strictly ration it—and this fact reenergizes me.

I'm proud of myself too. If I hadn't recalled the television program about people surviving in the wilderness, I might never have thought to scavenge the plane.

What a tragedy that would've been, to die from dehydration with two bottles of water and a container of grape juice mere yards away. I cringe when I consider the headlines reporters would've written about me.

COUNTRY MUSIC SUPERSTAR DIES
AFTER FAILING TO FIND WATER

or . . .

LAUREN MILLER, FAMED MUSICIAN,
SUCCUMBS TO ELEMENTS AFTER BEING AN IDIOT

Okay, so maybe they wouldn't have been quite that direct or insulting, but I know people would've considered me stupid and a complete failure if I'd simply lain down and died, literally feet from the items I needed to stay alive. I would've become the very stereotype I've been fighting my entire life—the brainless blonde girl.

But just as I'm about to lavish more praise on myself, I remember what caused me to think about the television program in the first place. It was Macy's request that I retrieve Mr. Pebbles. The little girl is owed some of the credit for our good fortune, and I don't begrudge her that.

Whatever it takes to keep both of us alive is fine with me.

I reach Macy, and I find excitement bubbling up inside me at the prospect of showing her the objects I've collected from inside the wreckage. "Look what I found!" I drop the two suitcases and backpack at her feet.

She claps her little hands and looks up at me, smiling. Her eyes are wide with anticipation. "Did you find Mr. Pebbles?"

"I sure did." I unzip my carry-on, reach in, and pull out the white-and-purple bear.

Her eyes light up and she takes the stuffed animal from me immediately, squeezing it in a fierce hug. She doesn't seem to care that Mr. Pebbles is dirty from the crash at all. "Thank you, thank you, THANK YOU!"

I chuckle softly. "You're welcome." Bending down, I unzip the backpack. "Look what else I found." I spread the snacks, juice, and water on the ground.

"Whoa!"

I pick up one of the bottles of water, unscrew the cap, and hand it to her. "Just drink a little, okay? We need to save as much as we can." She nods and takes two small gulps. As she hands the bottle back to me, I again want to drink the whole thing at once, but take only two modest swigs and replace the cap.

I return our food and drink items to the backpack and retrieve the package of moist towelettes. I wash Macy's face, arms, and hands, which are dusty and dirty from the crash, with one of the wipes. I pull the hairbrush from her suitcase and comb her hair too. I wish I could allow her to brush her teeth as well, but know we can't spare the water.

"I need to go to the bathroom," Macy tells me in a no-nonsense manner.

Great.

"Number one or number two?" I ask.

"Number two."

Uh . . . really great.

I sigh. "Okay." I offer her the package of towelettes and ask, "Do you need me to help you?"

"Probably. I've never gone number two in the woods before."

I laugh. "Neither have I." I take her by the hand and help her stand. The motion causes her to wince. "It'll be good to get up and walk around some more anyway," I add, gathering from her hesitant movements that her muscles are still sore. "Plus, we need to change your clothes."

From Macy's suitcase, I pull out the tennis shoes, socks, a pair of pink cotton sleep pants, fresh panties, and a white T-shirt with a dinosaur on the front to replace the vomit-stained blouse she has on.

Scanning the area around us, I search for a suitable location. For some reason, I haven't considered this issue arising before now, but I should've. Just because we're stranded in the wilderness, far away from a modern toilet, doesn't mean that normal biological processes cease.

A spot uphill from where we are sleeping during the night isn't an option, because if it rains again, water could wash the waste right back into our camp, so I lead Macy farther down the mountainside.

I'm again proud of myself. I thought through the problem and came up with the best solution available. I'm beginning to think like someone who's familiar with the outdoors, instead of what I really am—a pampered celebrity accustomed to staying in five-star hotels.

Forty yards down the mountain, far enough away that the odor won't be an issue, I find a small, relatively flat spot on the ground and stop. I help Macy take care of her business by placing my hands under her armpits and holding her off the ground in a squatting stance. As unpleasant as the chore is, it's a necessary one, and it pales in comparison to what I've just endured inside the plane.

She finishes, and I help her clean up and change her clothes, then put the tennis shoes on her feet. I tie her soiled garments around several nearby limbs on the off chance someone flying overhead will see them flapping in the breeze. It's certainly a long shot, but anything I can do to increase our chances of being found is worth trying. I leave the Mary Janes next to a pine tree because I see no further use for them out here, but if I need them later, I can always come back and retrieve them.

As I stand and begin to walk back toward our camp, a noise stops me in my tracks. I recognize it immediately. It's the familiar hum of an aircraft, not a jet, but a small propeller-driven plane.

My heart leaps in my chest. Someone is looking for us!

The hope that we may actually be rescued before we are forced to spend another cold, miserable night in the forest sends a burst of adrenaline through my veins. I grab Macy by the hand and pull her back up the mountain behind me. "Come on! Hurry!" I yell at her.

Her legs slip and flail through the wet leaves, but I keep dragging her, desperate to get back to the wreckage, where there's at least a possibility we'll be seen.

I gasp for air, my legs burning under the stress of towing Macy behind me, and I slip and fall to the ground. I scurry back to my feet and continue up the mountain. "Help! Help!" I scream into the air.

As I reach our campsite, I turn Macy loose and begin jumping up and down, waving my arms wildly above my head. Peering into the tree canopy, I search the small holes where the sunlight streams through, desperately hoping to catch a glimpse of the airplane, but all I see are empty patches of blue sky.

I pull off my dirty sweatshirt and twirl it above my head too, leaping around in only my bra. What a sight I'll be to anyone who might see me, but I don't care. I've long since abandoned any semblance of modesty. The important thing is to get the attention of the searchers.

"Help! Help! We're down here!" I scream again, although the absurdity of the idea that someone inside an airplane could actually hear my weak cries over the droning of the engine causes me to stop yelling. It's just a waste of energy. Instead, I focus my efforts on making large, visible motions.

Macy is standing a few yards away with her arms hanging at her sides. "Well, don't just stand there. MOVE!" I order her. She begins to run in circles, waving her hands in the air, imitating me, and yelling at the top of her small lungs. It's wholly inadequate, of course, and watching her reinforces the fact that I have no other adult to help me.

The high-pitched growl of the aircraft grows louder, flying closer to our location, but the forest and tree canopy is so dense that I know they won't be able to see us even if they fly right over the top of us. I need something that will be easily seen from the air.

A fire.

Racing over to the backpack, I find Adam's orange cigarette lighter near the bottom, grab it, and run forward a few feet. Falling to the ground, I gather the surrounding leaves into a pile with my forearms, and strike the lighter. Its sparks produce no flame. I growl with frustration and spin the metal wheel again with my thumb. This time, a flame springs forth and I touch it to the collection of leaves. Macy is still running through the woods behind me screaming uselessly for help as I watch the flame ignite the leaves.

Yes! Yes! Yes!

I blow gently on the infant fire, hoping to make it gain momentum and spread. A small amount of smoke begins to rise in pencil-thin tendrils.

Come on, baby! Go! Go! Go!

My spirits crash within me as I see the fire flicker and go out with one final gray puff of smoke.

Noooooo!

In desperation, I attempt to relight the leaves, placing my face low to the ground and blowing gently. A small flame forms once more, causing another thread of impotent smoke to rise, but it extinguishes even faster than the first one did.

What's wrong? Why can't I start a simple fire?

I reach down and grab a handful of the leaves.

They're wet. They still haven't dried out from the rainstorm that passed through the area the night of the crash.

The soft roar of the airplane's engine is still present, but it's becoming fainter. It's moving away from us. "No. No. Please no," I whimper. "Come back!" I stand and again twirl my sweatshirt in the air above my head.

But it's no use.

The once-hopeful sound gradually fades away until it vanishes completely. I've never felt so utterly defeated in my entire life. My sweatshirt slips from my hand and falls to the ground in a clump. I collapse in despair and exhaustion.

The plane is gone, and I have little hope it will ever return.

I've failed.

Frustration, anger, and hopelessness surge through me in a tidal wave that pummels my mind. I pull the smelly sweatshirt across my face and fall onto my back, covering my eyes as the tears begin to pour out.

It's all Macy's fault.

She pulled me away from camp to go to the bathroom. If I'd still been here when the plane flew near us, I might've had time to get a decent fire started. But I wasn't here—I was forty yards down the mountain helping a seven-year-old go number two.

I want so badly to lash out at her, to let her know just what she's cost both of us, but I don't say anything. What good would it accomplish to scold her? It wouldn't serve any purpose other than to waste my energy, so I just continue to sob into my sweatshirt.

"What's wrong?" Macy asks in a soft, worried tone.

I ignore her and keep my face covered. I don't want to see her right now, because I'm afraid her innocent face, looking at me as if nothing is wrong, will make it impossible for me to control my temper.

I lie on the ground for several more minutes, trying to compose myself.

Once my mind clears, I realize it wasn't Macy's fault that I was unable to signal the plane. She'd simply been a convenient scapegoat, someone I could cast blame on, instead of facing the fact that the failure landed squarely on my own shoulders.

It was *my* fault.

I should've been better prepared, should've foreseen that a plane might fly near us on a clear day like this one, but I spent too much time scavenging the wreckage instead of making preparations for such an event. That was my mistake and mine alone.

I can only hope it doesn't prove to be a fatal one.

I realize that my irrational feelings toward Macy are typical of the way I've acted over the last several years. My immediate reaction whenever something goes wrong is to blame everyone else around me, and to refuse to take any responsibility for my own failures. It's never my fault; it's always someone else's. My manager's, my record label's, my band members', Kelsey's . . . but never mine.

It's no wonder no one in Nashville wants to work with me anymore. Based on the way I've treated most of them, I don't blame them for wanting to stay as far away from me as possible.

I know I can't continue on the same path, especially out here in the wilderness, where I must weigh each and every move I make for potential consequences before taking action. Continuing to wrongly blame Macy for my own missteps will only make the situation worse by distracting me from the more important things necessary for survival.

Maybe the searchers will return tomorrow.

I hold on to that thread of hope, even though I know it's far from certain. There's no real evidence the airplane was even looking for us. On the contrary, it didn't circle the area, but flew in a straight line. That probably indicates that whoever was inside was simply flying from Point A to Point B, not conducting a search for a downed aircraft.

Maybe my hopes that they will return tomorrow are completely unfounded.

I wipe my eyes dry on the sweatshirt and remove it from my face. Macy is still standing a few feet away, staring at me with a worried and curious look on her face. "I'm fine," I say. "Just had to have a good cry."

"Hey, you're in your underwear!" She giggles and points to my red bra.

"Yes, I am . . . I sure am." Placing my weight on my elbows, I sit up, and another explosion of pain shoots through my body. I cry out.

"What's wrong?" Macy asks, again sounding worried for me.

"I'm just sore from the crash. But I'll be okay."

In all the commotion of dragging her back up the mountain and jumping around like a wild woman trying to get the pilot's attention, I must've aggravated my already stiff and aching muscles. All the adrenaline that was coursing through my veins sufficiently dulled the pain, but now that the excitement of the moment is over, the agony I experienced before has returned.

"Will you please hand me the backpack?" I ask.

She brings me the pack, and I retrieve the first aid kit from inside and open the plastic rectangular box. I take out one of the packages of Tylenol, close the kit back up, and return it to the backpack. I quickly tear the top off the paper package and pop one of the dry pills into my even drier mouth. I wash it down with a tiny sip from the bottle of water we drank from earlier. I offer the other pill to Macy. "Would you like some medicine to help with your sore muscles?"

"No, I don't think so. I'm feeling better already. Plus, Mommy said I shouldn't take things from strangers."

I smile. "I understand."

Since she doesn't appear to be in any real pain, I place the other pill in my mouth and swallow it with another small sip of water.

I lift my arm toward her. "Here, help me up."

She grasps my hand, grunts, and pulls back as hard as she can. She isn't very strong, but her help is enough to allow me to shift my weight onto the balls of my feet. I remain in that position a moment and rest. I slowly stand, consciously avoiding any sudden movement that might send another hot flash of pain down my body.

On my feet again, I gingerly move my hands behind my back and unclasp my bra. I hang it on a nearby tree branch.

This brings another round of giggling from Macy. She points at me with her little index finger. "You're naked!"

I smile at her and, in a playful voice, say, "Shut up. I'm hurt, okay?" It feels good to really smile again. I've become so accustomed to flashing fake smiles to photographers and fans, that I've forgotten how good it feels to smile simply because you feel like it.

I pull a blue T-shirt from my carry-on and put it on. It's dry and much more comfortable than the heavy sweatshirt I've been wearing. I also retrieve the black sequin dress I wore during the wedding concert from the suitcase because I have another purpose in mind for it.

The light is once again beginning to retreat from the mountains, signaling the approaching end of our second full day here. I spread my dirty sweatshirt on the ground and right beside it, the black dress. "Here, you take this spot," I tell Macy, motioning toward the dress. She takes a seat on my $3,000 designer dress, and I ease down onto the sweatshirt next to her. Three days ago, I would've never considered placing such an expensive garment on top of the wet, dirty ground, but what does it matter now?

Money means nothing in the wilderness, a fact I've learned quickly. All that matters out here is what you can use to survive. And the dress I wowed the crowd in, back at Larry's mountain estate, makes just as good a ground covering as my twenty-dollar sweatshirt. Both pieces of clothing will hopefully serve as a moisture barrier and keep us warmer than last night.

If they do, it will be worth every penny to destroy the $3,000 dress.

I attempt to get a fire going so we'll have heat and light during the night, but I give up because the wet leaves keep going out. All I have to show for twenty minutes worth of effort is a small blister on my right thumb where the flame from the lighter repeatedly licked at my skin. I don't want to waste any additional lighter fluid on a useless endeavor.

We'll just have to make it through the night without a fire—again.

Reaching into the backpack, I withdraw the package of Wheat Thins, the apple slices, the half-empty bottle of water, and the small container of grape juice. I twist the top off the juice and take a whiff of it. I'm not sure if it was supposed to remain refrigerated or not, but it smells okay. I take a tiny sip and it tastes fine, so I hand it and the apple slices to Macy. "Time for dinner," I say.

She claps with excitement, which brings another smile to my face.

I tear open the package of Wheat Thins and dig in, cramming five of the small square crackers into my mouth at once. My stomach is screaming at me for food, and I quickly chew and swallow the handful of meager treats. I glance over at Macy and expect to find her ravishing her food equally as fast, but I'm surprised when, instead, I see her hands folded in prayer.

"Dear God," she whispers, "thank you for this food. Thank you for my Mommy and Daddy, for Mr. Pebbles, and thank you for Miss Lauren too. Please help us get home soon. In Jesus' name, Amen."

I'm not sure what to think of this or what, if anything, I should say. Her display of thankfulness strikes me like a sledgehammer. How can she be thankful for a meager ration of food and juice when she is stranded in the middle of the woods without her parents? I just don't get it.

But her simple act of gratitude makes me feel about two inches tall.

We continue eating in silence. I savor the flavor of the wheat crackers, bland as they are, and the coolness of the water in my mouth. Macy shares a couple of small sips of the grape juice with me, and the sweetness of it invigorates my palate. I give her a few of the Wheat Thins, and she lets me have one of her apple slices. I consume my portion of the food quickly, excuse myself, and walk down the mountain to use the restroom.

I return a few minutes later and find Macy finishing her last bite of food and drinking the final gulp of grape juice. Seeing it makes me wish I'd taken more time to enjoy my meal also.

"Mmmm, that was great," she exclaims, shaking her head and causing her blonde curls to bounce on her shoulders.

I laugh. "Good, I'm glad you enjoyed it." I return to my seat on the sweatshirt next to her and stretch out.

She lies back on top of my fancy dress and sighs. "I'm tired."

"Me too."

"Do you think someone will come and help us tomorrow?"

"I don't know, sweetie. I sure hope so." My answer leaves room for Macy to maintain hope—I don't want to crush her spirit—but inside, my own faint glimmer of hope has all but gone out. I now have very little expectation that we will be found tomorrow, or even the day after that. When I stepped away after dinner to use the restroom, I had a few quiet moments to myself, and I thought about that very same question.

The conclusion I came to left me even more pessimistic about our situation.

I now know with certainty that, for whatever reason, there is no emergency transponder transmitting a signal that can be used to find us. Whether it wasn't on the plane to begin with or has simply malfunctioned, I don't know. It doesn't really matter. Either way, the result is the same.

Until tonight, I've been holding on to the smallest thread of faith that it was functioning correctly and our rescuers were simply being delayed for some reason. But now I know that isn't the case. If the beacon had been working as is should have since the crash, there's no doubt we would've been found today. I can't imagine any delay that could have possibly lasted this long.

And without the transponder to guide rescuers, what are the chances we'll be found?

Attempting to locate the wreckage of a plane that has been reduced to roughly the size of a large SUV, inside millions of acres of dense, tree-covered forest, is the equivalent of searching for the proverbial needle in a haystack.

No, it isn't.

It's much worse.

I have no doubt people are searching for us by now, but depending on how far off course we were pushed by the storm, they could be searching an area that's miles away from where we actually crashed.

LOST GIRLS · 109

And all of this leads me to the inescapable conclusion that it may very well be several days or even a week or more before we are found. I'm not sure we can survive here that long. I've yet to find a nearby water source, and all we have remaining from the plane is one bottle of water and the small pack of Teddy Grahams. I know I should've rationed better and not allowed us to consume so much of our supplies for dinner tonight, but we were both so thirsty and hungry that I felt I didn't have a choice.

And if we can't stay here and wait to be rescued, that leaves only one alternative. It's the same option I pushed out of my mind earlier this morning, unwilling to even entertain it as a viable solution, but now it seems it might be the only one left for us, and the one we are forced to undertake.

We can try to walk out of the wilderness and find help.

Setting out on foot in this rugged terrain comes with its own set of dangers, though, and I'm not at all certain it's preferable to remaining here at the crash site and just taking our chances that we can survive long enough to be located.

I don't know if Macy is capable of making such an arduous journey . . . and the truth is, I'm not sure I am either, given my current physical condition. Even after consuming the crackers and water earlier, I remain weak. On top of that, the stiffness and soreness I'm experiencing as a result of the crash would make such a trip grueling, if not downright impossible.

The enormity of what we'll face if we attempt to walk out of here is overwhelming.

What if one, or both of us, are injured during the hike and we find ourselves stuck and unable to move on? Then what? Will we simply be forced to lie down and wait to die?

What if we become lost and disoriented? Will we begin to walk in giant circles, no longer aware that our weary minds are making tragic decisions, until we just can't go on any farther and collapse from exhaustion?

No, there's certainly no guarantee that such a perilous undertaking will succeed.

But is it worth taking the risk anyway?

Is that our best—our only—chance to survive?

If we stay here at the crash site until the paltry rations I scavenged from the plane run out, will the decision be made for us? Will it be too late by then to even attempt to walk out?

I don't know. I don't know anything, really. My mind feels paralyzed, unable to make a decision.

I'm scared.

Maybe my brain is just as worn out as my body and, after a good night's sleep, the answer as to what I should do going forward will become clear to me. I hope that's the case. But if not, I'll still have to make a decision tomorrow. I can't put it off.

The single bottle of water and pack of Teddy Grahams we have left from the plane won't last us much longer.

13

As I continue to stare into the tree canopy, the light slowly fades from the sky and darkness descends on the mountains.

I take several deep breaths, allow all my muscles to relax, and attempt to banish all the stress from my mind. There will be plenty of time tomorrow to worry about what I'm going to do next.

Right now, both my mind and body desperately need rest.

But as soon as I set aside the worries about our survival, a new series of thoughts and questions enter my mind.

By now, newscasters across the country will have already reported that the country music star Lauren Miller has vanished and is thought to have been a passenger on a plane that may have crashed somewhere in the Smoky Mountains.

Surely someone must've connected the dots by now.

I suspect the reporters who are covering the story, despite portraying a false sense of hope on air, are, in reality, already prepping their obit pieces about me behind the scenes.

Of course they are. That's their job.

Are they telling their viewers how grim the situation is? How it's very unlikely there will be a happy ending? Easing my fans into the truth the newscasters are all so certain will eventually be revealed?

That I'm gone forever?

I imagine my name appearing in a red news ticker, scrolling across the bottom of a million television sets, the media giving hourly updates on the search for me. I've followed similar news stories in the past, and I know that once your name ends up in the news ticker along with the phrases *plane crash* and *extensive search*, it rarely ends well.

Everyone is thinking the same thing about me right now. They've already written me off as dead.

But I'm still here.

I'm still surviving.

I'm sure at this very minute, reporters are reveling in the huge impact my relatively short career has had on the music industry, all the awards I've won. And people I barely knew growing up in my hometown are giving television interviews, desperate for their own fifteen minutes of fame.

Isn't it always that way?

News programs are running pictures of me from different stages of my life. Snapshots of me as a kid back in Oklahoma. Goofy photos of me singing in run-down bars and county fairs when I first started my professional career. Videos of my latest multimillion-dollar tour.

Music producers and record label executives are issuing statements, noting what a valuable artist I am and how their thoughts and prayers are with me, my family, and my friends during this most difficult time.

I can't help but wonder if what they're really worried about is the money they're about to lose?

Or maybe I'll be even more valuable to them dead than alive? That sometimes happens. Nothing like the tragic and unexpected death of a young star to boost record sales.

My acquaintances in Nashville—I don't have any true friends—are relating whimsical stories about me on prime-time cable news programs, the majority of which will have been fabricated by my publicist, no doubt. I smile at that thought. Even after a client's death, a good publicist's work is never done.

And all of this, the whole evocative production, is being done in an effort to ease viewers toward acceptance of what the media already considers a foregone conclusion—that Lauren Miller will never sing again.

Maybe they're right.

Maybe I'm already as good as dead.

I let out an angry and exasperated sigh. Knowing what's being said about me at this very moment, knowing how many people have already written me off without even giving me a say in the matter, is both infuriating and depressing. It almost makes me want to give up, throw my hands in the air, and accept my inevitable fate.

Almost.

Yes, it pisses me off that people are already preparing obit pieces, and in the end, they may very well be proven right. But until they are, I'm going to keep fighting.

Because if there's one thing *everyone* can agree on about Lauren Miller, it's that she's not a quitter.

Just as I come to terms with my own thoughts on this issue, another strange idea enters my mind.

Once it's confirmed that a celebrity has died, there are always biographical television programs that memorialize their life—I've watched quite a few of them myself—and it seems to me that these shows often gloss over reality. They excuse away criminal behavior, addictions, and other personal failings. They ignore the people who were hurt by the celebrity's actions. And if the said celebrity was known to be difficult to work with and for treating the people around him or her like objects to be walked on, it's written off as just a side effect of their creative genius, which is, of course, what made them so special in the first place.

No one wants to speak ill of the dead, I get that, but being truthful is not a bad thing either.

I consider the way I've treated people around me for the past few years—since I *hit it big*, as they say. My actions haven't been what most people, including myself if I'm being completely honest, would consider decent and moral. If I want something, I get it, no matter who or what is damaged in the process.

But is my behavior any different than that of other celebrities? Even if it isn't, does that make my conduct okay?

I don't think it does.

Will my associates and so-called friends be forced to make excuses for my harshness and cutthroat attitude if I don't make it out of here alive?

Have I become someone others simply tolerate because of my money and fame, but no one really likes at all?

Am I just a horrible person?

And when it's all said and done, once the television programs are over and the last shovelful of dirt is thrown on top of my casket, will anyone really care that I'm gone?

I know the answer to that question, even if I'm reluctant to admit it, and the truth of who I am as a person makes me sick to my stomach and bores a hole through my heart. Sure, there'll be lots of fake sorrow, but the cold, hard truth of the matter is that few will genuinely mourn my passing.

The only people I know who will actually grieve for me are my parents and older brother back in Oklahoma. I haven't seen any of them since I left years ago. I've been too busy making a name for myself to bother going back to the small town in Northeastern Oklahoma where I was raised, even for a short visit. It didn't help that my mother and I never saw eye to eye, and after I left town without an explanation or even telling her goodbye, the gulf between us only widened.

But right now, lying on this cold, wet ground, I would give anything to be able to speak to her, to hear the encouragement I know she would give me.

What if I never get another chance to see my family, to talk with them and tell them I'm sorry?

Will they think that I abandoned them?

That I didn't love them?

That I *hated* them?

A whip-poor-will calls from somewhere in the distance and snaps me away from my thoughts just as my eyes fill with tears. Both my mind and body are utterly exhausted, and I feel as if I'm almost at the point of cracking.

"Miss Lauren?" Macy asks, interrupting the whip-poor-will's song.

"Yes?"

"Mommy and Daddy aren't asleep, are they?"

I can't breathe.

"We had a cat named Freckles," Macy says. "He had orange hair and I loved him. But he got sick and Mommy had to take him to the doctor. They said he was just too old." She sniffles. "Daddy buried him in our backyard." She pauses for what seems like an eternity and my tongue is frozen, my heart racing.

"Mommy and Daddy are in Heaven . . . just like Freckles . . . aren't they, Miss Lauren?" she asks, her voice soft and shaking.

Here it is, the question I've been dreading, the one I knew without a doubt was coming.

My heart breaks for her, and even though I know her little lower lip must be quivering, trying to hold it together, I can't bring myself to look at her. If I do, I'll go to pieces. I can't imagine how hard it's going to be for her to keep going, to simply maintain the will to survive, knowing that her parents are never coming back.

There are no words that seem even remotely adequate for the heartache I know she's experiencing. But I have to say something. I can't just ignore the question, as much as I'd like to. It isn't something I can push away and pretend never existed.

The question has, at last, been asked of me, and it demands an answer.

116 • J. MICHAEL STEWART

An honest answer.

No more skirting around the truth, no more glossing over the horror of what really occurred.

Earlier, I decided that when the matter was finally thrust upon me, I would just say whatever felt right in the moment, but now that it's staring me directly in the face, my lips won't move, my mind is blank.

But I've got to do it. There's no way around it. I have to rip the emotional Band-Aid off and just tell the girl the truth. Quickly.

I draw in a deep breath and clear my throat.

"Yes."

14

My third day in the wilderness dawns with a purplish-gray hue invading the sky above me, the soft light falling through the trees and kissing my cold cheeks.

The exhaustion that has plagued me since the crash proves even more profound and draining this morning. I don't want to move. Even though I count myself fortunate to have had *anything* to eat and drink yesterday, the persistent body aches and malaise I'm experiencing tell me the calories and hydration the rations provided weren't nearly enough.

Achieving any meaningful rest during the cool, damp night was impossible. Sleep came only in sporadic, restless fits.

The sweatshirt proved itself to be a horrible moisture barrier against the cold ground and offered no padding whatsoever. The small sticks and rocks that litter the earth dug into my back throughout the night. Mosquitoes and gnats and other tiny, unseen bugs again attacked my skin constantly and kept my hands busy in an effort to stave them off, which rarely worked.

The whole experience was absolutely miserable.

But it wasn't the poor sleeping conditions or my hunger or even the endless thoughts of how I'm going to survive that kept me awake most of the night—it was the little girl lying next to me.

After I told Macy the truth about her parents, she began to cry. She didn't sob or wail but wept with a soft and reverent elegance that seemed well beyond her years. I suspect she already knew the truth, but just wanted, or maybe even needed, an adult's verification of the fact that her parents were gone.

Hearing her struggle to come to grips with her new reality shattered my own feeble emotional strength. I felt useless, unable to offer her even the smallest amount of comfort in the most trying of circumstances.

Why is that?

Why can't I connect with people on a more personal level? Why do I always hold others at a safe distance?

Why can't I allow anyone to get close to me?

Maybe it's because of Oklahoma. Maybe all of my emotional problems and social awkwardness stem from the guilt I feel over what happened there. Maybe somewhere in my subconscious I view myself as unworthy of love, or even simple kindness.

Maybe I'm not worthy.

Is that why, no matter how famous I've become or how many thousands of fans surround me, I always feel alone? Why I've never wanted a family and dislike being around children?

It must be. That's the only reasonable explanation.

And how can I, burdened with my own life's baggage, be expected to offer any help or support to Macy?

But even if I were a trained grief counselor, I'm not sure there would be anything I could do for her. Is there really anything that would help ease her mourning process, especially given the trauma of a plane crash and her parents' bodies lying only yards away?

If there is, I don't know what.

Simply saying, "I'm sorry," and "It'll be okay," seems inadequate, although I spoke those exact words when she started to cry because they seemed appropriate for the moment, even if I did deliver them in a stale, robotic fashion.

It was what I was supposed to do, right?

But I know my words must've come across as empty platitudes to Macy because even I thought they sounded sterile.

Looking back, maybe it was a mistake for me to say anything at all.

After my ineffective attempt to comfort her last night, Macy continued to cry softly for at least two hours before she finally succumbed to her body's need for rest and fell asleep. I didn't blame her either. My inadequate words certainly didn't heal her broken heart.

Time is the only thing that can do that—if a broken heart can ever fully heal at all.

But I wish there were something more I could do for her, to genuinely help her in some way, but I've never been in a situation like this before, and I really have no idea how to handle it properly.

She's still asleep, lying on her side and facing me. I don't disturb her because she needs the rest, and I'm also afraid that once she wakes, she'll bring up the subject of her parents again.

I'm not ready for that yet.

My muscles are still sore and seem determined to continue fighting my every move as I slowly lift myself from the ground into a sitting position, though the pain is not as intense as it was yesterday.

At some point during the night, in between rounds of mosquito attacks I suppose, I finally made a decision about my next move. After hours of internal debate, rolling different courses of action and potential consequences around in my mind, I decided that the best decision is for us to stay here, at the crash site, one more day. It will give the searchers more time to find us, in the off chance they are searching near this area.

It seems the most logical choice.

But as *logical* as it may appear, I'm not at all certain I'm making the *right* decision. In fact, I might very well be sealing our fate by committing us to a disastrous course of action. Our rations are running dangerously low. Perhaps the single bottle of water and pack of Teddy Grahams would be better spent fueling a trek through the wilderness in search of help instead of keeping us alive here for a while longer, waiting for a rescue that may never happen.

There are no *good* answers, though. None.

But with the only other option a dangerous journey through the forest with an emotionally wrecked seven-year-old girl in tow, it seems only prudent to give the searchers just a little bit more time.

I just hope I've made the right decision, because our success or failure out here now rests squarely on my shoulders alone. Macy is dependent on me to keep her safe. I'm the only one she has left to lean on. She's *my* responsibility now. As much as I didn't want this job, it's been thrust upon me, and I'm determined to do the absolute best I can to ensure both of us make it out of here alive.

Since I've made the decision to stay here at the crash site another day, I need to make good use of this additional time and not waste it away.

What can I do to increase our chances of being found?

Trying to start a fire again is the obvious choice. But this time, I can't give up until I have one large enough so that the smoke will be seen from the air.

I stand gingerly and stretch, taking care not to move too quickly and allowing time for my tense muscles to relax.

There has been no rain since the night of the crash, but with the thick foliage blocking the vast majority of the sunlight and the oppressive humidity, the ground remains damp. It's frustrating beyond belief, but there isn't anything I can do about it. I'll just have to come up with a way to overcome the obstacle. My greatest chance for success will be to scavenge every piece of wood nearby that is even somewhat dry and hope for the best.

I begin walking around the mountainside and gathering the twigs and small tree limbs that have fallen to the ground. Most of them are still damp too, but I hope at least a few of them will be dry in the center.

It's slow work; my body simply won't move as fast as I want it to. Maybe it's the soreness or the dehydration or the sleep deprivation or maybe a combination of all three, but it takes almost all the energy I have to collect an armful of wood. Returning to the area where I slept, I dump the sticks on the ground in a pile, and head back out to look for more.

I continue working until my body screams at me that it needs a break. My guess is that I've worked for at least thirty minutes but, given my fatigue, it might not have been quite that long. It's hard to tell for sure when it's an intense physical struggle each time I bend over to pick up a stick. I dump my final armful of twigs and small limbs on the pile and sit down next to Macy, who's still sleeping.

The modest amount of labor has left me flushed and exhausted. The black backpack lying on the ground next to me grabs my eye. I want so badly to dig inside it, tear the lid off the water bottle, and drink. But even as dry as my throat is and as badly as my body needs water, it's simply not an option. We drank too much yesterday, so we must ration the remaining water even more strictly.

Finding more water continues to worry me more than anything else—even more than getting a fire started. Macy and I both need to consume substantially more than we are currently. I haven't urinated since before going to bed last night, but even worse, I haven't the slightest urge to go now, almost twelve hours later.

That's not a good sign—my dehydration is worsening with each passing hour.

Doubt again creeps into my mind that I've made the wrong decision by staying here another day.

If we aren't rescued today, will Macy and I be so dehydrated by tomorrow that our bodies will be seized with muscle cramps and spasms so severe we won't even be able to attempt to walk out and find help? If that happens, then what?

I know what.

We will die here.

A noise in the trees near the front of the airplane catches my attention. A large black vulture swoops down and settles on a limb a few yards from the smashed cockpit. Another one joins the first, landing in the adjacent tree and at a slightly higher elevation. The first one flies down from the limb and lights on the plane's crushed nose.

A chill runs up my spine.

I know what's about to happen, and I can't allow Macy to wake up and see the vultures feasting on the remains of her parents.

Kelsey's body is still inside the plane too. The vultures will eventually find her as well. An image of one of the massive black birds pecking at Kelsey's eyes and piercing them with its razor-sharp beak floods my mind. The idea of that makes me gasp, and before I realize what I'm doing, I leap off the ground and run toward the plane with one of the tree limbs from the woodpile in my hand. My sore muscles scream at me to stop, but I keep going, ignoring the pain. I fling the piece of wood at the bird that's now sticking its head through the destroyed cockpit window. The stick slams into the nearby sheet metal with a loud bang. The two birds shriek, turn, and beat their huge wings as they escape to another tree farther up the mountain and a safe distance away from me.

I pick up a rock from the ground and fling it up the hill. It lands harmlessly, yards from either of the vultures. "Get out of here!" I yell, but my voice trails off through the trees, weak and impotent.

The two black heads peer down at me quizzically, tilting to the right, then to the left. Their eyes bore into me, as if I'm robbing them of their rightful property.

I don't blame the vultures; they're simply doing what's ingrained in them, serving their natural purpose. But the people inside that plane mean something to me now, and I'm not just going to sit back and let the birds pull them to pieces.

I know I won't be able to hold them off indefinitely. Soon, they'll be back. And next time, they'll bring more of their friends to join in a revolting feast. When that occurs, Macy and I will leave here one way or the other. I certainly don't want to be forced to watch it happen, to hear the hellish noises they'll make as they gorge themselves.

Above all, I must keep Macy from seeing that.

I scream at the birds again and throw another rock, chasing them farther up the mountain. I lose sight of them and walk back down to where Macy is lying. She sits up as I approach her.

"What's wrong?" she asks, wiping the sleep away from her eyes with her hands.

"Nothing. Just watching some birds."

"But you were yelling at them."

I shrug my shoulders. "Yeah, I was just having fun with them. Guess I was bored."

"Oh," she replies, but the suspicious look on her face tells me she doesn't really believe my explanation.

I'm desperate to change the subject before she asks more questions. "Hey, I need some help gathering sticks to build a fire with. I thought maybe if we can get a big one going, someone might see the smoke from it. You want to give me a hand?"

She nods and stands, her small legs trembling slightly. "Okay."

I lead her around the mountain while we gather more sticks, holding her hand most of the time to make sure she doesn't lose her balance and fall. It's busy work. There's already enough wood to get a fire started, but if I can keep her occupied with something, anything, it'll be better than allowing her to sit idle and focus on the loss of her parents.

That's another thing I remember from the television survival show. The people who fared the best were the ones who kept themselves, and their minds, busy. Whether it was just writing in a journal or making some sort of craft, or even devising a simple game to play, the activity kept them from focusing on the isolation and the hardships of their situation.

So, if it means that in order to keep Macy's mind occupied I must hold her hand as we walk all over the woods, working on a project that might not even succeed, I'm glad to do it. I'll need her mentally strong if we're forced to hike out of here, and if she's consumed with the death of her parents instead of the monumental task ahead of us, it will become a major obstacle.

And the last thing either of us needs at this point is another obstacle to overcome.

15

Surprisingly, I find that I actually enjoy the time we spend together, focusing solely on the menial task of picking up sticks. It's certainly a departure from my normal aloofness toward children. Watching Macy, so eager to help me and trying her best to do a good job, allows my mind time away from the stresses and worries that have consumed me since the crash, and I'm happy about that.

I never expected to reach this point—actually appreciating her company—but I feel as if she and I are strengthening the bond that was formed between us the moment we survived the plane crash. I imagine any time two strangers go through a traumatic experience together, such as we have, there's a certain connection or even friendship that grows out of the knowledge that the two of you share something no one else ever can.

For as long as both of us live, we will be bound together by the shared experience of the plane crash. That's just a fact.

"You think that's enough?" Macy asks, pulling me away from my thoughts. Her right hand is full with another load of sticks and twigs, her left still grasping mine tightly.

"Yep, that should be plenty. Thanks for helping me." I pat her on the head and smile.

"You're welcome." She leads us back up the mountainside toward our campsite.

Macy dumps the last load of sticks onto the woodpile, which has grown significantly since I first started it earlier this morning.

I dust my hands off on my jeans. "I think we should see if we can get a fire going. What do you say?"

She smiles and lifts her arms in the air as if she's just won a race. "Yeah!"

I can't help but chuckle at her. The little girl I first viewed as a hindrance to my own survival is growing on me. There's no doubt about that. I enjoy her company, and I'm glad she's here, even if her presence does occasionally make things a bit more difficult for me.

I kneel and begin arranging the smaller sticks that will serve as kindling into a square formation that resembles the walls of a log cabin, except that it's open at the top where the roof should be. Surrounding that structure, I build a tepee with some of the larger sticks, the tops of which meet each other above the tiny log cabin. My hope is that if I can get the smaller sticks to ignite first, the flame will gradually grow until it lights the larger ones of the tepee. That's my plan anyway.

I only pray it works.

I gather a handful of the leaves for fuel to help get the small sticks burning. Normally, dead tree leaves would be easy to light, but these are still damp. Just as I'm worrying about whether or not I'll be able to get the leaves to burn, I have an idea. I remember the pine resin I used as nose plugs yesterday. Resin burns easily and will make a much better fire starter than damp leaves—I know, because I've seen it on TV.

There's another pine tree just a few feet to my left. I hurry over and search the trunk until I find a small ball of sap oozing from the bark. I roll the pine resin into a tight ball, divide it in half, and stick one piece on the front and the other on the back of the tiny log cabin. With one touch of the flame from Adam's cigarette lighter, the fire should begin to grow.

I'm proud of myself again. Thinking to use the pine resin was a good idea, a really great idea, actually, and one that wouldn't have even crossed my mind a few days ago. I'm learning.

"Okay, I think we're ready." I can hear the excitement and hopefulness I'm feeling inside bubble over in my voice. "Will you go get the lighter out of the backpack?"

Macy nods and scurries over to the pack.

As I'm waiting, I notice the forest seems to be darker than it should be for this time of day. I doubt it's even noon yet. I tilt my head back and gaze through the holes in the tree canopy. Thick, billowing clouds have invaded the same sky that only yesterday was clear and blue. While I was concentrating on gathering wood and keeping Macy's mind occupied, I failed to notice the weather change. But just because clouds have moved in doesn't necessarily mean it's going to rain.

Maybe we'll get lucky.

But probably not.

I need to get the fire started as soon as possible. There's a chance that another airplane will fly near us before the weather turns bad, and if it does, I want to be ready. "Macy, hurry up with that lighter. It looks like it might rain."

"I can't find it."

"What? It's in the backpack," I tell her, incredulous.

She has her face and arms buried inside the main compartment of the pack, but she's having no luck.

I walk over to help her, because I'm sure she's just overlooking the lighter. I take the backpack from her. "Here, let me have a peek." I suspect it slid past the other things in the pack and is hiding somewhere at the bottom, so I remove everything inside and arrange the items neatly on the ground until the entire compartment is clearly visible.

But the lighter is nowhere to be seen.

I shove my hand in and search with my fingertips, hoping it is hidden inside a crease along one of the edges, but I feel nothing except the rough synthetic fabric. The side pockets and the exterior front pocket sewn onto the body of the pack are empty as well. My stomach sinks. I must've forgotten to return the lighter to the backpack yesterday following my hurried attempt to start a fire while the plane was flying nearby.

I check the pockets of my blue jeans. Nothing.

Sighing, I look at Macy. "I can't find it either. It must be on the ground somewhere. Help me look for it."

We both begin to search through the leaves littering the area where I'd tried to start the fire. Hunched over at our waists, we scour the ground.

"Make sure you look at everything closely. It's orange," I remind her without looking up. I desperately hope it's not hiding underneath the blanket of leaves, because if it is, it may take us hours to find it. Just as that thought leaves my mind, I hear a violent cracking sound come from where Macy is searching. I straighten and look toward her. "What was that?"

"Oh no," she whispers.

I walk in her direction, but before I even reach her, I can tell by the devastated look on her face what's happened.

"I'm sorry. I didn't mean to. It was an accident! I promise it was." Her eyes are already filling with tears. At her feet, the remnants of the lighter are scattered on top of and surrounding a small rock, the orange plastic case cracked into a handful of small pieces. The fluid is running out and soaking into the ground.

My heart falls to my feet.

Our only chance to build a fire and signal for help is literally disappearing before my eyes. As much as I try to stop it, my anger boils inside my chest and burns a white-hot trail up the back of my throat.

How could Macy have been so careless? Doesn't she know the lighter was our last hope of being rescued?

I'm furious with her.

The desire—no, the *need*—to lash out at her grows so intense it feels as if there's a roaring furnace in my gut.

What are we going to do now?

Without a fire, there's no way we'll be able to signal anyone. Macy has ruined my plan. All the energy I spent this morning collecting the wood is wasted—and at this point, I don't have any to spare.

I throw myself to the ground, landing on my knees. The shattered lighter is in front of me, and I pick up the metal top. I spin the wheel feverishly with my thumb, trying to ignite the surrounding leaves that are wet with the spilled lighter fluid. A few tiny sparks fly out, but disappear into the air just as fast as they appear. "No, no, no. Come on . . . light. Please light," I whisper.

I try again, placing the striker directly against one of the soaked leaves, but my thumb slips off and I cut the inside of my hand against the jagged fragments of the plastic case. I hardly notice the pain. "You've got to light!"

I try again. And again. Nothing is working. No matter how I hold the lighter, I can't get it to ignite the leaves. Over and over I pull my thumb across the top of the striker wheel, to no avail. I keep trying until even the anemic sparks from the igniter cease.

Exhausted, I fling the broken, useless piece of metal and plastic to the ground.

"I stepped on it. I'm sorry . . . I really am . . . I just didn't see it," Macy says from behind me in a trembling voice.

I bite the inside of my cheek to keep myself from spinning around and screaming at her. I'm so angry that I'm afraid if I even let one word escape my lips, I'll launch a salvo of verbal bombs that will destroy her.

I'm mad—livid, in fact—but I don't want to crush her.

Three deep, calming breaths return my heart rate to normal. I sit, staring at the ground, not knowing what I should say or do.

Getting a fire started was our last hope of being rescued. And now that hope is gone.

It's beyond devastating.

As the anger slowly subsides and my mind clears, I realize that, just as the lack of preparation for signaling the airplane yesterday was my fault, so is the crushed lighter. Not Macy's.

Yes, the little girl accidentally stepped on it and broke it, but it shouldn't have been lying on the ground in the first place. After I used it yesterday, I failed to return it to the backpack where it would've been safe. That's on me, plain and simple.

My other mistake was that I should never have allowed myself to rest until I had a large, sustainable fire going. That was really stupid of me. Maintaining a fire for heat and the ability to signal potential searchers should've been my number one priority, not trying to sleep, which had proved pretty much useless anyway.

I should've stayed up all night and worked on getting a fire started. Why didn't I collect some of the leaves from around the plane that might've been soaked with fuel and use them to get a fire started? I don't know that it would've worked, but I should've at least tried. And why, just because I'm not a smoker, did I flippantly discard Adam's cigarettes without considering their other potential use? The burning tobacco could've made it easier to get the damp leaves and twigs ignited.

In hindsight, I should've done a lot of things differently, I suppose. But now, without the lighter, those things aren't even possible.

There's not going to be a signal fire—not now, not ever.

This bold, frightening reality forces me to acknowledge how truly foolish my decisions have been.

Everything's my fault.

The weight of my own carelessness crushes me. I don't know if I can keep going, keep struggling one minute to the next just to stay alive, when my own mistakes are sabotaging me and making survival seem an impossible task.

I turn from the pieces of orange plastic littering the ground in front of me and look at Macy. She's on the verge of sobbing, her eyes filled with tears. One of them spills over and runs down her cheek. I sigh and give her a soft smile. "It's okay. It's my fault anyway. I forgot to put the lighter back in the pack yesterday."

Her lower lip starts to tremble, and another tear slides its way down her rosy cheek. "I'm s-sorry," she says, her voice quaking and her breaths coming in short, rapid succession as she tries to hold herself together.

My own emotional dam breaks as tears stream down my face. I leap toward Macy and throw my arms around her, pulling her head to my chest. Her racking sobs flow through my own body. "It's okay . . . it's going to be okay," I tell her. "We *are* going to make it out of here. I promise."

Of course, I have no right to promise her any such thing. I have no idea if we can make it or not. Given my propensity toward idiotic decisions lately, it doesn't look hopeful. But it seems a promise I should make anyway, because I'm now more determined than ever to do my best, in order to ensure we both make it out of here alive. In the end, I may not succeed, but if failure is my destiny, I'll meet it with a clear conscience—because I'll have given everything inside of me to the cause.

Every emotion I've experienced before, during, and since the crash collapses on me in one giant tidal wave. It's as if my mental shoulders, unable to bear the load any longer, give way and allow the fear, the anger, the relief of still being alive, and the uncertainty of how I'm going to stay that way, to travel through my soul in one powerful surge. I pull Macy in closer and bury my face in the crook of her neck as my tears come faster.

It feels good to let it all go.

Thunder cracks overhead and the cloud-laden sky opens up. The rain begins to pelt the dense leaves above and quickly gains intensity until it climaxes in a violent roar. The wind howls through the forest, whistling past my ears. Both of us quickly become soaked, strands of our blonde hair intertwining in the downpour. But I refuse to let go, holding her tight to me.

We are both still sobbing.

I'm sure Macy is again thinking about the loss of her parents. She hasn't broached the subject all morning, even during our trek to collect wood for the fire. I can't imagine what she's feeling. But for her sake, I hope she's experiencing the same emotional cleansing I am right now.

She lifts her head off my shoulder. I grasp her face in my hands and stare into her innocent blue eyes. "It's going to be all right," I say. "I'm going to do the very best I can to get us out of here." I kiss her wet forehead.

She sniffles and nods, but doesn't speak.

"But I'm going to need your help, okay?"

Another nod.

"Good. You're going to do great, Macy. I know you will." My words are meant to reassure her, but I find comfort in them as well.

I tilt my head back and let the cool raindrops fall on my face and wash my tears away. In this instant, joy takes hold of me and I begin to laugh.

I'm not sure why I'm laughing in the middle of such a dire situation. We've lost any chance of building a fire. Any chance of signaling for help. Any hope of being rescued. Yet I find myself overcome with laughter so intense it overpowers the din of the rain battering the tree leaves around me.

And it feels even better than the crying did.

Maybe it's simply because I'm no longer scared of what lies ahead of me. There's no doubt it will be more grueling and tougher than anything I've ever faced, but I know I can do it. I have confidence in myself again.

The sobs purged my fears and anxieties.

But the laughter refreshes and rejuvenates my soul.

And it feels wonderful.

Raindrops shower my lips and I lick them off, opening my mouth wide to drink in as much of the refreshing water as I can. Macy copies me and opens her mouth to the sky too. She begins to laugh as well, and the musical, high timbre of her juvenile giggles ring in my ears.

It's the most soul-stirring sound I've heard in a long time—much better than thousands of fans screaming my name inside a packed coliseum.

I stand and spread my arms wide, opening my entire body to the rain and allowing it to soak the front of my T-shirt. I begin to jog in circles as if I'm a child playing in an open fire hydrant on a blistering summer day, just as I remember doing as a kid back in Oklahoma.

Macy joins me, and we both continue to giggle as we revel in the cool water falling from the sky. We suck the moisture from our clothes and our stringy hair, trying to satisfy our thirst and rehydrate our bodies. We rub our filthy arms and faces, cleaning them of the dirt accumulated there.

It's absolutely invigorating.

The rain showering me causes me to realize something else. My anger flared toward Macy over the broken lighter, but even if we had found it perfectly intact, it wouldn't have changed a thing because the rain would've made lighting a fire impossible anyway. The result of my well-thought-out plan would've been the same, and getting angry about the destroyed lighter was just as much a waste of energy as collecting the firewood had been.

But instead of depressing me, I find this new insight encouraging.

I've come to terms with the fact that I can't control much of what goes on out here in the wilderness, not the least of which is the weather, but I *can* control my feelings and, in turn, my reactions. I must be able to think through problems calmly and rationally if I'm to overcome the numerous obstacles I'll face.

As if on cue, I think about the empty water bottle I saved after dinner last night. It's lying in the collection of items I took from the pack while searching for the lighter. I rush over to it, twist the plastic cap off, and place it upright on the ground, holding it in place with three small rocks. A couple of green leaves from a nearby oak tree, their tips placed strategically into the neck of the bottle, serve as a makeshift funnel.

Any rainwater I'm able to collect now will delay the moment when we must begin to consume the last full bottle from the airplane.

I'm already thinking like a survivor.

16

We spend the rest of the afternoon huddled under the low branches of a nearby pine tree, wrapping ourselves around each other in a sideways hug to conserve body heat. Claps of thunder and brilliant flashes of lightning invade the forest with regularity. Even though I've weaved both the sweatshirt and sequin dress through the boughs above our heads to serve as a makeshift roof, we are still drenched, the soaked and muddy garments offering little shelter from the rain. All they do is slow the water down for a few seconds while it works its way through the filthy material and then drops on our shivering heads anyway.

Everything else is waterlogged too: my carry-on bag, the backpack, the extra clothes . . . all of it. I'm freezing, my entire body quivering against the frigid rain. I hold Macy close; she is shaking just as badly as I am.

The rain that rejuvenated my soul and felt so refreshing only hours ago, has now become my torturous and chronic companion. It infiltrates every crevice of my body and saturates my skin. My palms and fingertips resemble raisins, the skin white, drawn, and covered with tiny ridges. My teeth chatter ceaselessly, and my soaking-wet ponytail is glued to the back of my neck.

It amazes me how the mountain forest can be so warm and humid during the day, making you want to strip all your clothes off just to find some relief, but at night or during a rainstorm, its damp chill cuts right through you.

It's positively miserable.

No, miserable isn't the right word. Miserable isn't strong enough to accurately describe what I'm going through.

It's . . . pure agony.

There's only one other place that would offer us better protection from the elements than this pine tree, but that's not an option. There's no way I'm going to force Macy to see her parents' bodies. If she does, that vision will be burned into her mind's eye for the rest of her life. Something she'll never be able to forget, no matter how hard she tries. It will haunt her every holiday, birthday, and anniversary. Whenever she thinks of her parents, remembers what wonderful people they were and how much she loved them, the image of their death will overpower everything.

Absolutely not. No matter how bad the weather gets, how wet or cold I am, I won't even consider taking Macy to the shelter of the plane. No.

But stuck under this pine tree, with nothing to do except try to stay warm, I find myself again trapped with my own thoughts.

It dawns on me how different I feel out here. Everything has been taken from me. I'm naked, stripped of all the things that make me who I am. The luxury of my fame is gone—it means nothing to the trees that surround me. To them, I'm just another lost wanderer at their mercy.

No, the wilderness isn't going to do me any favors or cut me any slack simply because I'm famous back in Nashville. It couldn't care less.

I'm rich too. Very rich. I've made enough money to retire right now if I wanted to. I could buy an ocean-front mansion on a Caribbean island—where it would be a lot warmer than these rain-soaked mountains—and never work another day in my life.

But all my millions won't even buy a peanut butter sandwich right now.

My material possessions and fame can't help me now, and I finally see them for what they really are: meaningless. The sum total of it all is just as useless as a handful of the dead leaves that blanket the ground around me.

Yes, my life was turned upside down the second that plane crashed.

I think about Kelsey, her broken body lying inside the wreckage, her lifeless hands unable to wipe away the raindrops that fall through the torn sheet metal. Her icy, decaying body. Her swollen face and milky eyes.

And she is alone.

The pictures in my mind send a shudder through me so great that, for a second, it overpowers the effects of the cold rain.

It's my fault Kelsey is dead. She didn't want to get on the plane in the first place, almost as if she had a feeling something terrible was going to happen. But I insisted we board the flight because I had to get back to Nashville in time for my all-important studio session. Even after I realized how scared she was, I still made her get on that doomed plane. What Kelsey wanted, what she was feeling, didn't matter to me at all. All that was important was what *I* wanted. If I'd just exercised some patience, some understanding, and waited to travel back the following day, after my jet was repaired, Kelsey would still be alive. It hurts to admit this to myself, but I know it's true.

But I wasn't willing to wait. I had to have things my way, just as I'd always done in the past—placing my own wants and needs above everyone else's. It was the same in Oklahoma, when I made that terrible, selfish decision. And it's a decision I've lived with ever since, but at the time, I was totally consumed with protecting my own self-interests and gave no thought to anyone else.

It's a sick, depraved pattern that I now realize I've repeated over and over throughout my life.

I think about the way I treated Kelsey—as just a hired hand, someone I could beckon with the snap of my fingers, a rude phone call, or a blunt text message.

Kelsey was just there to serve me.

To serve me?

That notion makes my stomach flip. Was that really how I'd thought of her? How I'd treated her?

I know that, sadly, the answer is *yes*.

The truth is, I treated all of my employees as nothing more than tools to be used at my discretion. I never asked about their families, their hobbies . . . their aspirations.

But Kelsey stood out from the others. Not in the way I treated her. She received the same treatment as the other employees did, sometimes worse. However, she was unique in that she had the backbone to stand up to me when she thought it necessary. She didn't have a problem speaking frankly to me, unlike most of the others around me. They would just tell me what they thought I wanted to hear.

We love you, Lauren! . . . That dress looks great! . . . Your new single is going to be number one on the charts in no time! . . . You're such a great person, Lauren.

I know they were all lies, especially the one about me being a great person, because I now see that I was far from that.

Kelsey, though, was honest with me when my outfit looked horrible or when a new song was just awful or, as was often the case, when I needed to cool my temper.

And while some others flocked to be close to me in order to further their own career goals or financial well-being, Kelsey wasn't like that. She actually wanted the best for *me* and was willing to tell me the truth, even when it wasn't what I wanted to hear. That's what made her so special, and it's the reason I'm going to miss her so much.

I was wrong before, when I thought I had no true friends in Nashville, only *acquaintances*.

Kelsey was a true friend.

But instead of reciprocating that friendship, I chose, instead, to treat her like crap.

And now my narcissism has cost Kelsey her life.

I'll never be able to forgive myself for that.

Tears begin to flow down my cheeks and mingle with the rainwater that's falling all around me. I lift my head and glance at Macy. The girl gives me a soft, warm smile as if she knows I'm going through something painful.

I'm amazed at how she's able to keep such an optimistic attitude after everything she's been through and the horrible conditions we're enduring. This little seven-year-old girl next to me is strong and tough and mature beyond her years, and her resiliency inspires me.

I've tended to the water-collection device I fashioned out of the empty plastic bottle throughout the afternoon, and so far, I've been able to glean about one gulp of water every hour, which Macy and I share. The rainwater tastes of the forest, earthy and bland, but it hydrates us, which I'm thankful for.

It's almost dark now, and the thunderstorms are moving out of the area, leaving behind only a light, steady rain falling over the mountains. The cloud bases have lowered to the point they appear to be touching the tops of the trees.

That's bad news.

No other aircraft have flown near us since yesterday, even before the storm set in, and I know that no air search will be conducted in the current weather conditions. If the clouds don't clear out of the area by morning, rescue seems a pipe dream.

The two vultures have returned, and this time, they brought along a friend. These three will soon be six, and the six will morph into twelve. Even in the rain, the scavengers aren't going to be denied their meal. I avert my eyes quickly. I don't have the energy to chase them away again, and I don't want to see what they're doing.

It occurs to me that perhaps I made a mistake by chasing them away earlier. If they were circling above, their presence might've caught someone's eye, but only *if* there were searchers nearby, which I doubt. Either way, I don't regret chasing the vultures away, and I would do it again right now if I had the strength.

At least it will be night soon and Macy and I won't have to watch the morbid spectacle.

There's no doubt in my mind now that my decision to stay an extra day here at the crash site was a mistake. What did it gain us?

Absolutely nothing, that's what.

No one came for us, and now I've wasted another day's worth of energy when I could've used it to begin the journey I now know is inevitable. What if the extra day costs us our lives?

It was foolish of me to risk so much on the scant hope of being rescued, and I can't afford to keep making mistakes if I ever want to see home again. The idea of crawling into my own warm, dry bed and sleeping without worry of when or where I'll manage to find my next meal, or the next mouthful of water, seems more than just elusive now—it seems impossible. Yet, I still hang on to that hope because it's all I have left.

But if I'm ever to make that dream a reality, I must start making smart decisions and stop making stupid ones.

The hunger is becoming a real issue for me. I haven't eaten anything since the small package of Wheat Thins and the single apple slice I had for dinner last night. Each time my stomach roars to be fed, or groans because it hasn't been, it reminds me that our situation is growing more desperate by the minute. We have only the one pack of Teddy Grahams left. It's currently inside the plastic medical kit, which itself is wrapped with a pair of Juliette's sweatpants and tucked away inside my carry-on. I hope my efforts will keep the small amount of food and medical supplies we have dry through the night.

Macy has to be just as hungry as I am, and I desperately want to dig into the carry-on and tear open our last package of food.

But as unbearable as the physical hunger is, I have no choice but to leave the bag of snacks tucked securely away in its hiding spot. We'll need the meager calories more tomorrow than we do now.

I get up and retrieve the rain-collection bottle and bring it back to our spot under the pine tree. It won't catch as much water here, but I'll be able to find it quickly in the dark.

There's no doubt that I need sleep as badly as I need food, but with the light rain continuing to fall all around me, I know I'm in for another restless night.

My mind is slowing down. I can feel it. It takes me longer to complete a series of thoughts or analyze a problem. It's as if my mental abilities are bogged down by a ghostly fog that I can't see, yet know with certainty is there.

I wrap my arm around Macy's shoulders again and pull her close, then lower my head to shield my face from the constant drops of water that continue to slip off the pine boughs above and stream down onto my head. It's as if I'm undergoing Chinese water torture, the incessant dripping driving me closer to the brink of insanity with each passing second.

It's going to be a long, agonizing night.

But if there's a bright side to being forced to hunker under a leaking pine-bough roof for hours, it's that I've finally made the decision I should've found the courage to make yesterday. I have no way of knowing whether or not it's the right decision. It very well could be another mistake and end in complete disaster, but I feel as if it's my only remaining option.

Our only hope of surviving this.

Tomorrow, I'll embark on the most frightening journey I've ever attempted—a journey that has only two possible outcomes.

Either way, my time as a castaway in the Smoky Mountains will soon be coming to an end.

17

As soon as the first hint of daylight slithers its way into the forest, I emerge from underneath the pine tree.

I was right about one thing—it was indeed an agonizing night.

It was so bad, in fact, that if I'd had the benefit of a flashlight,
I would've gone ahead and left and just done my best to navigate
the steep terrain in the dark. Anything would've been better than
what I instead endured—immobile and freezing under the tree
while the raindrops continued to torture me. The minuscule beads
of water seemed insistent on robbing me of the little body heat I
had left as they slowly traversed my skin on their journey down
to the ground. I kept my legs pulled tight to my body throughout
the night, my shivering chin resting against the top of my knees,
in a feeble, unsuccessful effort to stay warm. I prayed for daylight
to return, but time seemed to pass at a slumberous pace—minutes turned to hours, hours to days. Other than a handful of times
when I nodded off for a minute or two, only to be jerked violently
awake by my shivering body, sleep eluded me.

So even though I'm still wet and cold, I'm thankful to be
standing upright again. My mind is anxious to get moving, to
start working toward a goal, but my body—my muscles, joints,

and tendons, all of which must function properly if I'm to make it out of the wilderness—is still lethargic.

Macy crawls from underneath the tree and walks to my side. "Did you get any sleep last night?" I ask her, but one look into her blue eyes reveals the answer. The poor girl looks exhausted, with drooping eyelids and a dirty, forlorn face. If I look half as beaten down and worn out as she does, we're in real trouble.

She shakes her head. "No, not really."

"Me either." I take a deep breath and hold it in for a few seconds, hoping it will chase the weariness away, but it has little effect. The rain stopped a few hours ago, but now the mountainside appears as if it's a frigid sauna, wisps of cold mist moving over our bodies and ensuring we stay just as wet as we were throughout the night.

The sky is completely overcast by a dull, featureless cloud base. I can't even see the tops of some of the taller trees now, their leaves hidden inside a milky fog of dense water particles. No matter which way I look, I'm surrounded by the grayish-white soup. It isn't what I wanted to find this morning, and it's utterly depressing.

I was hoping for sunshine.

Feeling as if I've been run over by a freight train and knowing that Macy must be experiencing the same thing, doubt creeps into my mind about the decision I've made.

Is it really the right thing to do—to try to walk out of here?

What seemed like the bold and correct decision last night, while the rain was battering me under the pine tree, now doesn't seem like such a good one. It's fraught with potential problems.

I'm not even sure that, in our current physical shape, we can survive the hike. There's no way of knowing how long we'll have to walk to find help. It may take several days. Or longer.

And then there's the possibility that we're only able to travel a mile or two before becoming so exhausted we can't move any farther. Then we'll be stuck with absolutely no hope of being found. At least if we stay near the plane, we have a *chance* of being found, remote as it is.

But if we stay, the single bottle of water and the pack of Teddy Grahams we have left will be gone within a day, two at the most. I can probably stretch the pack of snacks to three days, but those few calories over that time period will be basically no help to us anyway. And now that the rain has stopped, I won't be able to collect rainwater any longer, although we might be able to glean a small amount today by licking the moisture from the tree leaves and branches. But that won't sustain us for very long.

And with each day we remain here without proper supplies, the weaker we will become, until eventually, the lack of sufficient food and water will render us so feeble that the option of walking out will no longer be available to us. There will be no second chance.

I don't know what to do. Should we stay or should we go?

It's frustrating because I'm sure others, who have much more outdoor experience than I, would know immediately which decision is correct in this situation—which one gives us our best chance at survival—but I seem, once again, paralyzed by indecision. I think it's because my celebrity lifestyle doesn't require me to make life-or-death decisions that affect not only me, but someone else as well. The reality is, Macy will have to live with the consequences of whatever I decide.

And the last time I made a decision of this magnitude that affected someone else, I totally blew it.

The burden of my dilemma settles on my shoulders like a millstone, and I feel as if I might collapse under its weight.

But as I continue to consider the two available options, one of the vultures returns and lands on the broken windshield of the plane, the outline of its body diffuse and ghostlike through the mist, like something from a horror movie.

I take it as a sign, and the decision I first settled on last night solidifies in my mind.

We have to go.

If I don't take a chance, if I don't make at least an effort to save Macy and myself, then I might as well just give up now and watch as the vultures feast on Adam, Juliette, and Kelsey, then wait to die so they can feast on me.

I have to be bold in this situation—I can't follow the safe course. I didn't do that in Oklahoma, and I won't do it now.

What if I'd been afraid of leaving my small hometown to venture into the world and chase my dreams of stardom? What if, paralyzed by indecision, I'd simply accepted the status quo, made the easy, the safe choice? The choice that required no sacrifice, no fortitude.

I know what my life would've become had I failed to be bold. I would still be stuck working a minimum-wage job, probably living in a run-down trailer park, just struggling to get by.

And now, faced with a life-and-death struggle much more serious than just a career choice, I know I must act.

I cannot allow myself or Macy to become indecision's next victims.

I turn to her. "We have to start walking and try to find help."

She doesn't respond, but she stares at me with sleepy eyes that seem to say, *Are you sure this is the right thing to do?*

I can only imagine what she must be feeling at this moment, and I find myself overcome with sympathy for her. Her whole life was torn to shreds mere days ago when the plane crash robbed her of the people who loved her most, the people she loved with the kind of wholehearted, consummate love only a child can give. And now, on top of all that, she finds herself stranded in the middle of nowhere with a woman she barely knows, who is asking her to embark on a terrifying journey.

I reach over and hug her, pulling her close in an embrace. The warmness between us supplants the cool dampness of the mountain air for a moment. "I know you're scared. I'm scared too, but we have to do this. We have to try to find help," I whisper. "Do you understand?"

Her head nods against my shoulder. I pat her on the back and draw away so I can look into her eyes. "We're going to be okay. Both of us. I promise I'm going to do my absolute best to take care of you and keep you safe, okay? It's going to be hard, but I know you can do it."

She nods again and, this time, smiles softly. She appears buoyed by my confidence in her.

I just wish I had as much confidence in myself. I'm not at all sure that we're going to be *okay*, but verbalizing my doubts and fears to her at this point would only be detrimental.

Over the next few minutes, we sort through everything that I scavenged from the airplane, setting aside the most necessary items and consolidating those into the black backpack. I rule out trying to take along either of our suitcases because their weight and bulk would just slow us down.

Macy is still wearing the dinosaur T-shirt and pink sleep pants I put on her the day after the crash, and when I look at her outfit, it prompts me to remove my soaking wet blue jeans and exchange them for Juliette's pair of gray sweatpants. The cotton fabric, even when wet, won't cling to and chafe my skin like the denim does and will make walking up and down the steep slopes much easier. It feels a little odd wearing a dead woman's clothes, but it's necessary in this situation, and I try not to think about it.

I complete a final inventory of the backpack to make sure I haven't overlooked anything we may need. The small pocket on the right side of the pack contains my cellphone. Inside the main compartment is the first aid kit, the package of moist towelettes, two pairs of socks and underwear for each of us, the full bottle of water, the package of Teddy Grahams, and two extra T-shirts, one for me and one for Macy. I toss in the empty water bottle as well, thinking that I can use it to collect rainwater again if the opportunity presents itself.

"Here," Macy says.

I look up and see that she is holding Mr. Pebbles.

"Will you put him inside the pack? You know, just so he'll be safe."

Smiling, I nod and say, "Sure." I take Mr. Pebbles from her—who is just as soaking wet as I am—stuff him inside the pack, and zip it closed.

I pluck my bra from the tree branch where I left it hanging and put it back on. I roll my jeans into a tight log, and I do the same with a pair I took from Juliette's suitcase when I scavenged the plane. I use the shoelaces from Kelsey's sneakers to lash both pairs of pants to the back of the pack. Even though the jeans are wet and heavy, I know I should bring them with us. Along with serving as a backup to our cotton pants, they can be used as a ground covering or shaped into pillows when we stop for the night. I should have thought of this last use for them earlier—a pillow would've been nice to have while we were trying to sleep out here.

I'm going to leave everything else I took from the plane behind, even my sweatshirt and sequin dress that remain woven in the boughs of the pine tree we huddled under last night. The trip itself will be grueling, and I surely don't need the burden of carrying the extra weight of items I can do without.

Satisfied that I haven't forgotten anything, I slip my arms through the padded shoulder straps and lift the pack onto my back. The load isn't bad, probably less than ten pounds, but the bigger issue is the bulk of it. I worry it will make it difficult to pass through the thick underbrush I'll encounter, but there's nothing I can do to change that, so I'll just have to manage the best I can.

The low cloud cover continues to obscure my view of the surrounding terrain, and I realize that after all my internal debate about whether we should stay or leave, I've failed to consider one very important question.

Which direction should we take?

I feel stupid for not thinking about this issue until the moment we are ready to leave, but now I'm faced with another decision that, either way, will have enormous consequences.

Should we go left? Right? Up the mountain? Down?

I have no idea.

If I make the wrong choice we might travel for days and only move deeper into the wilderness and farther away from help with each step. I try to recall what the area looked like the day after the crash, when the weather was clear.

Down the mountain and in front of us, I'd seen only a rugged wilderness that seemed to stretch on forever, a sea of mountaintops extending to meet the distant horizon. To the left and right, high ridges extended up, creating almost a bowl effect, and behind us the mountain rose to its peak. I don't remember how far away the top of the mountain appeared. All I recall seeing in that direction was a sea of tree trunks with patches of dense, green underbrush interspersed among them.

Perhaps there's a house or a road just on the other side of the mountain we're on. If not, maybe from the higher elevation I'll at least be able to get a signal on my cellphone and call for help. Going downhill would be easier. Or would it? One thing I've learned since the plane crash is that nothing in the wilderness is easy—everything is hard.

The fact is, I don't know what's at the bottom of the mountain. There might be nothing at all down there that will help us, and weighing that scenario with the possibility of getting cell service at the peak, makes my decision a fairly easy one.

"Are you ready?" I ask Macy.

She frowns and settles her doubt-filled eyes on me once more. "Are you sure we should leave?"

"Yes, I'm sure. I know it's scary, but we have to do this, Macy." I pause to give my words time to sink in, to let her digest the seriousness of our situation. I gaze at her face, but instead of comprehension, all I see is more uncertainty. Her eyes shift past my body, gazing into the forest at something behind me. It's clear she's avoiding looking me in the eyes. Her head drops and she stares at the dead, wet leaves between our feet.

Perhaps she's ashamed of her fear, her hesitance to follow me into the wilderness. I get that. In fact, I don't blame her at all. Even after all my careful deliberation, even *I'm* not one hundred percent sure it's the right call. But we must do something. We can't just sit here and wait to die.

I need her to understand why we must leave and to be in agreement with the plan, because if she isn't, it'll just make everything more difficult. I want her to *want* to go with me. If I force her to come along, I'll only come across as a dictator and she'll resent me for it.

That won't go well for either of us.

I sigh.

Until this moment, I haven't even considered the possibility that she might refuse to go with me. But what if she does? I certainly can't leave her behind. I'm not a monster. If she doesn't trust me enough, if I'm unable to convince her to follow me up the mountain, then all my internal debating and problem solving will have been for naught—I'll still be stuck right here, next to the crashed plane, with only the slimmest hope that someone will find us before it's too late.

My own fate will be taken completely out of my hands.

I kneel so that I'm at eye level with Macy. Maybe I simply haven't been direct enough. Maybe I've tried to shield her too much. She seems mature for her age. Perhaps a frank, honest discussion about the harsh reality of our situation is the best course of action.

I take a deep breath and pause another few seconds to gather my thoughts. I put my hand under her chin and gently raise it until she's looking at me. "Macy, I've thought *a lot* about this, and I really think we need to leave. I've been hoping that someone would find us, just like I know you have been . . . but no one has.

"And the fact is, we can't wait any longer. If we stay here too long and help doesn't come, we might—" I stop midsentence and contemplate whether or not I really want to be this blunt with the girl. I know what I have to do, though, and I see no reason to delay the inevitable or sugarcoat the truth. "If we don't find help soon, we might die. That's just the way it is. I'm sorry things have turned out like they have, but I just want to be honest with you and help you see why we must try to walk out of here and get help."

My statement is firm, yet simple enough to be clearly understood by a young girl.

Macy's lips are pencil-thin and drawn inward. Her wet bangs are matted to her forehead, her blonde locks plastered to her shoulders. She drops her eyes back to the ground, and her chest begins to heave in and out as she takes deep breaths. I know what she's doing because I used to do the exact same thing when I was a little girl—she's trying to keep herself from crying. "Do you understand what I told you, Macy?"

She lifts her head and nods, but her eyes are now full of tears. "I just don't want to leave . . . Mommy and Daddy. They're still in the airplane." She motions with her hand toward the twisted wreckage behind me.

"Oh, sweetie." I wrap my arms around her. Sobs reverberate against my chest, and her tears dampen my neck. "I'm so sorry," I say.

She keeps crying . . . and I let her. She needs to.

As her sobs begin to subside, I pull away a few inches so that I can look into her eyes. "I can't imagine how hard this is for you, but you know something?"

"Wh-what?" Her voice is broken by a trembling amalgam of sharp inhalations and sniffling.

"If your parents were still alive, they would want you to do everything you could to get out of here and to have a long, happy life. They wouldn't want you to stay here with them."

"They wouldn't?"

"No, honey, they wouldn't." My own eyes fill with tears. One escapes and runs down my right cheek. I quickly brush it away.

"Are you sure?"

"Yes, I'm positive. They would want you to go with me and try to find help. I know it's scary leaving with someone you just met, but we've gotten to be friends, right?"

She wipes away her tears with the backs of her hands and nods. "I . . . guess so."

"Sure we are." I give her an encouraging smile. "It's going to be okay, I promise, and I'm going to help you and do my absolute best to make sure you stay safe . . . but I need you to trust me, okay? Is that a deal?"

She hesitates for a few seconds, as if she's carefully analyzing the terms of an important business arrangement. "Deal," she finally replies and sticks her small hand out toward me.

I laugh and take her hand, shaking it. "Deal." I'm once again impressed at how resilient and tough she is. It's admirable, and I find myself wishing that I could be more like her. I pat her on the shoulder. "You're going to do great. I just know you will."

She nods again. "Okay."

I stand and readjust the backpack on my shoulders. "You ready to get going?"

"I guess so . . . but—" The doubtful look has crept back on her face.

"What is it?" I prod her.

"Can I see Mommy and Daddy one more time before we leave? You know, just to tell them goodbye?"

An intense heat attacks my chest at once, and I bite my lower lip to keep from breaking out in sobs. My eyes fill with tears for the second time, and I have to look away from her questioning face to keep from totally losing it.

How am I going to explain this? How am I going to tell her she can't see her parents again? How am I going to make her realize that by denying her simple request, I'm actually trying to do what's best for her?

I take a deep breath, wipe my eyes, and kneel again so that we're eye to eye. "Macy, I'm sorry, but you can't. I know that you might not understand this, but I just can't let you do that."

"Why not?" Her brow furrows with confusion.

Dropping my head and staring at the ground, I fight to find the right words, the words that will help her understand why she can't see her parents one last time, but also won't further scar her emotionally. "Because . . . they don't look the same as you remember them, sweetie."

"They don't?"

I again stare into her eyes and shake my head. "No, they don't."

"What do you mean?"

I sigh, struggling to find a way to explain something no girl her age should ever have to deal with. I have to be completely honest with her, I decide. There's no other way.

"When people die, their bodies change, and it's not something that you want to see. You just have to believe me about this, okay?" I speak softly, hoping my words will resonate with her. "I promise, I'm not trying to be mean to you by not letting you see your parents. I'm just trying to protect you."

"But I want to see them, just once more before we leave. Please?"

I sigh and shake my head. As I'm considering what else to say to her so she'll understand, I recall something she told me earlier about her cat that died, and it brings forth a memory from my own childhood. "Macy, I want to tell you a story and see if that will help explain what I'm talking about, okay?"

She nods. "Okay."

"When I was a little girl, about your age, I had a pet dog named Jenny, and I loved her very much. But one day, Jenny was playing outside and she ran into the road in front of our house. A man in a truck came by, didn't see her, and hit her. He didn't mean to do it, it was just an accident. When the man stopped his truck, I looked behind it and saw Jenny lying in the road. Without thinking about what I was doing, I ran over to see if I could help her."

"And did you help her?"

I shake my head. "No, it was too late. She was already dead by the time I got to her."

"She was?"

"Yes, she was . . . and she didn't look like herself at all. Her hair was all messed up and she was bleeding a lot."

"That's sad."

"It was sad. But do you want to know what the worst part was?"

"What?"

"After she died, when I would think about her, I couldn't remember all the fun we had together, playing in the yard or in the creek behind our house; all I could remember was the way she looked on the road. That made me really sad for a very long time and, even today, I wish I hadn't gone over and looked at her after the truck hit her, because that memory, the way she looked, is still in my mind and it blocks out all the good times we had."

I pause and study Macy's face. Her solemn expression tells me my words are having the desired effect.

"I don't want the same thing to happen to you, Macy. I want you to be able to remember your mom and dad like they were before the plane crash, when they would take you to the park or play with you in the backyard. Does that make sense?"

She wipes a tear from her cheek. "Yes, I guess so."

"Good. I know you may not understand everything right now, but one day you will, and you'll be glad you have all those happy memories of your parents."

"Can I at least tell them bye before we leave?"

Her request brings a smile to my face. "Absolutely. I think that's a great idea."

She turns around, holds out her little arm and waves toward the wreckage of the plane. "Goodbye, Mommy and Daddy." She stifles another sob. "I love you, and I'm going to miss you bunches. I promise I won't forget you."

Standing silently behind her, I realize that even if I wanted to speak now, I wouldn't be able to.

A tornado of emotion flows through me, and it's all I can do to hold myself together. I mourn the loss of Adam, Juliette, and Kelsey. I'm filled with trepidation about the journey ahead of us, and awestruck by the display of pure love Macy has just shown.

I stare at the plane in front of me. It seems so long ago that I crawled inside it back at that small airport in Georgia. It's useless now, just a mangled mess of sheet metal that will never fly again.

But I feel different also. It's as if my own soul has been torn apart and rearranged just like the aircraft's body. I'm not the same person who boarded the doomed flight just days ago, desperate to get back to a career that no longer seems so important to me.

I'm not really sure *what's* changed inside me, only that *something* has.

I close my eyes and let my heart speak silently.

You were a good friend to me, Kelsey. The only true friend I've ever had. I'm so sorry I caused this to happen to you. Please forgive me. I will miss you. I love you. Goodbye.

I open my tear-filled eyes, take Macy by the hand, and we begin our journey up the mountain with a single step.

18

Only an hour into the journey, I'm seriously considering turning around and returning to the crash site.

Maybe my plan to set out for the top of the mountain wasn't such a great idea after all.

The terrain is brutal, so steep that we often find ourselves on our hands and knees, literally crawling, a few inches at a time, toward the summit. The ground is covered with wet, slick leaf litter that makes it nearly impossible to gain, or maintain, any significant traction.

Whenever we do manage to move three or four consecutive steps forward by tearing into the soil with our fingers or grasping a nearby bush for support, we soon lose our footing on the slippery leaves and slide back down the mountain half the distance we just covered. The whole process is so mind-numbingly slow, so infuriatingly difficult, that I scream out in frustration every couple of minutes.

I don't know if we'll ever reach the peak.

Even if we do, I'm sure we'll both be so exhausted we won't be able to move another inch. We may just collapse and die right there.

The only positive aspect of our journey so far is that Macy is able to keep up with me, much to my surprise. She isn't lagging behind at all, as I feared she might. Her smaller frame and the fact that she isn't carrying a backpack like I am make it easier for her to navigate through and around the underbrush and tree limbs that often block our path.

"You doing okay?" I glance over my shoulder to check on her again. She's still within an arm's reach.

She gives me an affirmative nod. "Yep." Her chest is heaving from the strenuous exertion that climbing the mountain demands, and her face is glistening with beads of sweat, but overall, she looks good.

I'm gasping for air too, and I wipe my wet brow with the back of my hand. "Let's stop for a few minutes and take a break."

Moving to the uphill side of a large oak tree, I sit down and place the soles of my feet against the trunk to keep myself from sliding back down the mountain. My shoulders are burning from the strain of carrying the backpack. Even though it felt light and very manageable when I first put it on back at the crash site, walking up this steep incline, with gravity fighting my every move, even the relatively insignificant weight of the pack has become a burden. I slide my arms out of the shoulder straps and let it fall to the ground.

The knees of my sweatpants are already black from crawling on the wet earth. My feet hurt, and I can feel a blister beginning to form on my right heel. The humidity is so thick I taste it with every breath I take. My shirt is soaked through with perspiration and clings to my skin as if it's glued to me. My throat is on fire and crying out for just a sip of water.

Other than all that, I'm doing just peachy.

I unzip the pack and grab the bottle of water. I take a small sip and hand it to Macy, who has taken a seat at the adjacent tree. "Don't drink a lot. We need to save as much as we can."

She nods and drinks her tiny ration. "Thank you."

"No problem." I take the bottle back and return it to the pack. "Are you sure you're making it okay? I know it's hard."

"Yeah, I'm fine," she says.

I lean back against the slanted terrain. "Let's take just a few minutes to rest."

The thick cloud cover is still over us, and it appears to be getting lower the farther up the mountain we travel. That makes sense, though. I'm not sure how much elevation we've gained, but it has to be a substantial amount. When I made the decision to climb up instead of down the mountain, I hoped that by reaching the summit I would be able to spot a house or road, but unless the cloud cover lifts, that's not going to be possible.

My body doesn't want to move. I'm beyond exhausted. The sleep deprivation, combined with the lack of food and water, has left me without energy. I'm in good physical shape, my body toned by a five-day-a-week workout regimen and a balanced diet, but this is tougher than anything I've ever faced before. Normally, this hike up the mountain, while still difficult, wouldn't leave me totally spent. But that's exactly how I feel now.

My tank is empty.

But there's no way I'm turning around and going back. We've already worked too hard and come too far to give up now. I just hope we reach the top soon.

The amorphous cloud hanging above me has almost a hypnotic quality. My eyelids grow heavy and slide shut. A short nap would be nice. Right now, given the choice between a big, juicy cheeseburger and six hours of uninterrupted sleep, I'd take the sleep without hesitation—and I'm *very* hungry.

I take several deep, relaxing breaths, and my mind and body begin to slide into slumber.

"Are you ready to go?" Macy asks loudly.

My eyes snap open. "Uh . . . yeah, I guess so." I'm aggravated at her for disturbing me, but I know she's right—we have to keep moving.

Rolling onto my side, I push off the ground with my elbows. My body feels as if it's been frozen in ice, stiff and sore. I slip my arms through the backpack straps and stand slowly. The pack seems even heavier than it did when we stopped to rest just a few minutes ago. It's not, of course, but it's just another sign that my body is becoming progressively weaker by the second.

"Ready?" I ask.

"Ready."

I plant my foot uphill, grasp a nearby branch, and we continue our arduous ascent.

19

I'm ecstatic when I finally see the summit come into view. It's been over four hours since we left the crash site, and the realization that we're almost to the top of the mountain sends a surge of excitement and adrenaline through my body, overpowering my crippling exhaustion and causing me to move faster than I have the entire climb.

"We're almost to the top!" I shout.

"Good, I'm ready for another break," Macy says from right behind me.

I grab a nearby tree limb and pull myself the final few feet up the mountain. Standing on the summit, an overwhelming sense of accomplishment and joy comes over me. I raise my hands skyward, fists clenched, in triumphant celebration. "Yes!" I yell into the clouds.

Macy follows me, but slips as she takes her final step and goes to her knees, so I quickly bend over, grasp her forearm, and pull her up to the top with me.

We embrace, laugh, and dance around in the dead leaves as much as our worn-out bodies will allow. It's really more of a shuffle than a dance, but it feels wonderful and invigorating just the same.

"We made it!" I scream.

"We made it!" Macy repeats. The smile on her face is wide and infectious.

The top of the mountain isn't a craggy summit like one might find in the Rockies, but rather a gently rounded mound covered with large oaks and pines. The front side we just climbed and the back side of the mountain are both steep, the terrain dropping precariously downward, but to the left and right, long ridges slope gently down in either direction, and these seem much more conducive to foot travel.

It's a scant bit of good news in a situation that hasn't been lacking in bad, and it makes me feel better about my decision to climb up the mountainside.

The cloud cover has lifted a bit, because I'm now able to make out the treetops above me, but I'm disappointed because I can't see anything beyond the mountaintop I'm standing on. There's no way to know if there's a highway or even houses in the distance because the long-range view remains obscured by the thick clouds.

I remove my pack and retrieve the cellphone from the side pocket. I hold the power button down until I see the screen come to life. Waiting for the phone to boot up is torturous and seems to take forever. I'm anxious to see if there's cell service up here.

The selfie I took at the Nashville coffee shop finally appears, but my eyes don't focus on the happy girl in the photo. Instead, they go immediately to the upper right corner of the screen.

My heart sinks.

There's no signal, and even worse, my battery life is down to eight percent now.

No! No! NO!

I don't understand; there has to be a signal up here. I'm high enough now that there should be at least marginal service. But, as I've already learned, these mountains are full of surprises. Maybe there isn't a cell signal for miles. My heart still pounding in my chest with disappointment and fear, I tell Macy, "Wait here."

I begin walking away from her while holding the phone skyward, hoping that I'll move into just the right spot and be able to make a phone call or send a text message.

I circle the entire mountaintop and never once get a signal. To say that I'm discouraged is an understatement. It's worse than that, much worse. I'm devastated. Getting to a higher elevation was my best shot at finding cell service. If I can't get a signal here, then there's no hope. We can't stay up here indefinitely, and once we leave, there will be no chance of calling for help.

I'm not willing to give up just yet, though. There's a large oak tree standing at the center of the rounded top, near where I left Macy, and it appears the branches are low enough that I might be able to climb it.

I make my way over to it and have Macy push up on my butt as I struggle and wrangle myself onto the lowest limb by placing my feet against the tree trunk for leverage and grasping on to the limb with my hands. The process causes the pain to return to my chest and shoulders, but I fight through it.

I stand slowly, gingerly placing my weight on the shaking limb, which, thankfully, doesn't collapse and send me tumbling back to the ground. Wrapping my left arm around the massive trunk for balance, I raise the phone skyward in my right hand and move it in a slow arc, my eyes glued to the signal meter on the screen. The smallest bar illuminates, indicating the faintest of signals, and my heart jumps in my chest.

Yes!

I attempt to hold that position, but it's a challenge. My body is so weak now that my arm begins to shake from just the weight of the phone in my hand. Out of frustration, I scream loudly into the air.

"What's wrong?" Macy asks.

I ignore her question and continue to focus on the screen. The bar is still lit, but I'm afraid if I move even an inch it will disappear. By carefully maneuvering my thumb, I'm able to pull up the telephone dialer and enter 9-1-1. I press the green telephone icon at the bottom of the screen, which commands the phone to begin dialing the number. I hold my breath, hoping that the signal is strong enough to establish a connection.

A violent tremor shoots through my arm, and I watch in horror as the phone slips out of my hand and crashes to the ground below me.

No, this can't be happening!

"Macy, pick up the phone and toss it to me. Hurry!" I scream.

She lobs it toward my chest and miraculously, I pin the phone against my body with my right hand. I pull it away and hold it toward the sky again, but it's no use. The call has been dropped, and the single signal bar is no longer illuminated.

Crushing defeat envelops me, and I feel as if I'm going to have a complete meltdown at any second.

But instead of giving in to my despair, I stay focused. Sweeping my arm side to side again, I attempt to reacquire the signal, but my search is fruitless. No matter which direction I move the phone, I'm unable to find the signal again.

Please . . . please . . . come on!

As if answering my internal pleas, the bar flashes on for a split second and I gasp with excitement. But my hopelessness returns in a tidal wave as the faint signal leaves just as quickly as it reappeared.

I keep trying, unwilling to give up, until the battery finally dies and the phone shuts itself down. I toss it angrily to the ground and scream again, anger and sheer frustration coursing through my body.

Macy doesn't ask why I screamed this time.

I lower myself from the tree and walk away, leaving her standing alone next to my discarded phone. Having a conversation is the last thing I want to do right now. I need some time to myself to clear my head, and she must recognize this because she doesn't follow me.

I walk to the edge of the mountaintop and lean against a tree. With the chance of signaling for help now gone for good, the adrenaline leaves my body, and the toll of the difficult climb from the crash site pummels me with full force. It's not only my arm that is shaking now, but my whole frame.

I develop a severe, pulsating headache, the effects of dehydration and sleep deprivation intensifying their assault on me. My skin is filthy and covered in bug bites that itch incessantly. The pungent aroma of soured body odor stings my nostrils.

I want out of this wretched place with every fiber of my being.

Not only am I physically exhausted, but I'm now an emotional wreck too. The hope I had of being able to signal someone for help once I reached the top of the mountain has vanished, and it seems there's nothing else, no other sliver of optimism, to hang on to. The cellphone dying put the final nail in my mental coffin.

I'm finished. Done. I can't go on any longer.

Ever since the crash, I've been holding myself together with the faint hope that everything was going to be all right. But now, that tiny thread of optimism is on the verge of snapping in two. I kept telling myself that I'd find a way to make it through this, but I've reached the point where I no longer believe my own lies.

Unable to continue fighting against the constant emotional strain any longer, I break down. Sobs rack my body, and I bury my head in my hands as my body slides down the tree trunk, the rough bark clawing at my back. If I weren't so dehydrated, I'm sure tears would be streaming into my palms, but they're not.

Why is this happening to me?

I'd give everything—my money, my fame, my hit songs, all of it—to be out of this brutal wilderness right now.

I just want to go home.

I'm not even sure it's worth trying to continue. I'm so exhausted that I can't go on another day. There's just no way.

Maybe I was never meant to make it out of here alive.

For the first time, I genuinely consider the possibility that I may not survive. Sure, I've thought about the prospect of dying out here before, but it's never been as real as it is right now.

I may never again walk the streets of Nashville on a warm summer day or enjoy a cup of coffee on my back deck during autumn when the air is crisp and clean and the trees are exploding with vibrant colors.

I want to live, to be able to enjoy those things again, but if I'm honest with myself, I have to admit that at least a part of me wants to lie down on this mountaintop, call it quits, and simply wait to die. And I might actually consider that a viable option . . . if it weren't for Macy.

The promise I made to her—that I would do my best to take care of her and keep her safe—rings in my mind. If I quit now, I'll be breaking that promise. No, I can't give up. Not for my own sake, but for hers. Until I'm physically unable to move a single inch farther, I must keep going.

I needed a good cry—I guess everyone does sometimes. Crying has a way of cleansing one's body and soul. But there comes a time when you just have to pick yourself back up and keep going.

That time is now.

I slowly stand and walk back toward Macy. She's still standing next to the big oak tree, waiting patiently for my return, gripping my discarded cellphone in her small hand.

She lifts her arm toward me. "Here's your phone."

I take it from her. "Thanks, but the battery is dead. It's useless now."

"Oh."

I return the phone to the side pocket of the backpack. Why, I'm not sure. Like I told Macy, it's useless now. It's nothing more than an inoperable collection of electrical components, glass, and plastic, but for some reason I still want to hang on to it.

There's still plenty of daylight left, enough that we could walk for several more hours, but I'm too exhausted to keep going any farther today, and I know that Macy has to feel the same way.

I take Mr. Pebbles from the backpack and hand him to her. She pulls the stuffed animal into her chest in a robust hug and kisses him on the face.

"Thanks," she says, smiling at me.

"No problem."

I sit down and pull the bottle of water and pack of Teddy Grahams from the pack, along with the last dose of Tylenol from the first aid kit. "Let's eat," I say and motion for Macy to sit beside me. She takes a seat, and I open the bag of snacks. I take only a few out for myself and hand her the rest.

We consume all of the tiny bears within a minute—it's hardly a sufficient meal for either of us.

I have no idea when we'll be able to eat again.

The water bottle is already half-empty because we were forced to stop several times during our ascent to rest, and we both took a small sip each time to keep us going. We also sucked the water from wet pine boughs when they were within easy reach, but each offered only enough moisture to wet our mouths.

Even though my thirst is so intense it overpowers everything else I'm feeling, including my splitting headache, I drink only enough water to wash the Tylenol down, and hand what's left to Macy. "Drink this . . . all of it." She looks at me with a questioning glare. She's a smart girl. She watched me drink and knows I didn't take my full ration. "Just do it," I tell her firmly.

She raises the bottle to her lips and turns it up. The water slowly drains from the clear plastic container. As I watch the final sip slide into her mouth, I mark the passing of this monumental event with nothing more than a quiet sigh.

Our water is gone.

"Thank you," Macy whispers as she hands the bottle back to me.

"You're welcome." I take it from her and return it to the backpack, placing it next to the other empty bottle I brought along from the crash site. Hopefully, we'll be able to find a water source tomorrow and refill both of them.

If not, we're going to be in serious trouble.

It occurs to me that if we had stayed with the airplane, we would've been able to make the small amount of water stretch for at least a couple of days, but the strenuous hike we undertook to reach the top of the mountain forced us to consume the entire bottle in just a short time period. Doubt again creeps into my mind as to whether I made the right decision, but I quickly chase it away because it no longer matters. What's done is done. I can't go back and change it, so why bother worrying about it now?

I remove the lashing from the pack and grab the two pairs of rolled-up blue jeans. I hand Macy hers and I take mine, placing the makeshift pillow behind my head as I stretch out on the ground. A cold breeze blows across the mountaintop and nips at my skin, causing me to regret leaving my sweatshirt and dress hanging in the pine tree back at the crash site. I reach back into the pack and pull out the extra T-shirts I brought along. We both put one on over the shirts we are already wearing, but even two layers of thin cotton does little to stop the chilling effect of the wind.

I close my eyes and try to rest, hoping that the Tylenol will soon take effect and dull the throbbing pain inside my head. The whisper of the wind sliding through the tree leaves is peaceful, and as I concentrate on the sound, I begin to feel as though sleep may at last come to me.

In an instant, the fear and anxiety about what lies ahead of me return with a cold blast of the wind. A shiver runs down my body.

Macy's tiny hand reaches out and grasps mine. "It's going to be okay, Miss Lauren," she says softly.

20

It was just before I left my home in Oklahoma that I did the thing that has robbed me of sleep so many times.

Even back in my own comfortable bed in Nashville, it haunted my nights.

The memory of it is with me here in the wilderness too, once again overpowering my intense need for rest. Over the years I've learned that I cannot outrun it or hide from it. Wherever I go, no matter how doggedly I strive to focus on present things and forget the past, it's always with me, hiding somewhere in the shadows of my mind.

As hard as I've tried to escape its grasp, it remains.

The decision I made, the one that's gnawed at my conscience ever since, was thrust upon me just before I graduated high school, though the road that led to it began much earlier.

Growing up, my parents and I never really got along. They were good parents. They never mistreated or abused me in any way; we just had diametrically opposing views on life. They were both straitlaced, no-nonsense types. They rarely allowed themselves time to relax so they could slow down and enjoy life. I don't remember them ever taking a vacation. They found meaning in life by working hard, paying their bills, and just being all-around good, productive citizens.

My brother was cut from the same mold they were, never questioning rules or authority, just plodding through life as if he were a robot, programmed to do only what he was supposed to do, nothing more.

But I was different. I found my joy by living free, outside the set of moral boundaries that seemed to trap everyone around me. Even at an early age, I rebelled against this strict, conformist lifestyle. I didn't care what others thought about me. I didn't need, or even want, for that matter, my parents' or society's approval.

This clash of personalities often led to arguments between me and my parents. My mother and I usually butted heads the hardest, because my father generally stayed out of it and let her handle my acting out.

Once, in the fifth grade, I asked her if I could dye my hair purple. When she asked why on earth I would want to do such a thing, I told her, "It's my hair and I can do whatever I want to with it." That didn't go over so well. She flipped out and grounded me for a week for back talking. As soon as the week was over, I sneaked off to Walmart, bought the dye, and did it anyway.

That earned me two months in my room.

I didn't care, though, because I valued my independence, or at least the appearance of it, above all else. If that meant I had to spend countless hours locked up inside my room to maintain it, then I was more than willing to pay that price.

And I'm glad I held on to what made me different. Because that sense of fierce individualism is what spurred my creative side and led to my career in music later in life.

I continued to challenge norms once I began high school. I never was part of the *in-crowd*, but instead of trying to gain acceptance, like most others would have, I went the opposite direction—I intentionally dressed and acted differently just to make myself stand out.

I guess I've always liked being the center of attention, even back then. But it wasn't because I sought my classmates' approval or friendship. It was just my way of saying, *"Screw you, world. I am who I am, and I don't care what you think about me!"*

I wore shorter skirts than any of the other girls and the lowest-cut blouses. Sometimes I even dressed Goth with a full black ensemble and lipstick the shade of coal. That sure caused whispers and odd stares from the rednecks and preachers' daughters my town was full of.

Of course, my parents would've never let me leave the house looking like that, but I would just hide the outfit *I* wanted to wear inside my backpack and change once I got to school.

Everyone, my family included, assumed I must've been hanging around the wrong crowd. In reality, I was a loner. Not many of the country kids wanted to hang around with the weirdest girl in school. I soon found out that Northeast Oklahoma wasn't exactly a bastion for free-thinking individuals like me.

I dabbled with drugs too. Nothing hard, just marijuana, but when my mother found a joint inside my sock drawer when I was a sophomore, she came to the instant conclusion that I was the leader of a national drug cartel, pushing dope to every child and adolescent in our small town. She threatened to send me away to an all-girls reform school in Tulsa for that crime. My father eventually talked her off the ledge and, thankfully, I was allowed to remain in the house.

Being blessed with a great voice was probably the only thing that kept me from going completely rogue and setting fire to my entire life. Singing was the only thing I did that everyone approved of. My mother heard me in the shower when I was twelve, belting out a Reba McEntire hit. She proclaimed at once that I had been gifted with "the voice of an angel," and the very next day she marched me down to the choir director at the local Baptist church we attended.

And I was there singing almost every Sunday after that, right up until I left town.

Out of pure hardheadedness, I argued with my mother every Sunday morning about having to sing. Although it was true that I didn't like the idea of being *forced* to sing in church, I grew to love being in front of a crowd. But I kept up my charade of hating it because it was most important to me that I maintain my reputation as a rebel. I wasn't about to admit to my parents that they'd been right about something.

To say I was strong-willed would be an understatement.

I blossomed into an exceptional singer, and I found it was really the only thing in my life that gave me genuine joy. I hated school and didn't have much in common with the other teenagers in my town, but I could sing better than any of them. Knowing that I was the best at something was redemptive. Hearing others' applause and verbal encouragement was a drug to me, and I became hopelessly addicted to it. I knew that becoming a performer was what I wanted to do with my life, what I was destined for. I determined that one day I would escape the sleepy Oklahoma town I called home and make my own way in the world, my voice propelling me to fortune and fame.

I met Logan the middle of my junior year. His family had moved into the area from California, and he was different from most of the other guys in our town. He didn't drive a pickup truck, chew tobacco, or wear a hat. He had long, brown hair that fell below his shoulders, which caused him to endure more than a few verbal insults from our fellow students. He had dark hazel eyes, and the first moment I saw him, I thought he was the hottest guy I'd ever seen. The fact that he also seemed to be rebelling against society only increased my attraction.

We quickly struck up a friendship because we were like-minded individuals who both shared an interest in music. We often talked between classes and after school and eventually began to date.

My parents didn't approve of Logan, as I knew they wouldn't, and I guess that was one reason I liked him so much. My father hated his long hair, and my mother thought that he had no future. I knew they wanted me to marry a local boy whose family owned a profitable cattle ranch or other business so that I would have financial security. That was the last thing I was concerned with. Their opposition only spurred me on, and rather than try to hide or downplay my relationship with Logan, I threw it in their faces every chance I got.

The summer before my senior year, we spent a lot of time together and our relationship grew. I fell in love with him as he did with me—at least, that's what he told me, and I believed him.

So I was crushed when, right before school started again, he told me that his father had lost his job with the local bank and the family would be moving back to California. I begged him to stay with me, but he said that he had to go, that he couldn't stay in Oklahoma without his family.

I tried to understand, but I couldn't.

He was the only person in my life that I felt actually understood me, and I didn't want to lose that connection. But as much as I didn't want him to go, there was nothing I could do to stop him.

The day before his family was to leave, Logan and I spent one last night together, parked next to the small lake just outside of town. I still remember every detail, what he was wearing, his cologne, the way his lips tasted of the peppermint gum he chewed. I don't think I'll ever forget that night. He promised to stay in touch with me after he returned to California, and I promised the same.

I never heard from him again.

In September I discovered I was pregnant. I was terrified at the prospect of becoming a mother at such a young age and what that would mean for my dreams of becoming a famous singer. I was even more worried what my parents would do to me if they found out.

I didn't know what to do.

I couldn't afford to pay for an abortion, but even if I could've, it wouldn't have mattered anyway. I didn't have a friend I trusted to drive me to the clinic in Tulsa and then keep my secret. No, that wasn't an option.

It's a well-known fact that residents of a small town have an intelligence gathering operation that would make even the CIA proud, its headquarters usually being located at the beauty salon or local church. So there was no way I could tell anyone about the pregnancy. If I had, rumors about me would've been flying all over town in a matter of hours. My parents would've certainly heard them too, which was the last thing I wanted to happen. Sure, I was rebellious, but even I didn't have the stomach for that type of scrutiny.

I decided to keep the pregnancy a secret as long as I could, hoping that I could figure something out before the time came that I could no longer hide it.

During the first few months, I dealt with morning sickness and general lethargy, but I managed to keep up the appearance that everything was completely normal for the most part. Once, my mother did find me puking my guts up in the bathroom one morning before school. She wanted to take me to the doctor, but I adamantly refused. I knew if I went to see the doctor, one of his nurses would blab to the receptionist what my real issue was, and, in turn, the receptionist would report back to one of the senior intelligence officers in town—who also served as her Sunday school teacher—in the form of a prayer request for me. Then the truth would come out, and everyone around town would know.

I blamed my upset stomach on a bad taco I ate the previous day and, thankfully, my mother let the subject drop.

As the weeks passed, the morning sickness gradually abated and I began to feel better. I was relieved that my stomach wasn't growing as much as I'd expected, and I hoped that this might enable me to hide my condition for another month or two.

It seemed that I thought about the new life growing inside of me every single minute. It was all my mind could focus on. I didn't know what I was going to do once the baby arrived or how it would affect my plans for my future. My dreams of leaving town and pursuing a singing career were gone, that much I knew. There's no way I could move away with a newborn in tow.

I was going to be doomed to spending the rest of my life in the small town, relying on my parents for help, with no hope of ever escaping.

The longer I thought about what I faced, the more I began to resent the unborn child because of what it represented—my dreams being crushed into a million tiny pieces.

Strangely, I wasn't angry at myself or even at Logan for being irresponsible; instead, I was livid at the baby inside me who was screwing up my entire life. All my aspirations for the future were being stolen from me. I knew if I didn't find a way out, my life, for all practical purposes, would be over at the ripe old age of eighteen.

By spring of my senior year, I was still able to hide my enlarged belly with bulky shirts and loose-fitting clothes. I lived in fear that one morning I would wake up looking as if I'd swallowed a beach ball, but it never happened. I just kept dressing so that the changes to my body remained hidden, and no one was the wiser. I was thankful for that, because if someone at school had suspected anything, rumors about me would've been flying all over the place.

With my body working with me to conceal the pregnancy, I began to seriously consider the possibility that I might be able to hide it altogether. I'd seen TV programs and news reports about young women who had successfully hidden pregnancies from everyone around them, including their closest friends and family members, and I'd even seen a few cases where women were shocked when they gave birth because they had no clue they were even pregnant.

I wondered if I might be one of the fortunate ones who could keep it all a secret.

Counting from the last night Logan and I spent together, I calculated that my due date would be sometime during the middle two weeks of May. Of course, that was just an educated guess, but I felt fairly confident that it would be around that time.

In April, I began devising a plan.

I needed to find somewhere private to give birth, without the fear of being discovered. After some thought and scouting different locations, I decided on an old barn that sat on a sprawling farm outside of town. The old man who owned the property had attended the Baptist church where I sang every Sunday, and I remembered that he had passed away about a year earlier. From what I heard, he had left the farm to his son and daughter, but both of them had long ago moved away from Oklahoma and had no desire to return, so they put it up for sale. Fortunately, the property was still vacant, and I decided that it would offer me the best chance at successfully implementing my plan.

I researched online about what to expect during the birthing process, what supplies I should have on hand, and how to know if there was a complication that needed immediate medical attention. The whole process was petrifying.

Every possible scenario I read about brought new worries and new problems that I had to plan for. I put together a duffel bag of necessities—feminine hygiene items, medical supplies, and clean towels—and I kept it in the trunk of my car at all times, ready to make the dash to the barn whenever the time came. I also made sure that my cellphone was always charged and that I always had it with me. If a problem arose, like a breech birth or something else, I would at least be able to call for help. I desperately wanted to keep my secret, but I wasn't willing to lose my life for it.

My biggest fear during that time was that my water would break while I was walking down the hallway at school and then everyone would know at once. There would be no way to hide anything if that happened. Because of this, I left school on more than one occasion and headed to the barn just because I felt something strange that I thought might be a contraction, but they all turned out to be false alarms.

I doubted that I could pull the whole thing off, but I was determined to give it my best shot—my future rested on it.

It was during the last week of school it finally happened. Having passed all my final exams, I was preparing for my upcoming graduation, but unlike most of my peers, who were looking forward to a carefree summer, my mind was consumed with anxiety about the approaching birth. I knew it was coming soon. I could feel it.

On Tuesday evening of that week, I was home alone, which was unusual, as both of my parents were homebodies. But on that particular night, they decided to accept the invitation of another couple they were friends with and join them for dinner. My older brother had moved out the year before so he wasn't there either.

I couldn't have asked for better timing.

I'd gone to the restroom and when I stood up, my water broke. I panicked at first, and I almost picked up the phone to dial 9-1-1 right then and there, willing to toss all my careful planning and my hopes for the future out the window in exchange for the comfort and safety of a modern hospital.

But within a minute, I gained control of my emotions and put my plan into action.

Scrambling to get out of the house before my parents returned, I quickly cleaned the mess off the bathroom floor, then stuffed the soiled towels into a garbage bag. I changed out of my pajamas and into a pair of sweatpants and a comfortable T-shirt. I took three bottles of water and a large Gatorade out of the refrigerator, then pulled an extra clean towel out of the hall closet.

Less than ten minutes after my water broke, I placed the drinks and the bag of dirty towels into the trunk of the beat-up Toyota Corolla my parents had purchased for my brother and me to use during high school. I placed the clean towel on the driver's seat to protect it, slid behind the wheel, and headed to the abandoned barn. At the first stop sign I fired off a quick text message to my mother: I'm going out to grab a bite to eat. Be back later.

The contractions were already intense by the time I pulled the car up to the steel cattle gate that blocked the entrance to the farm. I was relieved to see that the padlock I'd cut a week earlier with my father's heavy-duty bolt cutter hadn't been replaced by the realtor. Once I opened and drove through the gate, I closed it to avoid suspicion. I parked the car at the rear of the barn so no one would be able to see it from the gravel road that ran along the front of the farm.

I hurriedly retrieved my bag of medical necessities from the trunk, along with the water and Gatorade, and made my way toward the barn using the flashlight I kept in the car. The drumfire of a thousand cicadas welcomed me, and a multitude of fireflies hovered over the old field, showering it with brilliant flashes of neon green. The May air was warm and humid, and I began to sweat profusely within the first minute of my arrival.

The old building was dark and dank, with spiderwebs hanging off every constructed angle. I walked straight into a large, sticky one and had to fight to clear it from my face. The half-rotten floorboards creaked against the worn nails with every step I took. It smelled of musty hay and old leather.

The barn was a creepy place at night, like something from a horror movie. If I hadn't already been there several times in the daylight, during the false alarms or while I was preparing and scouting it out, I would've turned around and run away as fast as I could just out of sheer terror.

It was a lousy place to bring a new life into the world, but I didn't have any other option.

Just as I reached the corner of the barn I'd determined would be the most comfortable place to go through labor, a violent contraction hit me like a sledgehammer to the stomach. I went to my knees with a deafening scream. My voice echoed off the old wooden walls and reverberated in my ears.

I'd selected this location specifically because of its remoteness, but the sound of my agony was so loud I feared that someone might hear me from the gravel road if they happened to drive by. I removed my T-shirt and quickly rolled it into a tight log and bit down on it. I could feel my jaw muscles tense every few seconds from the pain, but at least the mass of cotton in my mouth muffled my cries. I took a blanket from the medical bag and spread it over the old hay that still covered the dirty wooden floor.

I'd worried that I might suffer in labor for a long while, and I'd given myself a timeline of four hours, deciding that if I labored for that long without delivery, which many women do, then I'd be forced to call for help.

But I could tell that the baby was coming quickly.

I removed my sweatpants and underwear and sat down on top of the blanket, leaning back against the corner of the barn. The wood was rough and pricked at my bare back and shoulders. I propped the flashlight up on a nearby board so that I would have enough light to see.

Another contraction came, and I clenched down on the T-shirt until my jaw felt as if it were going to break in two. I tried to remember everything I'd learned online about giving birth, when to push and when not to, how to breathe, and relaxation techniques, but the pain was so unbearable that my mind went blank. I couldn't focus on anything but the agony I was experiencing—it felt as if my insides were about to be ripped from me in one terrifying, violent explosion.

After thirty minutes, I grabbed the cellphone and started to call for help, but just as I was about to dial, my thumb froze in place. I knew I couldn't give up. I'd already come too far and invested too much into the plan to just abandon it, no matter how much I was hurting. My future was riding on enduring this and successfully hiding the pregnancy.

I knew that if I called for help, it would all be over.

Even though I'd watched lots of videos online of women giving birth and read countless articles about the process, trying to
prepare myself for what I should expect, I was shocked by the intensity of the pain. I soon found out, suffering in the corner of that
dirty Oklahoma barn, that watching a video or reading an article
and going through the same thing myself were two entirely different things.

I was so naïve . . . about everything.

I took deep breaths and tried to calm down. I told myself that,
somehow, I would get through it.

It was excruciating, and several times I thought I was going to
pass out. I poured half of one of the bottles of water over the top
of my head to cool off and took a quick drink of what was left to
moisten my dry throat. I kept working through the pain, hoping
that I wasn't going to die on this dusty, hay-strewn floor.

Breathing in rapid bursts, then bearing down and pushing
when I felt I needed to, I managed to progress to the point where
I could feel the baby crowning when I moved my hand between
my legs to check.

Ten more minutes of pushing and the baby's shoulders broke
free. I reached down and grasped it. It was wet and slick and my
hands slipped off, so I grabbed a clean towel out of the medical
bag and placed that over the body for a better grip. With the next
contraction, I pulled at it firmly as I pushed.

When the legs popped out, I let out a sigh of relief, feeling as
if I'd just been unburdened of a great weight. I quickly reached
into the medical bag and retrieved the two zip ties I'd taken from
my father's tool chest and secured both of them tightly around the
umbilical cord about an inch apart, then cut the cord in the middle with a pair of large scissors I'd taken from a kitchen drawer.

I wiped the baby off with the towel, and turned it over. I
grabbed a suction bulb from the bag and drew the mucus from
the mouth and nostrils, just as I'd seen in the videos online, but it
still wasn't crying. At first, I thought it might be dead.

I picked it up by the ankles and dangled it out in front of me, then smacked it several times on the back and bottom. At last I heard a sharp cry erupt from its lungs. I placed it back on the blanket, and only then did I realize that I'd just given birth to a little girl. I checked to be sure everything looked as it should; she had two arms and two legs, ten toes and ten fingers. Her face and ears were normal.

She appeared to be perfectly healthy.

I retrieved another clean towel from the bag and wrapped it tightly around her. By this time, she was crying loudly and, without even thinking about it, I placed her against my chest and rocked her.

I didn't expect what happened next.

As I cuddled her, I felt an overwhelming sense of love envelop me. Tears began to run down my sweaty cheeks. I laughed and cried simultaneously. This precious little life that had grown inside of me for the past nine months, and that I'd come to resent, now elicited nothing but complete joy in me.

Although I'd just met her, I loved her with a pure, all-encompassing love as if I'd known her my whole life. I pressed her against my breast and nursed her. Her blue eyes focused on me, and I just knew she loved me too.

Unlike others in my life, she accepted me just the way I was. She didn't see my faults, my mistakes. To her, I was simply her mother, nothing else.

The afterbirth passed without complication a few minutes later, which was another huge relief. I was weak and trembling from the experience, so I drank the Gatorade, hoping it would help replenish my body's nutrients while she continued to nurse.

After I'd spent an hour with her, I cleaned myself up, dressed, and collected everything I'd brought with me in an effort to leave as little evidence as possible of what had occurred there. I packed it all back inside the trunk of my car and then held my daughter in my arms as I drove off.

When I was a mile away from the farm, I stopped along the gravel road and retrieved the black garbage bag from the trunk and tossed it into the woods. Inside it were the dirty towels I'd used to clean up the bathroom at home and protect the front seat of the car, along with the blanket and towels from the barn.

Once I made it to the state highway, I prayed I wouldn't be stopped by the cops. Holding a newborn in my arms versus having her properly restrained in a car seat would certainly raise some questions.

I didn't need any questions.

I drove west for forty-five minutes. The place I'd chosen was far enough away from my house that I hoped any media attention that might be generated would be directed away from the town where I lived. I'd already driven this route from the barn a couple of times in order to familiarize myself with the roads, turns, and any hazards I might encounter. Getting into an accident on my way there would've screwed everything up.

As I pulled into the parking lot of the library, I began to have second thoughts about the whole idea. After leaving the barn, I'd gone into execution mode, completing the plan I'd played out in my mind a hundred times before that night, detached and robotic—I was a soldier on a mission.

But once I arrived at the library safely, staring out the windshield at the fire department across the street, then back down into my daughter's eyes, I wasn't sure I could really go through with it.

Or even that I *wanted* to.

The overwhelming feelings of love and acceptance I experienced back at the barn returned. I hadn't counted on those affecting me the way they did. It was new to me, that feeling of unconditional love, and I found it fulfilling in a way that I couldn't even explain to myself.

I'm not sure why I thought that having a baby and then abandoning it would be as simple and emotionless as running an errand for my parents. But that's how I'd looked at it—just something that had to be done. I'd made checklists and completed dry runs of everything that would take place leading up to and after the birth, and all my preparation had paid off. Everything had gone just as I'd planned.

But the one thing I hadn't planned on was my emotions getting in the way.

I found that I really didn't want to leave her. I wanted to drive across the country with her beside me and start a new life *together*, to leave Oklahoma and everything it represented behind, once and for all.

But as the tears started to flow down my cheeks once more, I knew that wasn't a possibility at all. It was only a fantasy.

I had no job, nowhere to go, no way to support my daughter. My dreams of becoming a successful recording artist would be history too. What was I going to do, drag her along with me while I struggled to make it? Of course not. That wasn't realistic.

My plan had been the right one all along.

I knew what I had to do, and I decided that the quicker I did it, the better.

I lifted my head and dried my eyes with my shirt. I didn't look at her face again. I couldn't.

I went to the trunk and took out the cardboard box I'd been carrying around for the last couple of months. I made sure she was still wrapped tightly in the towel, then I placed her gently into the box.

I checked for traffic, but it was getting late and the small-town street was empty. Pale yellow light shone from the three windows along the front of the fire department. During the initial stages of my planning, I'd considered dropping my child off at the town's only hospital, but quickly ruled it out once I discovered there were numerous video cameras covering the parking lot and all the entrances. I would've been recorded, along with my car and license tag, and I couldn't risk having the police or a reporter show up at my parents' house asking questions. The fire department was the next logical choice because I knew that someone would always be there, and there was only a single video camera that covered the front of the building, which I could easily avoid.

I checked a second time to make sure no one was walking or driving down the street and then hurried across the road. I ducked behind the corner of the fire department building, the brick exterior warm against my skin, and waited to see if anyone inside had spotted me running across the street. When no one emerged to investigate, I rose from my hiding spot and walked briskly to the front door, making sure to keep my head down and out of view of the camera. I placed the box down, but wouldn't look inside it.

I was still afraid I might change my mind.

I took a deep breath, rapped firmly on the red metal door, then sprinted back across the street and climbed into my car, which I'd left running. I pulled out of the parking lot, then paused at the edge of the street and stared at the fire station and the cardboard box in front of it.

As soon as I saw the door crack open, I turned onto the road and stomped the accelerator.

I drove home in silence. I didn't even want the radio on. I cried and told myself I'd done the right thing, that now I was free to chase my dreams and that my daughter would be adopted by a rich, loving family that would take good care of her.

And then I cried some more.

Several miles down the road, I told myself the sadness I was feeling would eventually go away and that I'd accomplished what I set out to, which was the important thing.

I couldn't believe everything had worked out just as I'd planned. There were no complications during the birth, and I didn't get caught dropping the baby off at the fire station.

Twenty minutes after I left the fire station, I pulled into a convenience store and went straight to the restroom; I knew the way because I'd been there before too. I was careful not to look at the overhead video cameras I'd noticed on a previous visit or at the cashier, who was, thankfully, busy with another customer. I kept my eyes glued to the ivory-colored floor.

Once inside the safety of the bathroom, I washed my face, then changed into the skirt and blouse that I'd stashed inside my purse. I threw the sweatpants and T-shirt I'd worn to the barn into the trash receptacle, then covered them with a hefty pile of paper towels. I put on some makeup and fixed my hair as best I could, so that it would appear to my parents that I'd actually gone out to dinner.

I exited the store as quickly as I'd entered and, as far as I could tell, went unnoticed by the cashier and customers who were inside.

Once I returned home, my parents questioned me about why I'd been out so late, but I told them that I'd met a friend from school during dinner and we were going over graduation plans and that the time just got away from me. After some dubious looks, they accepted my explanation and effusive apology. I showered, then retreated quickly to the solitude of my room. I collapsed onto the bed, both mentally and physically exhausted.

I found out a couple of years later that Oklahoma has a safe haven law, and I could've saved myself a lot of paranoia and many scouting missions by just walking into the fire department or hospital and handing my baby to someone working there. I could've remained anonymous and wouldn't have been legally charged. When I first found this out, I felt stupid that I hadn't known such a crucial fact, but the more I thought about it, the more convinced I became that it wouldn't have changed the way I chose to handle the situation. I doubt I'd have had the courage to look another human being in the eyes as I abandoned my child.

During the following days, I tried my best to put the whole incident out of my mind, and I almost succeeded. It was over, and I didn't want to dwell on it. I purposely avoided watching the news or reading the local papers as well. I simply wanted to forget that it had ever happened.

The following Saturday night, I graduated from high school. My parents and brother all attended, and I flashed the same fake smile that I'm so accustomed to using now in my life as a celebrity.

No one suspected a thing.

On Sunday, I sang in church for the last time.

On Monday, I bought a bus ticket and left town without saying goodbye, headed to Nashville to follow my dreams.

21

When I wake, I'm still lying flat on my back, peering into the same cloudy sky, but the light inside the forest is different, softer and more diffuse than when I first lay down.

I realize that what I'm actually seeing is the breaking dawn, and it brings a smile to my face. I rub the sleep from my eyes and stretch my arms above my head. Much to my surprise, I actually feel rested, despite the cold, hard ground beneath me and the stiff pillow of my rolled-up blue jeans under my head.

I don't recall tossing or turning during the night at all. I remember thinking about Oklahoma, just as I've done so many times before bed, but after that, there's simply nothing. I've slept just as soundly as I would have on a bed inside a five-star hotel. I suppose that I've pushed my mind and body so far beyond their normal limits ever since the plane crash that they'd finally had enough and decided to take some downtime.

I'm glad they did, because I certainly needed it.

Macy is asleep beside me, with Mr. Pebbles pinned tightly against her chest by her small arms. She's lying on her right side, facing me, and I can see her eyes moving behind her closed lids. I wonder if she's dreaming, and if so, about what? Whatever it is, it must be pleasant because the muscles in her face are relaxed, and her skin is a warm, rosy color. She looks peaceful, and I'm thankful that she's gotten some much-needed rest too.

I sit up and discover that, despite the good night's sleep, the soreness in my muscles has returned with a vengeance. Everything hurts: my shoulders, my arms, my ribs, and especially my legs. The climb up the mountain yesterday probably stretched muscles inside my body that I didn't even know existed. I'm going to have to get up and move around to loosen up, just as I did when I was so sore following the plane crash.

I gently stand and shuffle away from Macy, trying not to cause myself undue pain by moving my legs too quickly. I walk around the mountaintop until my tense muscles begin to feel better. My thighs are still on fire, though. I'm not surprised; they took the worst of the punishment during the climb.

As stiff as my body is, I try to focus on the positive. I feel rested, which is a pleasant change. The migraine that plagued me yesterday evening is gone, and my mind seems clear and refreshed for the first time since the crash.

The urge to pee hits me, and I duck behind a tree and squat, but only a tiny, broken stream of urine leaves my body. The overpowering smell of ammonia assaults my nostrils.

Even though the sky is still overcast, the rain has stopped entirely; not even a light drizzle is falling anymore, so I must make finding a water source the number one priority for today. Of course, we have no more food either, but that's a secondary concern at this point.

Macy stirs as I walk back to her. "Good morning," I say.

She wipes her eyes with the backs of her hands. "Morning."

"How'd you sleep?"

"Pretty good," she says through a yawn. "Did you sleep okay, Miss Lauren?"

I nod. "I sure did." I look down at her and smile, but inside, I'm consumed with the fact that neither of us has anything to eat or drink this morning.

That has to change—today.

"You ready to get going?" I ask.

She nods and slowly gets to her feet. I can tell by her tentative movements that she's sore from the climb up the mountain too, but I don't raise the subject. No sense in dwelling on how much this sucks for both of us.

We remove the extra T-shirts we donned last night in our feeble attempt to stay warm. I'm confident that we won't need them once we get going. I place the shirts back inside the backpack and double-check to make sure everything else we brought along is still inside. Macy hands me Mr. Pebbles, and I place him inside for safekeeping. The two pairs of rolled-up blue jeans I again lash to the outside of the pack with the shoelaces, which seemed to work well yesterday.

I place my arms through the thinly padded shoulder straps and lift the pack onto my back, ready for another day of arduous travel.

If only the clouds had lifted during the night, I might be able to get a better visual reference of the surrounding terrain and gain a clue as to which way we should start walking. But I'm still unable to see anything past the top of this mountain, and I face another decision that I don't know the answer to.

But I *have* to make a decision, right or wrong, and act on it.

There's no way I'm going to head down the other steep side of the mountain, opposite the one we climbed yesterday. My body just can't take that amount of abuse right now. Besides, I might take only two steps off the summit before my weak legs collapse underneath me and send me tumbling end over end down the mountain slope for who knows how far.

That's definitely not an option.

So that leaves the two more gently sloping ridges that descend from the mountaintop. I turn so that one of them is in front of me, the other behind. I have no idea which, if either of them, is the best choice. But I've always believed in marching forward, not backward, so I head off in that direction, with Macy following close behind.

As we leave the summit and begin walking down the ridgeline, dodging large trees and small rock outcroppings along the way, I'm careful to watch every step I take. My legs feel limp, almost like wet dish rags, and I find that it's difficult for me to control them at times. I move slowly and with caution, making sure my feet are always on solid ground before placing my weight on them. The last thing I need is a broken ankle.

Macy and I talk as we travel, and although I'm not accustomed to conversing with seven-year-old girls, I'm happy to do it because it keeps my mind off my burning thirst and aching body.

She tells me about the school she attends, describing in detail every single one of her classmates, how they look, what they like to do, et cetera. She doesn't mention anything about her parents or her home life, and I understand completely.

I don't broach the topic either.

She asks me about my life, where I live and what I do. I purposely avoid the fact that I'm a celebrity, telling her only that my home is just outside of Nashville and that I work for a record company.

It's been obvious to me since the crash that Macy doesn't know who I am. She must've been half-asleep when I introduced myself to her mother and father at the airport. Maybe she wouldn't have recognized me even if she'd been wide awake, I really don't know—it doesn't matter either. Because the fact is, I'm enjoying just being plain old Lauren again, having a genuine, honest discussion with someone who's not afraid to be herself around me.

To Macy, I'm just the woman who was in the plane crash with her.

And I like that.

Being forced to spend time with her, being treated as a normal person, makes me realize how much my fame changes the people around me.

Sometimes the fans I meet backstage at a concert or those who recognize me in town when I'm shopping lose all dignity. They scream like kindergarteners and wildly snap pictures with their cellphones. Their hands shake with nervous excitement when they ask for my autograph. Others get lightheaded at just seeing, touching, or meeting me. More than once, a fan has passed out backstage or in an autograph line and paramedics had to be called. Some don't go that far, for sure, but almost all of them act or speak differently than I imagine they would in their real lives.

It makes me feel isolated, as if I'm trapped inside my own little cocoon that I'll never escape.

None of my fans are real to me. How can they be? How can I connect with someone who's afraid to show me their true self?

And the sad part is, I know I'm not real to them either.

Instead of seeing me as a person, a fellow human being, I'm only the living embodiment of an image they've seen on television or the voice they've heard on the radio.

That's all I am.

An image. A voice.

And I really don't get that at all. Because if you take away all the glitz and laser lights and smoke-filled coliseums, if you strip all that nonsense away, I'm just a normal person who likes to sing.

Not that I'm without guilt in this whole scenario—because I certainly am not.

I deserve no sympathy.

After all, I'm the one who wanted fame in the first place, who worked so hard just so people would recognize my name. I knew what I was getting into when I first started out, and I could've stopped at any time, but I didn't. I kept growing my *image*, determined to become a celebrity.

And I did, I was successful. More people know my name now than I could've ever imagined possible.

But I gave up my anonymity in the process.

People who've never been famous don't recognize what it's like to no longer be able to run down to the grocery store for a gallon of milk without having to stop for autographs and pictures with fans. Or to have to put on a smile and pretend you're deeply engaged in conversation when all you want to do is grab your milk and go home. I can never leave the house without considering how I look either, because someone is always taking pictures or video of me.

It was fun at first, but now it's just a huge pain.

So I enjoy the discussion with Macy, not for its great substance—learning the details of twenty first-grade students' lives isn't my normal area of interest—but rather, for its simple innocence and honesty. Listening to her and hearing the enthusiasm in her voice as she recounts numerous stories from school makes me feel like a real, normal person again.

I've missed that.

We stop to rest, and I look back toward the mountaintop where we spent the night—it's still easily within view. It seems we've been walking for at least an hour, and our lack of significant progress is discouraging. We're progressing at a painfully slow pace, but there's not much I can do about that; my trembling legs will only move so fast.

There's no water for Macy and me to share this time during our break, no Teddy Grahams to nibble on. So rather than remain motionless and dwell on our destitute condition, I quickly catch my breath, push off the tree I'm leaning against, and continue my slow, methodical trudge down the ridgeline.

Macy is quiet as we continue to walk. I guess she's run out of stories to tell me. As much as I enjoyed our conversation, I enjoy the respite from it as well. I soak in the silence of the forest, the only sound in my ears the muted plod of our feet against the mat of dead leaves that cover the ground.

The memories of last night return, and I begin to think about the baby I abandoned back in Oklahoma. It isn't unusual for me to dwell on her—I've done it a lot over the years.

What I did is a secret—and a burden—that I alone carry. I've never told anyone what happened, not even Kelsey.

No one.

I chose not to contact Logan after I discovered I was pregnant because I saw nothing good that could come from it. He was already over 1,500 miles away in California; how was he going to be able to help me? He was just a kid himself, the same as me. Perhaps if he'd called me at some point, I would've told him, but he never did.

It's hard going through a thing like that and not being able to talk with anyone about it. Occasionally, I have the desire to just walk up to a stranger on the street and spill my guts, just to get it off my chest, but I know I can't. Keeping the secret is just part of the price I must pay for the choice I made.

Sometimes I can convince myself that my decision to leave her behind while I moved to Nashville and chased my dreams was the correct one.

At other times, I regret doing it with every fiber of my being.

Some nights I even dream that I'm holding her in my arms again, only to wake up and realize I'm alone.

I often wonder what became of her. After I left town, I never tried to find out any details of what happened after she was found at the fire department. I just didn't want to know. I guess I still don't, really, but there's a part of me that can't help but think about it.

With every success I've experienced, every hit single, every jam-packed coliseum, I've thought of her. While I've been getting to live my dream, I've often pondered what she is experiencing.

Was she adopted by a loving family? Does she have a good life? A happy life? What does she look like now?

I imagine her going to ballet recitals and playing with her friends in the backyard of her family's large home, running and laughing and just being a joyful little girl.

That's how I try to think about her anyway.

But sometimes, the possibility that she ended up being shuffled among numerous foster homes, with no stability or happiness in her life at all, enters my mind. I try not to focus on such negative outcomes as that, though, because they only make me regret my decision even more.

Once, after I became successful and had plenty of money to take care of her, I considered trying to locate her, but I ultimately decided against it. I still feel the same way. If she's happy and living with a good family, I don't want to upend her life. The media would hound her relentlessly because of who I am, and that wouldn't be fair to her. I made the decision to leave her, and I should be the one who deals with the guilt of that choice. Not her. She shouldn't have her life tossed into disarray just because I regret what I did to her.

The funny thing is, even though we only spent the first two hours of her life together, I still love her.

And I guess I always will.

22

I still remember the day I first arrived in Nashville. It was dreary and raining.

I could've headed to LA or New York to try my hand at pop or rock music, but I'd grown up listening to country at my parents' house and it was, outside of the hymns at the Baptist church, what I'd sung most often, so Nashville seemed the logical destination for me. It was my best chance at finding success.

The long bus ride from Oklahoma had proved a miserable experience. The air conditioning was broken, which made the inside hot and muggy. Some of my fellow travelers smelled as if they hadn't seen a shower in months. I was exhausted and just wanted to breathe fresh air again and get some rest.

I'd purposely chosen to take the bus rather than drive the Corolla I used during high school because the car was registered in my parents' names. Had they reported it stolen after I left, the police could've arrested me and returned me to Oklahoma, but since I left it there and I was already eighteen, there was nothing my mother or father could do about my decision to leave.

I called them once I arrived in Nashville, just to let them know that I was okay and that they shouldn't report me missing. They begged me to come home, but I refused and hung up the phone.

I haven't spoken to them since that day. They've tried to contact me through my agent several times, but I've never returned their calls.

I tell myself the reason I haven't communicated with them is because I don't need them. I've made it fine on my own. I have no desire to listen to their advice or pleas to return home.

But if I'm completely honest with myself, I know that isn't the truth. The real reason I don't want to see or talk to my parents is far more complex.

Even though I often think about the daughter I left behind, I've been able to move on with my life, and I guess I'm afraid if I ever go back there or even communicate with my family, I'll no longer be able to compartmentalize that period of my life and the guilt will cripple me.

When I first came to Nashville, my life was far from what it later became.

I lived in a run-down apartment that had peeling paint on the walls and threadbare brown shag carpeting that appeared to have been installed in the '70s. I split expenses with my roommate, Alice, who was trying to break into the music business herself. After a year and a half, she gave up and returned to Georgia, penniless and heartbroken. There was a string of other roommates after her. Most stayed less than six months before they also packed up and abandoned their dreams.

The sad fact of the music business, one most people never hear about, is that for every singer who makes it and lands a major record deal, there are thousands who don't.

I was one of the lucky ones who made it.

Sure, I have a great voice, but so did all my roommates who ultimately gave up and returned to their hometowns. The thing that made me different, and ultimately what made me successful, was my sheer determination not to quit until I'd achieved what I moved there for in the first place.

Unlike my roommates, I had nowhere to retreat to if I failed. I knew I couldn't go back to Oklahoma, not after everything that happened there. That fact kept me focused on my goal.

I *had* to succeed.

I worked as a waitress at a local bar to pay my rent and living expenses. Some months I barely scraped by. I ate boxed macaroni and cheese dinners more times than I can count.

On my nights off, the bar owner would let me bring my guitar in and play for the crowd for tips. That's how I got started. Over time, I began to sing in other bars that were better known and had reputations for springboarding new artists' careers.

It took a long time and a lot of grueling work, perfecting my craft and writing new songs, but I finally got a record deal and landed my first serious, high-profile gig when I signed on to be the opening act for a nationwide tour.

It was all uphill after that.

Years after I left Oklahoma in the middle of the night with nothing but a dream, I was at last a country music superstar. My face was suddenly on magazine covers and billboards, websites and newspapers. My voice echoed from thousands of radio stations. There were countless TV interviews and other media appearances.

It was all a bit overwhelming at first, going from being a waitress to a star in a relatively short amount of time, but I wasn't complaining. It was what I'd always wanted, what I'd worked so hard to achieve, and I quickly grew accustomed to the fame.

And my stubborn determination to succeed is what made it happen.

I'm not saying that I didn't have some lucky breaks, because I did, but what often separates success and failure in the music business is whether or not you grasp, without hesitation, the opportunities that are placed in front of you.

I decided early on to be prepared and willing to walk through any opening that might present itself.

That's exactly how I got my first record deal—I seized the moment.

It was rare that I wasn't playing for tips somewhere when I had a night off from the bar, but on this particular Friday, I didn't have a gig, so I decided to splurge on myself and take in a movie.

Once I took my seat in the theater, I realized that I was sitting next to an up-and-coming record producer, whom I recognized. After nonchalantly striking up a friendly conversation, I handed him my demo CD—I always kept a couple in my purse to hand out whenever I ran into a producer or record label executive. He rolled his eyes before grudgingly accepting it.

I never really expected to hear back from him. I knew he probably had people handing him demos all the time, but to my shock, he called me two weeks later and wanted to set up a meeting.

That man was Larry, my current record producer.

Despite what I often told Kelsey, I didn't make Larry. Sure, my success was his success, and he's certainly benefited a great deal from my accomplishments, but he had a lot to do with my career getting off the ground. Without him, I may have never become a star. That's just a fact, as much as I hate to admit it sometimes.

It's funny how seemingly random meetings or events in one's life can alter it so spectacularly.

After all, if I'd just stayed in my apartment that Friday night instead of going to the movies, I might never have met Larry. And if I'd never met him, then I wouldn't have been singing at his daughter's wedding Saturday night, which means I wouldn't have been in the plane crash.

But such is life, I suppose. It's just one giant web, connecting us all in one way or another.

It's been a long time since I climbed aboard that sweaty, rancid bus in Oklahoma, bound to make my dreams a reality, but I'm proud to say that I've accomplished what I set out to do. I've released two albums, both of which went multiplatinum, and am working on a third. I headline my own concerts now, no longer relegated to opening-act status, and the money has poured in, making me wealthier than I ever dreamed.

If anyone should be happy with their life, it's me. And I am, for the most part. But sometimes I wonder, deep down, if all the money and fame are really worth what I had to give up in order to get them.

My time here in the wilderness has forced me to slow down and take stock of my life.

And while a part of me still wants to think that I did the right thing, for both me and my daughter, by leaving her in front of that fire station, there's a nagging voice in my heart that tells me I didn't.

That what I did was selfish and horrible and unforgivable.

Maybe both voices inside of me are right. Maybe it was the wisest decision to leave her behind where she could be adopted by a loving family that would care for her and could afford to raise her properly, and at the same time, a seriously flawed choice because it was ultimately the result of my own selfish ambitions. But, in the end, that line of reasoning makes no sense to me at all, because the two things are antithetical. It can't be both a wise and a selfish decision at the same time.

Or can it?

I just don't know for sure.

My guess is that it cannot, that I've just been whitewashing my feelings ever since I made my choice. I've told myself over and over through the years that the real reason I decided to leave her was because I wanted the best for her, that since I couldn't afford to take care of her she would be better off with someone else.

But walking through this vast wilderness, with nothing else to occupy my mind—no concerts or business meetings or numerous other things to distract me—I realize that I've just been purposely deceiving myself all along.

That I abandoned my daughter because I wanted what was best for *her* is nothing but a bald-faced lie.

I didn't leave her behind in Oklahoma because I was consumed with ensuring that she would live a good life. If that were truly the case, I would've gone through an adoption agency to ensure she was properly taken care of.

The truth is, I did it because I wanted to live *my* life, unhindered by the responsibilities of having a child and without the inconvenience of a lengthy adoption process.

I wanted to be free of her—that's why I did it.

It *was* selfish of me. That's all. Plain and simple. There was no part of my decision that was wise.

There's no way to gloss over the cold, hard reality of the choice I made any longer.

And it hurts to admit the truth.

Maybe one day, when she's an adult and can better handle the stress and media attention such a reunion would entail, I'll be able to meet her.

I hope so.

Because I still miss her.

23

My legs feel as if they are about to fail me at any second, weak and trembling more fiercely with each step I take down the ridge. There's a low saddle in the mountain a short distance ahead of us, and with that in view, I force myself to keep walking.

The terrain levels off once we reach the mountain gap, and I remove the pack from my sore shoulders and let it drop to the ground. I collapse in front of it, and Macy sits down beside me. "How are you doing?" I ask her.

"Okay. But I'm really tired, Miss Lauren."

She looks it. Her face is red, and beads of sweat cling to her forehead. I place my hand against her skin. She's warm, but not overheated. "Me too. Let's rest a few minutes."

I lie back and lean my head on the backpack. A breeze is blowing through the gap, and the coolness of it feels good against my skin. I close my eyes and take several deep breaths.

The gently sloping ridgeline we just traveled down should've been an easy walk, but I could feel the energy leave my body with each faltering step down the ridge, as if my legs were a giant leaking faucet, constantly dripping away the strength I needed.

My body is wearing down faster now—and I'm powerless to stop it.

I must find water soon.

To my right, on the opposite side of the saddle, the ridgeline turns back uphill, toward another peak. There's no way I can make that climb right now. I just don't have it in me, and I don't want to subject Macy to it either.

My only option is to follow the path of least resistance.

That's probably just as well, because there's no water up here anyway. At least, not that I've seen. Perhaps if we move lower we'll run into a small stream. But I really don't trust my instincts any longer. Maybe moving lower isn't the best decision. Who knows? Certainly not me.

I feel like such an amateur out here, and totally out of my element. I have no idea what I'm doing. If there's a playbook one is supposed to follow in this situation, I sure would like to sneak a peek at it right about now.

Maybe we would've been better off to travel downhill from the crash site in the first place. Perhaps we would've already found a water source if we'd set off in that direction—or maybe not. I only know that my decision to climb up to the summit yesterday in the hopes of getting cell service resulted in total failure. My rationale for doing it seemed logical at the time, and maybe it was, but in the end it didn't matter because my phone's battery died.

The frustrating lesson I'm learning out here is that even if I follow the most rational, well-planned course of action, I may still fail because of events that are completely out of my control.

And that makes me want to scream.

But I can't change anything that's happened. All I can do is keep going. Once I decided to leave the crash site, wise or foolhardy, I committed us to that plan. There's no going back now, only forward.

I'll continue trying to walk out of here until I either succeed or die in the process.

I'm again faced with two choices. Since I can't continue along the ridgeline, I must turn down the mountain, electing to descend either the side in front of or the one behind me. Neither appears as steep as the one we traversed yesterday, but both are sloped significantly more than the ridge we just walked down.

This decision, unlike some of the others I've faced, is a fairly easy one, and I make it without hesitation.

The route behind me will lead us back in the direction we've just come from, toward the plane. I don't want to do that because there was no sign of water down there. Besides, backtracking would crush my spirit, and probably Macy's too. All the energy we've expended getting this far would be wasted.

I slowly stand up and my head swims. Flashes of light erupt in my vision. I lose my balance and almost topple back to the ground. Macy sees me wobbling, jumps to her feet, and grabs my forearm to steady me.

"Are you okay?" she asks, her brow furrowed and her eyes wide.

I nod. "Yes . . . a little dizzy . . . I just need a minute." I take a deep breath and allow my body to regain its composure. The flickering stars slowly clear from my eyesight, and my head stops spinning. I smile softly at Macy. "Thanks for catching me."

"That's okay. But maybe you should rest some more, Miss Lauren."

I sigh. "I'd like to, but we need to get going."

My urgent need to find water soon overpowers everything else, including the rest I crave so badly. I haven't had anything to drink since the small gulp last night, and my throat feels like someone has taken a blowtorch to it. "I'll be fine," I assure her. "We'll just have to take it slow." I nod toward the edge of the ridge. "We're going to head that way."

"Okay. Let's just take our time and be careful." She picks the backpack up off the ground and places her arms through the straps. "I can carry this." The pack looks too big for her small frame, but there's not a lot of weight inside and she seems to be able to handle it without trouble.

202 · J. MICHAEL STEWART

Her maturity and unbreakable inner strength continue to amaze me. Even after everything she's been through, she's still hanging in there with me. Most kids would've been complaining ever since the crash, but she hasn't. She's been a rock—far from the hindrance I was initially afraid she would be.

I'm glad she's here with me.

I realize now that I need her just as much as she needs me. Her presence keeps me focused and forging ahead.

We ease off the edge of the ridge and begin our descent.

24

"If the pack gets too heavy for you, you let me know, okay?" I say over my shoulder to Macy, who's following close behind me.

She sighs. "I'm fine."

Her tone is one of defiance, as if there isn't any doubt about whether or not she can handle the weight of the backpack. I can't see her face, but I imagine she's rolling her eyes at me.

That makes me smile.

The terrain is steeper than it appeared from above, and it's obvious we are going to have to choose our steps wisely, lest we go tumbling down the mountain out of control.

I devise a method for descending the mountainside that seems to work fairly well. Placing my leading foot perpendicular to the slope, I dig the edge of my tennis shoe into the leaves and dirt in order to brace myself, then turn my body and place my trailing foot in front of the first, secure it into the terrain as I grab on to a nearby bush or tree for balance, and then I repeat the process. It's slow going, and my shoes slide on the moist earth often . . . but it works.

This entire journey would be much easier if I were wearing hiking boots, but of course, those didn't make my packing list for the quick wedding concert.

We continue our slow, careful slog down the mountain in silence. I'm too focused on where I'm planting my feet to engage in conversation, and I imagine Macy is as well.

As the slope of the terrain decreases the slightest bit, I take the opportunity to stop and rest. I estimate that it's taken us over an hour to safely traverse the steepest section of the mountainside. I lean back against a large maple tree. My legs are jelly, and I'm afraid that if I sit down, I might not get back up.

In front of and below me the wilderness stretches out into a spacious, wide hollow, full of mature oaks, pines, maples, and other species I don't recognize. A layer of thick, lush underbrush covers the ground, the bright green leaves contrasting against the brown forest floor.

Macy pulls even with me and rests against the adjacent tree.

"How are you doing? Is the pack too heavy for you?" This time I know she rolls her eyes at my question because I'm looking right at her as she does it.

"I told you I'm fine. It's not too heavy. I can do it."

I stifle a chuckle and nod. "Okay. Just checking on you." With that, I let her be. I certainly don't want her to think I'm implying she isn't capable of helping out. She's more than capable. I know that and respect her for it. The kid has spunk, and I like that about her. She reminds me of myself as a rebellious young girl.

I massage my thighs, hoping to breathe some new life into the lethargic muscles. The pressure against them feels good and, if only for a quick moment, refreshes them.

Bent over, continuing to work on my legs, I hear something odd, a sound I haven't noticed until now. It's faint, almost inaudible. I concentrate on it—a bubbling, dripping noise slightly below me and to my right. I straighten up so suddenly that the dizziness returns. I plant my hands against the tree trunk behind me and turn to Macy. "Do you hear that?"

She shakes her head.

I point in the direction I hear the sound emanating from. "Listen."

Her eyes go wide with recognition as an excited grin spreads across her face. "Water!" she screams.

I smile too, but refuse to allow myself the luxury of a triumphant shout. Not yet. I don't want to get my hopes up, only to have them crushed if I'm wrong.

Pushing off the maple tree, I tilt my head in the direction of the sound, praying that what I perceive is real, and not just a figment of my overtired imagination. I can still hear it, soft and quiet, the trickling and bubbling continuing to ring in my ears. I hurry toward it, suddenly unaware of my hurting legs. My laser focus urges me on toward what may be our salvation.

The sound grows louder as I draw closer, and even though I'm not thinking about my legs any longer, their weakness causes me to stumble and go to my knees. I don't bother standing back up, instead I scurry along the ground, plowing through the leaf litter and digging my fingernails into the soft dirt for traction.

There's a small outcropping of rock to my right, and I crawl toward it.

My heart feels as if it's going to explode with sheer elation as my eyes take in the sight in front of me. A small stream of water is trickling from the cleft of the rock and spilling to the earth, creating a tiny pool about the size of my fist.

Yes!

I press my face against the rock and open my mouth wide, allowing the tiny stream, which is smaller than the diameter of a pencil, to flow into my mouth. As the cold water touches my scorched tongue and slides down my dry throat, the fresh, sweet flavor sends my spirit soaring. It's the best thing I've ever tasted.

Thank you, God!

"It's water! We found water!" I shout.

Macy races down the hill, a huge smile on her face. "Good job, Miss Lauren!"

I throw my arms around her. "We're going to be okay, now. We're going to make it out of here," I whisper in her ear.

"I know."

The two of us continue to laugh and shout as we celebrate our amazing turn of fortune.

Finding the water couldn't have come at a more opportune time. I'm not sure how much longer I could've continued. My body was failing fast, but now there's new optimism and a reason to rejoice. The mental and emotional boost it gives me is so strong that I feel as if I could climb Mount Everest with my hands tied behind my back.

"Here, drink!" I tell Macy. She removes the backpack from her shoulders, which still appears overly large for her, and pushes her face forward. She giggles with excitement as the water first touches her lips and flows into her mouth.

As she continues to drink, I go to work clearing away the dead leaves from the tiny pool at the bottom of the rock. I remove sticks, a handful of dirt, and some small stones too, deepening the depression so it will hold more water. My actions temporarily muddy the pool, but I know that the dirt will quickly settle to the bottom, leaving behind a larger supply of cold, clear water.

Macy backs away and rubs her hand across her wet lips. "That's so good," she says, grinning.

The mile-wide smile still on my face, I lean in and take another turn under the natural spigot. This time I stay until my thirst is completely satisfied. Backing away, I dry my soaking face with the bottom of my T-shirt. "Hand me the empty bottles out of the pack," I tell Macy.

She retrieves the two water bottles from the main compartment and hands them to me. I take them from her and quickly unscrew the caps on both. I set one of them directly under the flow of the spring and buttress it with two moss-covered rocks about the size of my hand on each side. The sound of the water striking the bottom of the plastic bottle echoes through me and reinforces the fact that I've at least made one good decision since the crash. Instead of discarding the bottles, I decided to keep them, and now they are proving useful by providing us the capability to store the water.

I dip the neck of the other bottle into the small pool at the base of the rock. Even after my excavating, the depression is still only deep enough to allow me to fill the bottle a third full. I pour this water over my arms and scrub away the dirt and dried sweat. Just having a small part of my body clean is invigorating.

An intermittent series of small rock terraces stairstep down the mountainside below the spring, each one separated from the next by a heavy blanket of dead leaves that block and diffuse the stream of water. It appears that, at one time, the spring flowed with greater volume, perhaps swollen by heavy rainfall, and carved out the path. But now it's barely noticeable, and the series of tiny terraces disappears into the curtain of underbrush fifteen yards below me. I already wanted to stop for the day and rejuvenate next to the spring, and this discovery only fortifies my decision.

Perhaps the spring water trickling out of the mountain here eventually leads to a larger creek with even more water, but I'm unable to see far enough to know that for sure. But it's also entirely possible, I would think even likely, that the small amount of water is being soaked up by the earth and vegetation long before it leads to anything larger.

From the survival shows I've watched on TV, I know that if I'm able to find a creek, I can follow it downstream until I reach some sign of civilization like a hiking trail, road, or even a house. But I'm not willing to leave this spring and continue walking today based solely on the hope of finding a larger stream. No, we need to stay here for the rest of the afternoon and rehydrate ourselves as much as we can before we continue, just in case we don't find more water for another day or two.

The plastic bottle I placed under the spring is almost full, so I remove it and hand it to Macy. "Here you go, keep drinking. Just take it slow. We don't want to drink too much too fast and make ourselves sick."

"Okay."

"I know it's still early, but I think we should stop here for the day and rest. We can drink as much as we want and just relax. We'll start out again early tomorrow morning. Sound good?"

Macy has already placed the bottle to her lips and turned it up, but she cuts her eyes toward me and nods her approval. Even though I'd already made the decision about what *I* wanted to do, it felt important that I ask her opinion this time, rather than just telling her what we were going to do. She needs to feel important and valuable, because she is. From now on, I'm going to bounce all my ideas off of her before I do anything. She's a smart girl, and it never hurts to get a second opinion. After all, she might just keep me from doing something really stupid and getting us both hurt—or worse.

We spend the rest of the afternoon slowly rehydrating ourselves with the sweet spring water. We use one of the extra pairs of socks from the backpack as washcloths and bathe ourselves as best we can.

As the sun begins to retreat from the forest, Macy and I are lying on the mountain slope a few feet from the spring, our blue jean pillows beneath our heads, and Mr. Pebbles resting between us on a bed of pinecones Macy made for him. He's had a bath too; Macy cleaned his fur with one of the extra T-shirts and the spring water.

It's amazing how refreshed and strengthened I feel.

I'm thankful beyond words that we found the spring. It saved our lives, I'm sure of it. My journey was nearing the end. My body was wrecked, and I wouldn't have made it much farther, certainly not far enough to find help.

Just as Macy prayed and thanked God for her apple slices and grape juice after the plane crash, I say a prayer of thanksgiving for the sweet, clean water.

I now know exactly how she felt.

"Miss Lauren?"

"Yes?"

"Thank you for taking care of me and helping me out here. I . . . was so scared when you first found me inside the airplane."

Reaching over, I take her hand in mine and give it a gentle squeeze. "You're welcome, sweetie. I need to thank you too, though."

"You do?" she asks, apparently surprised.

"Yep. I sure do. You've been a great traveling partner. You haven't complained, and you've helped me out a lot. I don't think I would've made it without you."

"You're welcome. I could tell you really needed my help when I first met you," she adds with complete seriousness.

I'm not facing her, I'm looking into the tree canopy above my head, but her comment brings a huge smile to my face. It's true, what she said. I did need her—I just didn't realize it at the time.

We both continue to stare into the trees above us in silence. The cloud cover remains over the area, although the bases have seemed to grow slightly higher throughout the day, and I can now see well above the treetops. And though I haven't heard an airplane or helicopter today, I'm not discouraged. Whereas yesterday brought a feeling of utter discouragement and hopelessness with the failed attempt at reaching someone on the cellphone, today has brought forth a new feeling of resiliency and a certain assurance that we are both going to make it back home safely. It's only a matter of time now. I know this. We just have to keep plodding along, determined not to quit until we reach help.

As the sunlight slips away and the encroaching twilight blankets the wilderness around me, my mind is consumed once again with thoughts of my daughter.

I now realize that even as I fought so desperately to suppress it, to fill my life with money, fame, and other distractions, the smothering guilt I first felt as I drove away from the fire station that fateful night has remained with me ever since.

There hasn't been a single day when I haven't thought about what I did.

I wonder if the guilt will ever leave. I certainly don't feel as if I deserve to have the burden lifted.

And maybe I don't.

If I'd just chosen to give her up for adoption, or even let my parents raise her, despite the fact that we didn't get along, I could've lived with that decision, maybe even felt good about it, because I would've known she was being well cared for. But instead, I dropped her in front of a small-town fire station because I didn't want her messing up my career plans, and I don't have any idea what happened to her after that.

I hope she's okay. I hope she's somewhere safe, with someone who loves her and takes good care of her.

There's no doubt that the reason I've been such a choleric human being since I left Oklahoma is the gnawing guilt within me. It wasn't really the people around me who made me angry. In truth, I was angry at myself. But instead of facing my failures and admitting my mistakes, I chose to unfairly cast my own feelings of inadequacy onto others.

The plane crash was a horrible event. Three good people lost their lives because of it, and I wish it had never happened. But I also now view it as a turning point in my own life. I'd erected a multitude of meaningless distractions in my life to avoid having to deal with what happened back in Oklahoma, but the crash demolished all those walls. In one swift moment, everything was torn from me, and I was forced to finally confront the singular event that has dominated my mind ever since I left home.

So, even though the plane crash was a horrible thing, I'm glad that at least something good has come from it.

I don't know what the future holds, once I make it back home, but I'm confident that I won't return the same bitter, mean-spirited person I was before the crash, and for that, I'm thankful.

Macy sniffles, and I turn my head to check on her. Her eyes are filled with tears. "What's wrong?" I ask.

My question causes her to lose control, and sobs rack her body. She moves her hand to her face to wipe the tears away, but they are simply replaced by others. "What's the matter, Macy?"

"I miss Mommy and Daddy," she says through a series of broken, rattling cries.

I slip my arm beneath her shoulders and pull her close to me in a hug, her head resting in the crook of my left arm. "I know you do, sweetie. It's okay to be sad," I whisper, although I'm not sure my words comfort her at all. My heart breaks for her, but I'm not sure what else to say.

I don't say anything; I just keep holding her tight and let her cry into my T-shirt as she nuzzles her face to the side of my breast. Seeing her like this reminds me that, although she's mature beyond her years and one tough kid, she's still just a kid—one who has lost both of her parents and is struggling to cope with that harsh new reality.

Tears well in my eyes. My own sense of loss, the feeling of emptiness that comes from losing a child, plunges a knife through my heart, and I began to cry too.

We hold each other close as we sob, drawing comfort from one another. The shared experience of losing someone we love binds our hearts together in a beautiful moment that seems to transcend everything else.

Macy's weeping slowly returns to quiet sniffles as I wipe my tears away. We've had a good cry, one that we both needed, and I feel emotionally renewed by the experience.

"I'm scared," she whispers, her face still buried in my side.

"Don't be scared, sweetie. We're going to be all right. We're going to get out of here, I promise."

She finally lifts her face from my shirt and twists her body so that she's once again looking into the tree canopy. "I'm not talking about that."

"What are you talking about, then?" I ask, confused.

She sighs heavily and sniffles again. "I'm worried about what's going to happen to me once we get back home."

I'm still perplexed about what she means. "I'm sorry, I guess I don't understand. What are you worried about?"

She shifts her blue eyes directly toward mine. "Mommy and Daddy are dead." She pauses and takes a breath.

"Yes. Go on," I prod her.

"Who's going to take care of me? Where will I live?"

I haven't considered that question before now. But it's completely understandable that Macy would be worried about it. I imagine any child who lost both parents would be concerned about those things.

Once again, I find myself unsure of what I can say to her that might bring some reassurance and comfort. Maybe there's nothing I can offer that will convince her she's going to be okay after all this is over. But I have to at least try to help her.

"I'm sure you'll be fine. One of your aunts or uncles will take care of you, I bet. It will be hard, and I suspect you'll always miss your parents, but you'll be loved and taken care of. I'm sure of that."

"No," she replies flatly.

Her answer shocks me. Why is she so certain her relatives won't take her in?

"Why do you say that?" I ask.

"I don't have any aunts or uncles."

"Really?"

"Yes. There's a girl in my class named Sarah who's always talking about her Aunt Cindy and Uncle Jeremy and all the presents they buy for her. I asked Mommy one time why my aunts and uncles never bought me presents. She said I didn't have any aunts or uncles."

"What about your grandparents?"

"Mommy's parents died in a car accident when I was just a baby. I don't even remember them. Daddy's dad got sick and died a few years ago. His mom is still alive, but she's old. Mommy said she lives in a home where other people help her. She can't take care of me. I just don't—" Her voice cracks and she stops. She clears her throat and wipes her eyes again with her small hand. "I just don't want to go to one of those places where all the kids who don't have mommies and daddies go."

"You mean an orphanage?"

She nods and sniffles. "Yeah. I couldn't remember what they're called, but my church takes up pencils and paper and clothes and stuff every Christmas to give to them. It's so sad."

"Oh, sweetie, that's not going to happen to you," I tell her, hoping the certainty with which I made the statement will convince her I'm right. She doesn't respond, so I don't know if I've helped the situation or just made it worse.

But now I do understand why she's so concerned. The idea that there are no extended family members who can step in for her parents never occurred to me. I just assumed she had other relatives, but it sounds as though she really is alone. I'm sure that fact has been weighing heavily on her mind ever since the crash. However, she's just now found the courage to vocalize her fears to me.

Macy's anxiety about being left in an orphanage pricks my own guilt about what might've happened to my daughter. I hope with all my heart that didn't happen to her.

I'm positive everything will work out just fine for Macy, but I need to encourage her of that fact right now, assure her that someone will always be there for her.

"I'm sorry, sweetie, I know it must be scary for you, but trust me, there will be a whole bunch of great people who will want to take care of you."

"You think so?"

I roll onto my side and look her in the eyes. "I *know* so."

"But *how* do you know, Miss Lauren?"

Up until now, I've kept the details of my career a secret from her because I enjoyed the anonymity I've found in the wilderness, but now it's time to give that up for her sake.

"Believe me, when we get out of here, our pictures are going to be plastered all over television. Once this is all over, everyone in the country will know who you are. You'll be famous . . . because everyone already knows who *I* am, and the media will love the story of you and me surviving alone in the wilderness. Trust me, folks will be lined up to adopt you. There'll be so many mommies and daddies wanting to share their home with you that you'll have a hard time deciding whom you want to live with."

She sighs. "I hope you're right, Miss Lauren."

I pat her on the thigh. "Sure I am. You're going to be fine."

Her eyes narrow as if she's just now processing everything I've told her. "What do you mean everyone already knows who you are?"

"Have you ever heard the song, 'Because I'm Me'? It's been on the radio a lot lately." My guess is that she'll recognize the name of my latest crossover hit. The last time I checked it was number one on the country charts and number three on the pop.

Her face lights up. "Oh, yeah, I've heard that one. I like it."

"Well . . . I'm the girl who sings that song."

"What?" She stares at me with a look of disbelief on her face.

I chuckle. "Yep, that's me."

"Really?"

"Yeah, really. I'm a country music singer. I think you were too sleepy to recognize me when we first met."

"Yeah, I guess so. I just thought you were another lady from the wedding." She exhales loudly. "You're the *real* Lauren Miller?"

"Afraid so," I say.

"Wow!" Her eyes go wide, and a beaming smile lights her face. "Wait until the kids at school hear about this! I knew your name was Lauren, but I didn't know you were *that* Lauren! You never told me your last name."

"No, I didn't. To be honest, I liked that you didn't know who I was. It was nice to just be plain old Lauren for a while."

"You mean you don't like being famous?" she asks, with a hint of shock in her voice.

"I wouldn't say that, exactly. It certainly has its advantages. But—" I stop and sigh, struggling to come up with the correct words to properly convey how I feel. "I guess it's hard to explain. I used to think that all I wanted in life was to become rich and famous . . . and when it first happened to me, I absolutely loved it. I couldn't get enough. I liked the fact that people on the street recognized me and asked me for my autograph or wanted to take a picture with me. It made me feel so special. The money was nice too. For the first time in my life I could go into any store I wanted and buy *whatever* I wanted."

"That sounds awesome! I wish I could be famous when I grow up."

I cut my eyes at her. "Be careful what you ask for."

She furrows her brow and frowns. "Why?"

"I'll just say that being a celebrity isn't all it's cracked up to be."

"Huh? What do you mean?"

I chuckle. "It's just that sometimes I wish I could be a regular person again. I had no clue how much I would miss being able to go to a movie or a nice dinner or shopping without everyone recognizing me and wanting a picture or an autograph. I've tried wearing disguises, and sometimes that works, but most of the time it doesn't."

"You mean you dress up like someone else? Like I do on Halloween? I was a princess last year. Is that the kind of costume you wear too?"

I laugh. "Not exactly. I usually just put on a wig and wear dark sunglasses. As I said, it rarely works. Most people still recognize me."

"Cool," Macy says.

"Not cool," I reply. "It all gets very old, very fast. It's too much. After a while, you just seem to forget who you really are, if that makes any sense. You *become* the celebrity; you're not yourself anymore. It's sad, really."

"It is? Why?"

"Yeah, it is. Because I'm no longer Lauren Miller, a normal girl from Oklahoma. Now I'm Lauren Miller, the superstar. I'm afraid the simple girl from Oklahoma has been lost for good. Maybe I'll find her again someday . . . I hope I do anyway." I stop talking and realize that I've been speaking to myself as much as to Macy.

"Sort of like when I won the spelling bee in kindergarten and all the other kids kept asking me what it was like talking to a reporter. It was *really* annoying."

A grin erupts across my face, and I bite my tongue to keep from laughing out loud.

Macy sighs. "I'd still like to be famous like you are. I think it would be cool. At least for a little while."

I chuckle at her. "Well, you're going to get your chance, believe me. Once we make it out of here, the reporters will be asking you all kinds of questions. You'll be plenty famous."

"I've never been on TV before. That seems kind of . . . scary."

"Oh, it's not that bad. You just have to pretend the cameras aren't there."

She's silent, and I can tell the realization that she's going to experience her fifteen minutes of fame is sinking in.

"Will you be there with me, Miss Lauren? You know, when we have to do the interviews and stuff?"

"Sure, I'll be there with you."

She exhales, obviously relieved. "Good. I was hoping you'd say that."

I smile. "No problem. I'm an old pro at this point, so I'll give you all my secret tips."

"And you think once I'm on TV, there'll be a family that wants me?" she asks.

My smile vanishes, and I stare at her seriously. "Yes, Macy. I'm positive . . . you're going to be fine."

She lets out another long breath, but this time it seems more from worry than relief. "I sure hope you're right."

"I am. Don't you worry about it anymore, okay?"

She nods. "I'll try not to."

Night has almost taken over the wilderness now, and I'm exhausted. It's been a long, eventful day, and I want to get an early start tomorrow. I lean over and kiss Macy on the forehead. "I promise, everything's going to be all right. Now, try to get some rest."

She nods softly and closes her eyes. "Okay."

I roll onto my back, lay my head on the blue jean pillow, and stare into the black sky. My eyelids slide shut. In the background, the sound of the spring water trickling from the rock nudges me toward sleep.

25

I wake to find the new day dawning with optimism and a sense of renewed hope.

The clouds are gone, and the early morning sunlight filters through the trees with a brightness and warmth I haven't experienced in what seems an eternity. Birds are singing to one another, warblers I believe, from a dozen different perches scattered through the forest.

I need to pee again, which is a good thing. I've gone several times already since we found the spring yesterday.

Sleep came to me again last night, the best so far. I suppose my body is becoming accustomed to its bed being a patch of cold, uneven ground. Being hydrated again definitely helped produce a deeper rest too. Even my mind is working better this morning. My thoughts seem sharper, clearer.

It's amazing how the human body sets the correct priorities and focuses one's mind solely on the most pressing need. Yesterday, when I was in dire need of water, all I could feel was my parched throat and burning tongue . . . my hot, dry skin . . . my trembling legs, the muscles weak from dehydration and barely able to hold me up. I never once thought about food during our trek down from the mountain's summit, though I must've been fiercely hungry. But my body needed water more than food, so every physical sensation was tuned to reinforce that urgent need in my mind.

But now that my thirst has been satisfied, my stomach is roaring and growling inside of me with such vigor that it actually hurts. I feel as if I could eat the bark right off this tree that I'm lying next to. My last real meal was a grilled chicken breast with a side salad and small dinner roll I had on board my private plane on the way to the wedding.

That was almost six days ago.

Now, all I can think about is food. My mind is totally consumed with finding something, anything, to eat. The most frustrating part is that I'm sure there are numerous edible plants here in the forest, but I don't know which ones are safe to eat and which ones aren't, and without knowing for sure, the risk of poisoning Macy or myself is just too high to chance it.

Even though I probably shouldn't, I close my eyes and allow my favorite restaurants back in Nashville to fill my thoughts in a deluge of culinary desire.

A slice of pepperoni-and-cheese pizza from Gino's would be nice. Heck, forget a slice; I'm so hungry that I could eat a whole large pie by myself. Memories of the smoothness of the mozzarella, the tanginess of the tomato sauce, the chewiness of the New York-style crust, pepper my senses to the point I can almost taste it, almost smell the intoxicating aroma of a fresh, brick oven pizza as I draw in a deep breath.

For dessert I'd have a gigantic piece of the triple-layer red velvet cake from Becca's Sugar Shack, a piece so big it would take two plates to hold it. I close my eyes and remember the sweet, buttery cream cheese frosting, the silkiness of the moist cake against the roof of my mouth. I'd wash it down with one of Becca's dynamite cappuccinos too.

My eyes pop open, and I find myself looking at green tree leaves instead of a giant pizza or piece of cake. It won't do me any good to lie here all morning thinking about the foods I miss. If I ever want to eat them again, I have to get off my butt and get to work.

Now that Macy and I are both well hydrated, I want to make good progress today. I figure we should be able to cover several miles at least. My plan is to continue down into the hollow below us and, hopefully, there'll be a small creek at the bottom, which we can follow to some sort of civilization. That's my hope anyway.

Of course, I've learned by now that things rarely work out as one hopes in the wilderness.

I raise my head and glance toward my feet. Macy's arm is slung over my abdomen in a hug, her body nuzzled into my left side, with Mr. Pebbles scrunched between us. She's still sleeping, so I try not to disturb her as I pick up her wrist with my hand, gently move it off to the side, and sit up.

My bladder isn't going to wait much longer.

The black backpack is lying on the ground next to me, and I retrieve the package of towelettes from it. I stand, walk past the spring, and continue another twenty yards farther before I stop and relieve myself.

As I return to our sparse campsite, Macy sits up. She yawns and stretches her arms above her head, smiling. I laugh at her. Even though she's spent the night on the cold ground with only a rolled-up pair of blue jeans for a pillow, the look on her face says she's just woken up in the lush bed of a five-star hotel. I toss the package of towelettes to her. "Here . . . if you need them."

"Thanks." She hops up and walks away.

The two bottles of water I filled before bed last night are leaning against a nearby tree. I pick one of them up and sit down, leaning back against the trunk and giving my legs a few more minutes of rest before the start of what I expect will be a long and grueling day of hiking. I drink the water slowly while I wait for Macy to return.

Once I finish, I place the bottle back underneath the spring to refill. Macy returns and I hand her the other full bottle. "Drink this."

"But I'm not thirsty."

"Well, drink as much as you can. Just take it slow. You need to get as much water in you as possible before we leave, just in case we don't find more for a while."

She nods her head and reluctantly takes the bottle from my hand. "Okay."

As she begins to drink, I strap the two pairs of blue jeans to the back of the pack and do a quick inventory to make sure we are not leaving anything behind.

Macy hands me the bottle. It's only one-third full now. "Here you go. I'm sorry, but that's all I can drink right now," she says.

"Okay, that's fine." I gulp down the remaining third, refill the bottle with fresh spring water, and place it inside the pack along with the other full bottle. I pick up the backpack and slip my arms through the shoulder straps, ready to start walking again.

Macy looks up at me, eyeing the pack. "I can carry it again today if you want."

I smile at her. "Thanks, I really appreciate it, and you did a great job yesterday, but I feel much better today."

She shrugs her shoulders. "I can do it. I'm strong enough."

Not wanting to hurt her feelings, I add, "I'm sure I'll need a break later on, and then you can carry it. Sound good?"

She nods and grins. "Yeah, that sounds fine. Just let me know when you're ready for my help again, Miss Lauren."

Pulling a deep breath into my lungs, I smile at her again and pat her on the back. "Well, let's get going."

26

We begin walking down the mountain, and as we go, I keep a close eye on the ground to see if I can follow the flow from the spring. There are small puddles of water here and there, but there is so much leaf litter absorbing and concealing the small amount of water that I eventually lose the trail of it.

It takes us over an hour to descend the mountainside and reach the bottom of the hollow because we continue to take our time and place our steps wisely. Even though the terrain isn't as steep as it was yesterday, when we first left the low saddle, the risk of a misplaced foot causing a twisted or broken ankle is still very real.

At the bottom, I find that high slopes surround us on three sides. The one we just descended is on our right, with additional ones to our left and rear. We are at the head of a hollow, and directly in front of us the terrain slopes slightly downward, and the forest gradually widens between the mountains.

This decision is a no-brainer.

I walk straight ahead, once again taking the path of least resistance and following the natural contour of the land. I pray we find a creek soon, so that we can follow it out of here, but I haven't the slightest idea how long it will take us to find help. It could be today or it could be five days from now. My stomach growls again at that thought. The possibility of going that much longer without something to eat is downright depressing and scary.

We walk for at least another thirty minutes before we stop to take a break. I slide the backpack off my shoulders and lower it to the ground. We both drink just a sip of the spring water from one of the bottles. "How are you making it?" I ask Macy.

"Fine. I'm just ready to be home."

I sigh. "Yeah, me too. We will be, soon. I'm sure of it."

I wish I actually believed my own words. While I now feel confident that we'll make it out of this alive, I'm not at all positive that our ordeal will be over soon. But I don't want to crush Macy's spirits by telling her we may have to walk for several more days.

As I'm putting the water bottle back inside the pack, the methodical, thumping sound of a helicopter in the distance reverberates in my ears. It's faint, but seems to be growing louder. I jump up. "Macy! Do you hear that?"

She leaps to her feet. "Yes!"

I quickly pull the two extra T-shirts from the pack and hand one of them to her. "Here, wave this in the air," I tell her. Neither of the shirts is white, one is gray, the other brown—not exactly colors that will stand out inside a forest. There are extra socks in the pack too, which are white, and I grab two pairs and toss one to Macy.

We both dance and yell at the top of our lungs, waving the T-shirts and socks above our heads. I scan the sky with my eyes, desperate to catch a glimpse of the chopper, praying that whoever is inside will fly over our location and see us.

The tree canopy is just as thick here as it was at the crash site, where the airplane flew near us on the second day, so I'm not optimistic that we'll be noticed. We keep trying anyway. The sound grows louder still, coming from behind us and to our right.

A new idea pops into my head. I scramble back to the pack and fish out the dead cellphone from the side pocket. Maybe this is why I wanted to hold on to it.

Tilting it skyward, I aim it at the sun, hoping to use it as a signal mirror. I have no idea if the plan will even work, but it seems a better option than simply waving clothes in the air.

Just as I bring the phone into position, I catch a glimpse of a dark green helicopter through some distant trees well behind us and crossing the path we traveled earlier this morning. I fumble with the phone, trying to make it reflect the sunlight, but as quickly as the helicopter came into view, it's gone again.

It flies straight past us and doesn't circle. The sound grows faint until it disappears completely. I drop the phone to the ground, devastated.

Macy is still screaming at the top of her little lungs and waving the T-shirt and socks above her head.

"You can stop now," I tell her. "It's no use. They're already gone."

She lowers her arms to her sides and drops the T-shirt and socks. Her eyes well up and her chin begins to quiver. She looks as if her will to keep trudging forward is gone, her spirit crushed to tiny pieces.

I walk over and embrace her. "It's going to be okay. Don't worry about it. There will be another helicopter along soon, I bet. Besides, we're doing pretty well on our own. We'll find our way out of here before you know it."

She doesn't say a word.

I gently push her away but keep my hands on her shoulders as I hold her gaze. "Keep going. We're going to be fine." She nods, and I leave it at that.

I return everything to the pack, heft it back onto my shoulders, and we start walking again.

27

I put on a brave face back there, after the helicopter passed us by, as if watching it fly away without the slightest hint of slowing down or circling back didn't faze me at all.

But as I monotonously place one foot in front of the other and continue my grueling journey through the mountains, I admit to myself that my display of absolute confidence that we're going to make it out of here soon was all just an act. And the truth is, I'm not sure whom the spectacle was intended for more, Macy or me.

Despite my actions to the contrary, I'm just as devastated at the missed opportunity as she is.

It's heartbreaking.

After everything we've been through, all the trials and hardships we've endured, all the obstacles we've overcome to make it this far, to have something so promising dangled in front of our eyes only to have it snatched away at the last second seems utterly cruel.

The notion that this whole nightmare—the pain, the hunger, the thirst, the never-ending walking—is just one big swing of God's gavel, punishing me for Oklahoma, flares in my mind again.

What if my daughter, wherever she is, has suffered ever since I abandoned her? What if she goes to bed hungry or doesn't have clean clothes or anyone to help and love her?

What if she feels as lonely and scared as I do right now?

If only one of those things is true, then I deserve everything I'm experiencing.

But I can't keep thinking this way.

No matter what this is, whether some divine punishment or just a random event thrust on me, I have to keep going. I have to persevere, no matter how difficult or discouraging it is. Even if I'm not meant to make it out of here alive, I want Macy to survive. But beyond just surviving, I want her to truly *live*. I want her to experience her first kiss, learn to drive, and go to the prom. Enjoy her college years. Get married and have kids. Love and be loved.

It's the least I can do for her.

The leaves beneath my feet have become sopping wet, creating a slick walking surface, and my tennis shoes are having a difficult time gaining traction. I step five feet to my right, where it's a bit drier, and bend down to examine the ground.

Clearing the top layer of leaves away, I can see the faintest flow of water trickling over the earth. This means there must be another spring nearby, and I backtrack up the hollow searching for the source. I haven't gone fifty yards before I find it.

It isn't dripping like the first spring I found yesterday; the water is just oozing from underneath a small rock shelf I remember stepping over just two minutes ago. The flow is so slow that it could easily go undetected if a person wasn't specifically looking for it, which is why I missed it the first time.

I clear the leaves away and bend down to take a drink from the tiny pool. It tastes fresh and clean.

Macy walks up behind me. "What is it?"

"Another spring." I motion toward it with my hand as I back away. "Take a drink."

She drops to her knees, lowers her face, and draws the water slowly across her lips.

Even though we still have the two bottles of water in the backpack, I know it's best to drink as much as we can now and save the bottles for later in case this spring dries up farther down the mountain, as the first one did. We take turns drinking until we can't hold any more.

As we head off back down the hollow, Macy asks from behind me, "Miss Lauren, do you think the helicopter will come back again?"

"I don't know. Maybe."

"I sure hope it does. I'm tired of being out here."

"I know you are, Macy. I am too, but we just have to keep going. Okay?"

She sighs. "Yeah, I guess so."

I know she's exhausted, just as I am, and wants nothing more than for all this to be over, but her comment stings a little bit, as if I'm not doing a good enough job getting us out of here quickly enough.

Doesn't she know that I'm doing the best I can with the situation we've been given? Immediately, I recognize that I'm overreacting. My own weariness at being stuck out here has frayed my nerves to the point that Macy's words register as a complaint, though I know she doesn't really mean it that way. I take a deep breath and, when she doesn't say anything else, I let the subject drop.

As we continue on, the flow of water next to us gradually becomes more distinct and develops into a small stream that's swift enough to clear a trail through the dead leaves, revealing a bed of hand-size rocks and smaller pebbles below the inch or two of moving water. Rather than the flow becoming dispersed to the point that it vanishes, as the first spring did, this one just keeps growing in size the farther down the hollow we travel. I also spot a few other small trickles of water feeding into it from each side.

We keep walking, and the stream only continues to grow. Now, it's large enough that I would classify it as a small creek. This makes me confident that I've found what I'd hoped to—a watershed that we can follow until we reach some form of civilization.

The terrain bordering the creek on each side narrows, squeezing the water into a more constricted path, which increases its speed and depth. The topography also becomes markedly steeper, creating small cascades and knee-deep pools of water, as the creek continues its descent down the mountain.

All of this, of course, causes our progress to slow to a crawl. With only steep hillsides on either side, we are forced to wade down the middle of the creek. The water is frigid at first, but eventually my lower legs and feet become numb to it.

The current is now swift, and seems to become more so with each slight drop in elevation, making traversing it difficult and tedious. We have to navigate over large, moss-covered boulders and squeeze under trees that have fallen across the creek. Bugs and gnats swarm around me, hoping for a quick, easy meal, and my arms are weak from just trying to swat them away. Dense patches of rhododendron and mountain laurel overhang the small creek and, at certain locations, their leaf-laden branches become so thick that they almost block our path. It's a battle to work our way through them, the rough, flexible limbs creating interwoven obstacles that spring back and slap us if we make the mistake of removing our hands too soon. Since I'm leading the way, I take the brunt of the punishment. Three times a recoiling laurel branch smacks me square in the forehead. All of this while struggling to remain standing against the rushing water. We each slip and fall several times, but, thankfully, have only a few bruises to show for it.

Whoever said mountains were peaceful and beautiful never had to travel down this rugged creek!

But with a little experimenting, Macy and I come up with a system we're able to use over and over with only hand signals and nods to one another. I clear the way and hold the branches back while she wades close enough to grasp them, thus stopping them from recoiling against her. Whenever we come to a small water-fall, I go over first, then turn and help her stay sure-footed as she traverses it by giving her my hand for support. In the especially swift sections, I wrap my arm around her to steady us against the current.

As we make it down a difficult drop and into a large pool of water below, I realize just how exhausted I am. We've been trav-eling for hours, and I can tell by the sun's diminishing angle that it's well into the afternoon. The day seems to have flown by, but as I drag myself to shore, I can feel the effect of every tiresome second in my sore muscles and cold bones.

There's a small, level patch of dry gravel on the left side of the creek, where it appears the topsoil was washed away during a flash flood, and I stumble toward it. I practically throw the backpack off my shoulders as I wade ashore and collapse onto the bed of tiny rocks that have been ground smooth by the water.

After trudging through the swift creek for most of the day, fighting with everything I had just to stay upright, finally having the weight off of my feet feels heavenly. I remove my tennis shoes and soaking wet socks and toss them next to me as Macy walks up.

"Wow! That was really hard!" she says between deep breaths.

I somehow find the energy to smile at her. "Yes, it was. At least we made it. And we're safe."

My feet are so sore it hurts to even move my toes, and the skin on the bottom is white and deeply wrinkled from walking in the water for so long. A few places have started to peel. I begin to mas-sage them carefully with my hands. Macy sits down a few feet to my left. She moans as she stretches her legs out. "Sore?" I ask her.

She nods. "Yep."

"You need to take your shoes and socks off."

She stares at me with annoyed, narrow eyes. "Why?"

Uggghhh. I want to scream. Why can't she just do what I say without requiring an explanation?

But I keep forgetting she's just a kid and kids need a reason for everything. Even though I certainly don't feel like explaining myself, I do it anyway, although I try to make the consequences of not heeding my advice sound horrible enough that she won't question me again.

"Waterlogged feet can cause you all kinds of problems if you don't let them dry out. Eventually the skin gets so nasty from all the moisture that it begins to fall right off your feet, leaving behind only raw, unprotected flesh. Your feet become so irritated that it's too painful to even stand up. Does that sound like fun to you?"

Her eyes go wide, and she shakes her head. "No."

I cut my eyes and snap my head toward her sopping wet shoes. "Then off they come." She removes them without another word, which I'm thankful for, because I don't have the energy to argue with her.

This small patch of dry gravel is the first level ground I've seen in a good while, and I have no urge to leave it any time soon. "I don't know about you, but I'm exhausted. I say we stop here for the day."

She nods. "Sounds good to me." She sighs heavily and adds, "I'm tired too."

I pull my sweatpants off as well, wring them out, and hang them on a nearby branch, along with my socks. I'm under no illusion that they will dry sufficiently in the humid air next to the creek, but at least they're away from my chilled skin, if only for a while.

My arms are so covered in scratches from the rhododendron and mountain laurel limbs they look as if I've just gone twelve rounds with a feral cat. My legs don't look much better, despite the fact that they were somewhat protected by the thick sweatpants.

Copying me, Macy wrings her socks and cotton sleep pants out and hangs them on another nearby tree limb.

The extra socks, underwear, and shirts I've been carrying inside the backpack are wet too, the result of several frigid baptisms when my tennis shoes lost traction on slick rocks and sent my legs flying out from under me. I wring out and hang all those items as well.

We consumed the rest of our drinking water while we traveled down the creek, so I retrieve the empty plastic bottles from the pack and wade out into the pool to refill them. The small rocks at the bottom of the stream poke at my tender feet, and I step carefully to keep from taking another bath.

Untreated water, even water that appears crystal clear, as this does, can harbor parasites. The risk of becoming sick from drinking contaminated water is real. I know this, but we have no choice. We'll just have to take our chances and hope for the best. Not drinking after we've expended so much energy today isn't a viable option.

I walk to where the water is spilling over the rocks at the head of the pool, thinking that moving water will be safer to drink than the still water from the edge of the pool, although I'm not positive my assumption is valid. Maybe I heard this on one of the survival shows I watched late at night after a concert, or maybe not; I'm just not sure. Either way, I fill and cap both bottles and turn to walk back to shore.

Something slender and black shoots through the pool of water like a torpedo, the sudden movement startling me. I gasp, but quickly recognize what it was.

A fish.

Just the idea of having something, anything, inside my stomach makes my heart beat faster.

As I take another step forward, a second small fish darts off and circles behind me. I have no idea how, or if, I can even catch one . . . but I want to try.

I have no fishing line, no bait. Even if I do manage to get one of them out of the water, I have no way to cook it. Our only lighter was crushed into tiny pieces back at the crash site. I've seen people on TV make fire by using a bow drill or other friction device, but that requires lots of practice and something else I don't have . . . dry wood. Trying to find wood dry enough to start a fire using friction here, in what is essentially a rain forest, would just be a waste of time. I might as well be rubbing two candy canes together. Maybe an expert could pull off such a feat, but not me.

But why would I even have to cook the fish?

Over the past few years, I've developed a fondness for sushi. Take away the rice, vegetables, and wasabi and sushi is just raw fish. In fact, the finer restaurants in Nashville charge a hefty sum for it. So the thought of eating an uncooked mountain trout, which is what I assume these lightning-quick fish are, doesn't disgust me at all. Actually, I'm so hungry right now, I would gladly eat a dozen of them, given the opportunity.

If I can only figure out how to catch one.

Again, I lean on my encyclopedia of late-night television knowledge that has proven helpful to me time and again since the plane crash. I remember that on one show a guy fashioned a spear out of a forked branch, which he then used to pin a fish to the bottom of a stream before quickly flinging it onto dry ground.

That might actually work.

As I walk back to shore, I'm both hopeful and reserved. Trying to catch one of the fish for dinner might be just an immense waste of time and energy. The small, wiry trout could prove impossible to corral. Still, my growling stomach tells me I must try.

Scanning the bank, I find an oak tree that has a low-hanging forked branch that should serve my purpose nicely. I have to tip-toe to reach it, but with a little effort, I manage to grasp it firmly in my right hand. I pull and twist until it rips free of the tree, leaving a torn and jagged butt end. I clean off the leaves and twigs until I hold in my hand a two-pronged spear about the diameter of a quarter and three feet long.

Macy gives me a suspicious look. "What are you doing?"

"Going fishing," I respond as I wade back into the water.

I make my way toward the center of the pool where the water is swiftest and position myself so that I'm facing the shore. Macy's eyes are glued to me. I wonder if she thinks I can actually pull this off. If she does, she's got more faith in me than I do.

Tilting my head down, I peer into the dark pool. The water comes to the top of my knees, which will make it difficult for me to move quickly. I'll have to wait until one of the fish swims almost directly below me. I stand perfectly still.

It seems to take an eternity before a small fish swims into range. It faces upstream and comes to a hover right in front of me, its body undulating gracefully against the current. I thrust my makeshift spear downward in a violent motion, and at the same time, a primal growl involuntarily escapes my lungs. The prongs of the spear crash against the bottom of the creek, which causes an eruption of silt and muddies the water. I hold my position and wait for the murkiness to clear away.

It only takes a few seconds for the current to sweep away the particulates so that I again have a clear view of the bottom. The shaft of my spear is wedged between two small rocks and the points are buried in the silty bottom—but there's no trout.

Discouraged, but not defeated, I wrench the spear loose and raise it for another try, this time holding the prongs just a few inches off the bottom so there will be less distance for them to travel the next time I jab at a fish.

Another one swims close by, and I deftly move the spear over its back. I thrust it downward with another loud growl, and this time, I succeed in pinning the fish against the bottom for a split second, but my wet hands slip on the shaft, and I lose my grip.

The trout scurries away completely unharmed.

Angry, I throw the spear back into the water toward the escaping trout.

Macy laughs at me from shore. I can't really blame her; I'm sure I look like a bumbling idiot out here attempting to catch a fish the length of my hand with nothing but a wooden stick.

"Keep trying, Miss Lauren. You'll get it." She giggles again under her breath.

I raise my eyebrows at her. "Thanks," I say sarcastically, but I smile a little too.

I lower my head and ready the crude spear for a third go at it. Another miss.

And another.

I keep trying for at least thirty minutes without success.

At this point, I'm well aware that I've burned more calories attempting to catch one of the small trout than the fish itself will provide. Perhaps I should accept that it's irrational to continue such a fool's errand, but in my mind, a net loss of calories doesn't matter at all anymore.

It's a personal battle now.

One I have every intention of winning, if for nothing more than my own pride's sake. It's just the two of us . . . mano a mano . . . me against the fish.

Scanning the water slowly, I spot another trout just ahead and to my right, its tail moving in a slow rhythm as it waits for its next meal to come floating by. I slide my feet slowly across the slick rocks of the creek bottom, being careful not to spook it, and ease the spear farther into the water.

My eyes narrow, focusing on the slender black figure hovering above the streambed. My grip tightens on the wooden spear. My heart begins to race. The two of us are locked in a bizarre show-down, two Old West gunfighters circling one another, hands hovering above pearl-handled pistols, eyes searching for the slightest movement from our opponent.

I'm done waiting.

In a flash, I thrust the forked point of the spear toward the fish and drive it into the rock and silt with such force my shoulders burn with the strain of it.

Another primal grunt.

Without a second's hesitation, I dive chin-deep into the water and, while still applying downward pressure against the spear with my right hand, grasp the forked end of it with my left.

Something slick wiggles against my skin.

The fish!

I dig my fingers even farther into the silt to get beneath it and lay my thumb across its back. In one violent, sweeping motion, I bring the spear and fish out of the water, as an Olympian throwing a discus, and hurl both of them onto the shore.

I run, my pumping legs throwing cold water into my eyes and mouth, hurrying to pounce on the trout before it can flop back into the creek. Stones poke at the soles of my bare feet. I grimace at the sharp pain, but don't slow down.

"You did it!" Macy yells. The sound of her small hands clapping together echoes through the mountain air.

I throw myself ashore and scramble on my hands and knees the rest of the way to the fish, which is flopping and writhing on the ground. Grasping its slick body with my left hand, I pick up a nearby rock with my right and raise it above my head.

"Wait!" Macy yells just as I'm about to bring the hammer down on the trout's skull.

My hand freezes in midair, and I snap my head toward her. "What?"

Her hands are clasped together, dangling at her waist. Her eyes are wide and glaring at me.

"What?" I repeat sharply.

A breeze blows her blonde hair across her face, and she raises a hand to clear it away. "You're not going to kill her, are you?" she asks in a worried, tense voice.

I huff, irritated at Macy's question. "Of course I'm going to kill it. We need to eat. What did you think I was going to do with it?"

She takes a few steps forward and stares down at the trout pinned under my hand. "I thought you were just going to catch her and play with her. I didn't know you were going to *kill* her!

Can't we just let her go so she can swim back to her mommy and daddy?" She points at the fish beneath my hand with her index finger. "Look how pretty she is!"

You've got to be kidding me.

I consider explaining to her that a fish won't swim back to its mommy and daddy, that nature doesn't work that way, but I know that argument will prove futile, so I don't even attempt it. "Macy, we *need* food! Don't you understand that?"

She glares at me and shakes her head. "I'm not hungry."

"Well, *I* am! I'm starving!"

Her eyes narrow in defiance, and she crosses her arms over her chest. "I'm not."

The urge to scream at the top of my lungs hits me again. After all the work I've put into trying to catch one measly little fish—something to help us survive a bit longer—she's going to stare me down while I knock it over the head with this rock as if I'm a corrupt judge sentencing an innocent man to the electric chair.

"Please? We don't need to kill her. We should send her back home . . . I bet her parents are missing her already." She pauses. "She might even have a brother or sister too."

I sigh deeply.

I know when I'm beat.

Looking down at the trout, I realize for the first time how small it is. It's skinny and only five or six inches in length. Hardly enough to constitute a real meal.

And Macy's right about one thing—it is a beautiful creature. Its back is overlaid with a moss-green design in the form of a maze. Its sides are populated with a multitude of crimson and golden spots, and the crimson ones are even encircled with a blue halo. The bottom fins are reddish orange, with brilliant white accents on the leading edges. I'm not sure what species it is, but I'm positive it isn't a rainbow trout. I've seen those before, and they don't look like this one.

Its gills are opening and closing rapidly as it struggles to breathe. It doesn't appear hurt. I pick it up in the palm of my hand and show it to Macy. "Okay . . . we can let it go."

"Yay!" She claps and jumps up and down with a childlike enthusiasm that makes me feel good about my decision, even though my stomach is growling in protest as I stand and walk back to the edge of the creek. I lower my hand into the water until the small trout is fully submerged. Macy walks over and peers over my shoulder. She's smiling, and that makes me happy.

"Go on, fishy. Swim away!" she says.

I chuckle and glance back down at the trout. Its gills are still moving, and its tail begins to work slowly back and forth. I gently remove my hand, and we watch as it shoots back out into the center of the pool, happy and healthy. "Okay, it's gone. It's swimming back to its family," I say.

Macy lets out a huge sigh. "Thanks, Miss Lauren."

I stand and pat her on the back. "You're welcome."

Since we have no food to eat, we drink a lot of water, which fills my stomach but doesn't quell my hunger pangs. I could be angry about having to release the fish, but I don't regret my decision. Seeing the trout set free and swimming away made Macy feel good, and if any little girl in the world deserves a measure of happiness right now, it's her.

We bathe ourselves in the creek as best we can, even though we have no soap, and then spend the rest of the afternoon chatting. I hear more stories about her first-grade classmates and the minute details of every school field trip she's taken. She asks me more about my job, and I regale her with stories of sold-out coliseums and exciting cities and locations where I've performed. We gossip about other celebrities I've met, the ones I like and the ones I don't care for. She seems to enjoy this the most.

I feel myself growing closer to her.

As the sunlight continues to fade from the sky, I unlash our blue jean pillows from the backpack and we stretch out on the rocky shore. The air is warm this evening, so we leave our cotton pants hanging in the trees to dry some more throughout the night. A breeze rustles the thousands of green leaves that surround us. The sound of the creek rushing by is melodic and relaxing. I stare up into the clear sky and let the wind blow across my face.

If we weren't trapped in such a dire circumstance, this would really be a glorious place.

"Miss Lauren?"

"Yes?"

Macy sighs, and I get the feeling something is weighing heavily on her mind. She doesn't say anything else, so I prod her to continue. "What is it, Macy?"

"Well, it's just—" Another sigh. "I'm still worried about who will take care of me once I'm home."

"You don't need to worry about that, Macy."

"I can't help it."

"I told you that there will be plenty of nice families who will want to adopt you once this is all over. I promise there will be."

"I don't want to live with strangers. What if I don't like them?" She stops, and I have a feeling I know what is coming next. She draws in a deep breath and says, "I like you. Can I just live with you?"

Ever since I learned that Macy has no living relatives, other than a grandmother living at a retirement home, I've been afraid this issue might come up. I've been considering how I should handle it, suspecting it was only a matter of time before she asked, but even after working through the scenario numerous times in my mind, I'm still not entirely sure what my response is going to be.

It's not that I haven't grown fond of her—because I have—or even that I don't want her to live with me. It's just that I'm not sure it would work out, considering the career path I've chosen. A young girl like her needs a stable family environment, especially after everything she's been through, and that's something I can't provide. With my insane travel schedule and other commitments, I wouldn't be able to give her the time and attention she deserves.

As if reading my mind, she says, "I promise I won't be any trouble. I do well in school, and I can help you do chores too."

"Macy—"

"Well, don't you like me?" she interrupts, prodding me for an immediate answer.

I take a deep breath before I begin to speak. "Of course I like you, Macy. And it's not that I wouldn't love to have you come live with me . . . it's not that at all . . . but I just don't think it would be the best thing for you right now."

"Why not?" she asks, obviously peeved by my answer.

Of course she wants an explanation. I don't want to hurt her feelings, but I also need to ensure she understands why such an arrangement wouldn't be good for her. It would be wrong of me to allow her to get her hopes up, only to be disappointed in the end. "It's just that I travel all the time, and I'm so busy that I don't really have time—"

"I can go with you," she interrupts again. "That way I could see all those cool places you told me about. It would be so much fun!"

"No."

"But why?"

There's a sadness in her voice now that tears my heart out, and as much as I want to say yes, I know I can't. Living with me would not be the best for her. I know this, even if she doesn't, and I can't let my emotions or her pleas convince me otherwise. I clear my throat to steady my voice. "Because it just wouldn't work out."

"Yes, it would. It would work out just great."

"No, Macy, it wouldn't."

She huffs. "You just don't want me."

I turn my head and search her face. She appears hurt, her feelings not just wounded, but utterly crushed by my words. "That's not true, and you know it," I say. "I think you're awesome, but you need a family that can give you a good, stable life. You don't want to be traveling all over the country with me. You need a place you can call home, where you can make friends and focus on your education."

"But I don't want another family. I want to stay with you," she whimpers.

I sigh. After everything we've been through together, I just don't have the heart to hurt her feelings any further, and it's obvious she isn't going to change her mind. "Okay, how about this? If there isn't a great family who loves you and wants to adopt you when this is all over, then I'll try to make it work out. No promises, though. How does that sound?"

She smiles. "Deal."

I nod. The smile on her face tells me that she has taken my small capitulation as a guarantee she will get to stay with me, but I don't correct her misconception. I'm just too tired. "Okay, try to get some rest. We'll have another hard day tomorrow," I tell her.

Despite my best efforts to convince her otherwise, she's beaten me again—and I know it. But I'm confident that she'll never have to come stay with me in Nashville because, just as I told her before, as soon as we make it out of here and our story is splashed all over television, wonderful families will line up wanting to adopt her. Why wouldn't they? She's a great kid. And once she gets settled back in and gets used to her new family, she'll be happy and will forget about wanting to live with me.

With the emotional crisis averted, I stare back into the evening sky and close my eyes.

"Miss Lauren?"

"What?"

"I'm hungry."

Oh, for heaven's sake.

28

I'm awakened by a bloodcurdling scream that slices through the forest and shatters the peaceful, low roar of the creek rushing past me.

My eyes snap open, and I jerk my head off the rolled blue jeans. It's not completely dark yet, and I realize I've only dozed for a few minutes.

Macy is gone.

I jump to my feet just as another earsplitting scream reverberates in my ears. It's coming from behind a small patch of underbrush just a few yards down the shore from where Macy was lying. I rush forward, desperate to find her.

My heart pounding, I burst through the underbrush and find her standing next to a small pile of rocks. She's crying, shaking, and screaming uncontrollably. "Macy! What's wrong?" Tears are running down her terrified face, her legs trembling. "What's wrong?" I yell again, panic in my voice.

Between screams she points to the ground.

My eyes follow her small finger and I gasp.

Coiled and almost perfectly camouflaged on the dry leaves, is a snake. And it's one I recognize.

A copperhead.

I know for a fact that's what it is because I found one outside my home in Tennessee a year ago. It was hiding in my flower garden under an azalea bush. I didn't know what to do, so I called animal control. Two men came, identified it, and took it away.

This snake looks the same as the one in my garden. It's rust-colored, with dark brown hourglass-shaped bands across its back. It has the same triangular head too. The coal-black slits of its pupils stare me down. Its head cocks back, poised to strike again.

Without thinking, I pick up a nearby stick and wallop the copperhead across the head. The stick is rotten and breaks off in my hand, but the blow is enough to frighten the snake away. It retreats quickly, and I watch as its slender, black-tipped tail disappears into the forest.

Snatching Macy up in my arms, I race back to the creek shore. I set her down on the gravel, struggling to control my own fear. "What happened? Did it bite you? Are you okay?" I yell in rapid-fire succession, my panicked voice shooting through the air with the shrillness of a tornado siren.

She doesn't answer me, but she's screaming in pain, so I know she must've been bitten. I frantically scan her legs and, although the twilight makes seeing difficult, I make out two red puncture marks where the fangs entered her body on the side of her right calf, two inches below her knee.

My stomach sinks as if on a carnival ride. I was hoping that Macy was just frightened, that her screams weren't those of pain, but of terror. But now there's no longer any doubt—the snake struck her squarely in her calf muscle.

I jerk her T-shirt off and check her arms, back, and abdomen too, just to make sure she hasn't been bitten more than once. Those areas are clear.

My heart hammers in my chest with such force and speed that I feel as if it might seize up and stop working at any second. My breaths come in short, rapid gasps. My head spins. I can't believe this is happening, and I feel as though I'm going to pass out.

Calm down, Lauren. You've got to get it together, I tell myself.

"I-I'm sorry," Macy says between body-rattling sobs. "I just needed . . . bathroom . . . and—" Her broken speech is cut off by another scream of agony, but I comprehend enough of what she's saying to understand what happened.

I want to scold her for not waking me up to help her, for just wandering off unattended, but that won't do either of us a bit of good right now. I struggle to focus my brain and subdue my runaway emotions.

Finding the copperhead in my own flower garden back home unnerved me. Afterwards, I did some research online, trying to find a way to keep them far away from the house and what to do if I was bitten. I rack my brain, trying to remember everything I read, while at the same time trying to get Macy to stop crying, but she's hysterical and obviously in a tremendous amount of pain.

Gradually, what I learned comes back to me. I remember reading an article that said you should actually avoid a lot of the things people used to think you should do if you were bitten. You aren't supposed to try to suck the poison out or cut the wound or use a tourniquet. What you are supposed to do is get to a hospital as soon as possible.

Great. There's certainly not one of those around here.

Then another fact I'd come across during my research sears my mind. While copperhead bites are rarely fatal to healthy adults, people with compromised immune systems, the elderly, and young children, just like Macy, are more susceptible to serious complications if they don't receive prompt medical attention.

The flesh surrounding the bite on her leg is already red and beginning to swell, which I'm afraid indicates she was injected with a full dose of venom. There's only one thing I can do, and that's try to find help.

But there's no one to help us out here. No one.

I've never felt more alone and helpless than I do at this moment.

244 · J. MICHAEL STEWART

I have to leave . . . right now . . . in the dark . . . and pray I can find help before it's too late.

Leaving at night and traveling down this rugged mountain creek is dangerous in and of itself, and the idea of even attempting such a thing terrifies me to my very core, but I have no choice. I have to go. Now.

I spring to my feet and hurriedly begin making the necessary preparations. I pluck my sweatpants from the tree and put them on. I grab a nearby pair of socks and wrestle them over my worn-out feet. I don't even waste time looking for the driest pair because it doesn't matter, they'll be soaked in a matter of minutes anyway. I quickly put on my tennis shoes and lace them tightly against the tops of my feet.

Macy is still crying as I put her sleep pants back on, hoping they will protect her legs from the rough branches overhanging the creek. I don't worry about shoes for her because she's not going to be walking.

Racing back to the pack, I grab the two packages of Benadryl and tube of antibiotic ointment from the first aid kit and one of the bottles of water, which I refilled prior to lying down for the evening. With these items in hand, I hurry back to Macy.

I tear open one of the packages and pop the two small Benadryl pills into her mouth. I make her take a sip of water and force her to swallow. Hopefully, this will lessen her body's reaction to the venom. I'm not sure of this, but figure it can't hurt. At least the medicine will make her sleepy and hopefully allow her to rest. I wish I still had a dose of the Tylenol to help ease her pain, but I took the last of it on top of the mountain for my migraine.

I raise her pant leg up and apply a generous amount of the antibiotic ointment to the area of the bite. I seriously doubt this will help anything either, but I'm just trying to do everything I can think of that might possibly be of benefit. I shove the tube of ointment and the remaining dose of Benadryl into my bra.

I move frantically around the campsite, mentally running through everything we have available to us, trying to determine if I can use anything else. I grab the shoelaces I've been using to lash the blue jeans to the pack and, when I notice Mr. Pebbles lying near where Macy had been stretched out on the rocks, I pick him up too.

Everything else will have to stay behind, including the backpack and medical kit. I just can't carry any of it and Macy too. I'll need my hands free to navigate down the creek channel.

I rush back to Macy. She's shivering, and I'm afraid she's going into shock. I double the shoelaces and loosely tie her wrists together, about twelve inches apart. It's certainly not ideal, but it's the only thing I can think of that will keep her from falling off my back. I place Mr. Pebbles in the crook of her arm and she squeezes him against her body.

She's still crying as I kneel, slip my head behind the length of shoestring, and lift her onto my back. "It's going to be okay, Macy. Just try to relax and be brave," I tell her.

Darkness has fully engulfed the wilderness as I wade out into the water and turn downstream.

Please, God, don't let this little girl die.

29

I've traveled less than fifty yards when my feet slip on the slick underwater rocks and send me flying face-first into a pool at the base of a cascade.

My left knee slams against the craggy bottom, shooting pain up my leg. The frigid water shocks my body. Scrambling to my hands and knees, I push my head above the surface and gasp for air. The length of shoelace between Macy's hands goes taut over my throat and makes it even harder for me to catch my breath. I slip my fingers underneath it and pull forward, creating enough slack in the line so that I no longer feel as if I'm being strangled. I tilt my head over my right shoulder to check on Macy. "You okay?"

She doesn't answer, but the shrill cries that have assaulted my eardrums since the snakebite continue unabated. I know the pain must be excruciating for her, but I can't help hoping that her lungs will eventually tire out and she will cease her piercing screams. The annoying noise grates on my nerves and only serves to disrupt my concentration.

And if there's one thing I need while wading down this stream in the dark, it's the ability to concentrate on every move I make.

Maybe this wasn't such a good idea, after all. Maybe I should stop and wait until daybreak to continue.

I'm already exhausted from today's travel and my weariness only exacerbates the difficulty of this task. My legs are weak and trembling under Macy's weight on my back. I'm unable to see where I'm placing my feet, so I'm forced to *feel* the creek bottom with my tennis shoes, which leads to missteps such as the one that just sent me plunging headlong into the cold water.

If I keep going and twist my ankle thanks to a poorly placed foot or, even worse, break a leg, then neither Macy nor I will make it out of here alive.

But is stopping and waiting for daylight really an option?

No, it's not.

Macy needs to get to a hospital as soon as possible, I know this. Even though my energy reserves are completely drained, if I stop and try to rest, I know I'll be unable to. My mind, consumed with worry for her, will not allow me to sleep.

Stopping will serve no purpose other than to extend the amount of time we must spend in this infernal wilderness.

I continue on.

30

I've been going now for two or three hours, I guess. I'm not exactly sure. Time has a way of crawling by out here, and it's easy to lose perspective of it. For all I know, it's only been forty-five minutes since I left our campsite and it just seems as if I've been toiling for hours.

Even though the moon is now casting a small amount of pale light over the landscape, allowing me to just make out the boulders and fallen trees that often block my path, I so wish I had a flashlight to help me see where I'm going, and I wonder why there wasn't one inside the airplane. Maybe there was one and I just didn't find it. If so, it was a terrible oversight on my part. Without adequate light to guide my path down the creek, my progress is mind-numbingly slow. I have to carefully weigh the potential consequences of every reach of my hand, every slide of my foot, before taking any action, which makes the whole process extremely exhausting—both physically and mentally.

Macy has become sick several times since we left and vomited down my arms and back, the pungent smell adhering to my T-shirt and skin. The first time it happened, and I smelled the foul odor and felt the hot liquid slide down my back, it took me by surprise and I leaned over and retched myself, emptying my stomach contents into the creek.

I'm sure her throwing up is a reaction to the snakebite, and each time it happens, I'm forced to stop long enough to make sure she's still coherent and that she isn't choking on her own vomit.

Her cries have now slowed from continuous to frequent. Even though I'm sure the pain is still intense, I think her body is just too exhausted from the constant screaming to keep up the same intensity and pace as before. Her warm breath on the back of my neck lets me know she's still hanging in there. I talk very little, trying to stay focused on my own movements, only speaking when I need to check on her or when I try to console her after she tells me how much she's hurting, which she's done several times.

Despite my best efforts to concentrate on getting through the creek safely, we've tumbled and fallen into the cold water numerous times. Fortunately, other than some scrapes and bruises on my arms and legs, the mishaps have resulted in no serious injuries to either of us.

The pools of water keep getting deeper and the rapids swifter the farther down the mountain we go, which increases the amount of energy I have to expend. I can feel the strength ebbing from my body with every step of my legs, every reach of my arms, and I wonder if this torment will ever end.

Just hours ago, I was so certain we were both going to make it out of this that I began to make plans for my first few days back in Nashville. I see now that was a mistake. The same fear I faced after the crash returns.

We may never get out of here.

All those things I planned to do once I returned to Nashville—all the apologies I intended to make—well, they simply may never happen.

I have to face that fact. As much as I don't want to, I must. It's not that I'm giving up, not at all, but I feel as though I must prepare myself emotionally in case the worst happens. How will I face death, I wonder? With fear? Or with courage and dignity?

I've never really pondered that question before. Even during the times over the past several days when my spirits were at rock bottom, like when the airplane flew near us and I couldn't get the signal fire going in time, or at the top of the mountain when my cellphone died before I could call for help, even in those desperate moments, when I thought I might not make it, I never allowed myself to think about what my final moments might actually entail.

Maybe, somewhere in my subconscious, I was too afraid to think about it. But now I'm consumed with what the end might look like, and I can't help dwelling on it.

I hope that Macy goes before I do. That thought seems odd to me, maybe even cruel, though that's not my intention at all. It's not because I'm greedy or uncaring. In fact, it's just the opposite. If I were only concerned with myself, like the old Lauren would've been, I would wish a quick and easy death for myself. But I can't do that, because that's not the way I think now. It isn't all about me, not anymore.

The reason I hope Macy goes before I do has nothing to do with me at all; it has to do with her.

It's because I don't want her to have to die alone.

I want to be able to hold her in my arms and tell her I love her and what a great friend she has been to me, how much she's helped me and made me into a better person, as she takes her last breath. I'll sing to her too. It's what I do best . . . and she deserves my best.

Her parents can't be here to offer her comfort, so I'll have to fill that role, no matter how difficult it is.

But for now I'm still going, and as long as I have an ounce of energy left inside of me, I'll keep going.

Macy wouldn't give up on me, and I'm not going to give up on her either.

I can't. I won't.

I must dig to the very core of my soul and draw on every ounce of fortitude within me. I have to view myself as I am. Not as I was six days ago onstage at the wedding, but as I am now—hardened and tested.

I'm Lauren Miller.

Not the country music superstar, but the woman who gave birth by herself, with no pain medication, inside an old barn in Oklahoma.

That girl was tough.

And she's still inside me somewhere.

31

Dawn breaks, kissing the mountains with the first signs of a new day. Songbirds chirp and call to one another. A deer eases to the water's edge a hundred yards downstream and takes a drink before retreating into the forest.

I greet it with boundless delight.

After spending hours wading and oftentimes even crawling through the cold waters of the creek in darkness, just being able to once again see what's in front of me lifts my spirits.

Although my mind is buoyed by the sunlight, my body isn't. While the desire to keep going is still strong within me, my body is so battered I feel I might collapse at any moment, never to stand again.

The front of my neck is raw from being rubbed by the shoelaces between Macy's hands, and it causes excruciating pain every time her weight shifts backward and digs the laces into my skin. I wish I had brought along one of the extra socks we had back at our last camp as a guard for my throat, but I didn't think about it. I was in too big a rush to leave, desperate to find help for Macy.

My back and hips are screaming for relief from the extra weight, the muscles surrounding my spine burning with pain and quivering with intermittent spasms.

My arms are covered in deep, red scratches and huckleberry-colored bruises where I was whacked with a rebounding laurel bush or bounced off an ill-positioned rock. I imagine that, underneath my sweatpants, my legs are in even worse shape. I'm too tired to reach down and look, though.

My quadriceps are on fire from the constant pummeling they've taken, straining to hold me up against the surging current and propelling me over large boulders and fallen trees in my path. I can no longer lift my legs more than an inch or two, so I'm forced to just scoot my feet across the creek bottom, which is painful, because the continuous rubbing of my wet legs together has caused severe chafing on my inner thighs.

Macy hasn't cried or gotten sick in an hour or so, but I can still feel her warm breath against the back of my neck, so I know I must keep going. I'm unsure if she's asleep or unconscious. It doesn't really matter, I suppose. Either way, I have to get her to a hospital soon.

I hope her breathing doesn't stop, because I know if it does, I'll stop too. The will to keep myself alive is no longer strong enough to keep enduring this agony.

Macy is the only reason I've been able to go this long.

I'm not positive how many hours I've traveled, only that I've been walking since dark last night, so I'm guessing that's probably eight or nine. As long as that is, it feels so much longer—as if I've been walking since the beginning of time itself.

As badly as I want to press on for Macy's sake, I'm just not sure how much longer my body will be able to keep taking steps forward. I've had no sleep since we left the first spring yesterday morning, other than the few minutes I dozed just before Macy was bitten by the snake, and my mind has become noticeably more lethargic. It seems to be swathed in a dense fog that even the new sunlight can't chase away. My reactions are delayed and sluggish, as if my brain is having great difficulty communicating the simplest of tasks to my body.

It's a second-by-second battle to keep myself on track and away from the solid ground of the shore that seems to be beckoning to me with ever-increasing fervor to just come and lie down for a little while. I know if I do that, if I listen to the voice inside my head that wants me to quit, I'll never get back up.

I focus on the girl in the barn, how she'd found the strength to persevere through that.

That girl was me.

I can make it through this too. I know I can.

Because I'm a survivor.

"Just keep going, Lauren. One step at a time. One breath at a time. You have to," I whisper to myself.

"It still hurts so much," Macy mumbles in my right ear, her voice hoarse and cracking from the sustained crying.

"I know it does, sweetie. Just hang on a little longer, okay? I'm going as fast as I can."

"Okay," she whispers.

The sound of her voice spurs me on. I take another sliding step forward and then another.

I keep going.

32

Each time there's a bend in the creek, I focus on it and tell myself that help is just around that corner, if only I can find the strength to reach it. When I round the bend and discover there's nothing but more of the same unending wilderness, I fix my eyes on the next turn in the channel and tell myself the same lie all over again—and I believe it every time. I have to. It's the only way I can find the will to keep moving.

I slip and fall again, slamming my already beaten knees and shins against the submerged rocks, which causes me to shriek in pain. I somehow struggle back to my feet even as the swift water fights to knock me down again.

And I take another step forward.

The creek makes a sharp turn to the left just yards in front of me, once again concealing what's ahead behind a thick wall of hardwoods and underbrush. It taunts me with the same false hope I've fallen for numerous times already. But just as with all the previous instances, something inside of me *has* to see what's around the bend. I continue shuffling my feet as I make my way toward it.

As I round the corner, I see a glorious sight. It isn't a search party or even another helicopter flying overhead, but it's something I haven't seen in days.

A road.

Well, calling it a road is an overstatement. It's not a road any longer, that much is obvious, but rather an old and abandoned roadbed that meanders down to the water's edge. The heavy blanket of dead leaves that covers it and the multitude of small trees growing on top of it make it clear it hasn't been used in decades.

But it's the first sign of civilization, even if a minor one, that I've seen since before the plane crash, and I rush toward it with joyous enthusiasm. In my haphazard scramble to shore, my concentration is broken and I make a misstep, lose my balance, and fall hard onto my knees. I quickly recover and crawl on my scratched hands and scraped knees the rest of the way.

I collapse onto the dry ground, thankful to finally be out of the water. After my hours-long battle against the creek's unrelenting efforts to sweep me off my feet, having something solid beneath me is a glorious change. I bury my face in the dirt and leaf litter of the old roadbed and pull the earthy, organic smell of the soil into my nostrils.

The overpowering desire to remain in this resting position grips me with such ferocity that my eyelids close automatically. I want so badly to sleep, if only for a few minutes, just to rest my sore feet and let the burning muscles in my legs relax.

Macy moans and the sound startles me, my own mind so clouded by exhaustion that I've forgotten she's still hanging on to my back. I groan and roll to my side and, as her weight slides off me and onto the ground, I sigh with relief. I pull the shoelaces from my neck and over my head to free myself of her.

I need to check her condition. Now that it's daylight I'll be able to see if the area around the snakebite has gotten worse. But I'm so tired that it's a war just to open my eyes. I pry them open with my muddy fingers and sit up.

I'm surprised that somehow, during the entire trip down the creek through the night, she has managed to keep hold of Mr. Pebbles. He's still tucked securely under her right arm.

But her physical appearance disturbs me. Her face is pale, and her lips, which had been so pink and full of life yesterday, have now lost all color. Beads of sweat cover her forehead. Her eyes are closed, and I anxiously stare at her chest to see if she's still breathing. I let out a sigh of relief when I see it slowly rise and fall. I tap her cheeks repeatedly with my hand. "Macy, wake up. Can you open your eyes for me?"

She grumbles and groans incoherently. Slowly, her eyelids flutter open and her blue eyes fix on me. I wonder if I look to her as I feel—beaten, worn out, and on the verge of death.

"How are you feeling?" I ask.

She doesn't answer; instead, she quickly tilts her head to the side and retches again. Only a small amount of thick saliva drips to the ground. She's already dehydrated again. Having left the plastic bottles back at our last campsite, I have nothing to carry water in.

I prop her up against the trunk of a nearby tree and crawl the few feet back to the creek. Cupping my hands, I scoop some water up and carry it back to her. Most of it leaks out from between my fingers during the short trip, but I manage to hold on to enough of it that she's able to take a small sip. "You want some more?"

She shakes her head.

It's not a good sign that she doesn't want to drink. I go back to the creek and get another handful of water anyway. I return with it and try to coax her to drink, but she just shakes her head again and turns her face away from me. Her eyelids slide shut.

I raise the leg of her sleep pants so that I can examine the snakebite. The appearance of the area surrounding the two puncture marks in her right calf muscle makes my stomach drop. The skin has swollen to the point it has ruptured as if it's an overripe tomato, leaving a gap about a half-inch wide and two inches in length. Deep shades of red and purple indicate the tissue damage the toxic venom is causing.

"It hurts . . . so much," she mumbles.

"I know it does, sweetie. Just keep hanging in there, okay? We'll be out of here soon. I found a road, so we won't have to walk in the creek anymore," I say, trying to encourage her. Macy's eyes slowly open at the sound of my voice, but close again almost immediately. She's so lethargic that I'm not sure how much longer she's going to last without medical treatment.

My eyes well up, and a single tear runs down my left cheek.

I want desperately to help her, to do something for her to make her pain go away, but there's nothing more I can do, except keep going and pray that we reach help before it's too late.

As I'm wiping my cheek dry with the back of my hand, an idea pops into my mind. I carefully remove Macy's cotton pants and toss them away. Still on my hands and knees, I crawl back to the creek's edge.

Digging below the leaf litter of the old roadbed, I grab a handful of dirt, add water, and mix it in my palm until a muddy paste forms. I hurry back to Macy, dip the tip of my index finger in the mud, and scrawl the word *copperhead* on her upper right thigh.

My fear is that by the time we reach help—if we do at all—I'll be so out of it that I'll be unable to communicate adequately with anyone. At least if I'm babbling incoherently because I'm on the verge of death myself, the medical personnel will know what type of treatment Macy needs for her snakebite. I also decide not to put her sleep pants back on, because without them, there will be less chance that my rudimentary writing gets smeared away and her injury will be apparent to any rescuer.

I pull the tube of antibiotic ointment from my bra and squeeze what remains of it directly inside the crevice in her calf where the swollen skin has split. I don't dare try to rub it into the flesh, though, knowing this would only cause Macy excruciating pain. I gave her the last dose of Benadryl a few hours ago, although I'm not sure if it's helped.

Returning to the creek once more, I plunge my face in the water, and the iciness of it gives me a small boost of energy. The flowing water feels good against my warm face, but my primary purpose for coming back to the creek again is to rehydrate myself. There's no way for me to know how much farther I'll have to walk, and I certainly can't count on finding another spring, so I drink until my stomach feels as if it's about to burst.

I crawl the few feet to Macy, plant my back against her stomach, and slip my head underneath the length of shoelace that connects her hands. I grasp the back of her knees to steady her and slowly stand. A searing pain surges through my lower back as her weight once again settles onto my body.

"Hang in there," I say.

There's no response.

"Macy?"

Still nothing.

"Macy!" I scream and jostle her on my back, trying desperately to get her to acknowledge me. She finally mumbles something into my right ear, though I can't make it out. "Macy, you've got to stay strong for me, okay?" Hot tears stream down my cheeks. "Just don't give up." I take a deep breath and bite my quivering lower lip. My voice cracks as I struggle to keep my emotions under control. "Do it for me, sweetie. Please?"

"Okay . . . Miss Lauren . . . I'll try," she says in a weak, faint whisper.

I stare at the abandoned road beneath my feet . . . and pray that it will lead us home.

33

The old road is relatively flat and meanders next to the creek's shoreline. Even though I'm frequently forced to alter my course to navigate around the small trees scattered along the road-bed, I'm thankful to finally be on dry ground again and find the travel much easier than wading through the swift creek.

It's not much faster, though.

It seems to take an eternity just to cover a few feet, my pace glacial. On top of the fact that my exhaustion makes each step forward both a physical and mental battle, I'm repeatedly forced to pause and adjust Macy's weight on my ragged back.

She's been quiet since I began walking again. I'm worried about her. Really worried. I try to force the negative thoughts out of my mind and simply focus on placing one foot in front of the other and getting out of here as quickly as possible, but it's not easy. Worries about what might happen to Macy keep popping up, despite my best efforts to keep them at bay. I can't imagine how devastating it will be, after all we've gone through together, if I survive and she doesn't.

I don't think I could handle that.

I've gone no farther than a hundred yards down the road when it departs the creek channel and turns up the mountain at a rather steep incline, thus demanding another decision.

To my right, the creek continues to barrel down the mountain, creating swift rapids and deep pools. Even though I know getting back in the water and wading downstream will eventually lead me to some type of civilization, it isn't a viable option. My body is no longer strong enough to safely fight the current and navigate the boulder-strewn rapids.

Any attempt to do that would simply end in disaster.

So that leaves the roadbed as my only option. I don't relish the thought of having to walk uphill again, especially with Macy on my back, but I have no choice.

I can make out a ridgeline to my left and slightly above me. It doesn't appear to be far away. Hopefully the road will level out there or even turn downhill on the other side.

I grab the back of Macy's knees, lean slightly forward, and shift her weight to the middle of my back.

And take another step.

34

My guess is that it's taken me more than an hour and a half to reach the top of the inclined section of road. It doesn't lead to the high ridgeline on my left as I'd first thought, but instead is curving around the hillside halfway up. I'm thankful for that, because I doubt I could've made it to the top of the ridge. I'm so weary that walking even five feet takes every ounce of strength I can muster. But at least now the old roadbed has leveled off, which is a welcome change.

I stumbled and fell several times during my ascent and had to pause to catch my breath, before struggling back to my feet and taking another step. This process, repeated over and over, drained what little energy I had left.

Even though I drank as much as I could from the creek before I started the climb, simply making the trip up the road has left me with a ravenous thirst. And even though it wasn't that great a distance, maybe a couple of hundred yards, I feel as if I've just traveled a hundred miles across a scorching desert.

Maybe it was a mistake to choose the road instead of staying with the creek, where at least I'd have had plenty of water. But there's no going back now. I'm committed to this course of action, for better or worse.

I'm beaten.

Finished.

Done.

I collapse to my knees with a muted thud. Every emotion I fought so hard to suppress this morning comes pouring out in a torrent. There's nothing I can do to stop it, not that I even try.

I let go and just let what's going to happen, happen.

The fear, the desperation, the anger at our situation—all of it—flows from my body in a tidal wave of tears and soul-racking sobs. My elbows sink into the soft earth as I fall forward, and I bury my face in my hands. My cries reverberate through the vast wilderness that surrounds me, but as loud as they are, I know they're not reaching anyone else's ears.

I feel so alone. So empty.

Forsaken.

I don't even have Macy with me any longer. The weight of her is still pressing on my back, but she isn't really here. She isn't speaking at all now, only the occasional groan or incoherent mumble, and I long for just a single word to let me know she's doing okay.

Birds are chirping overhead, scattered throughout the green, vibrant trees. I'm surrounded by signs of life . . . but I feel as if I'm already dead.

Ever since the plane crash I've been a helpless passenger on an emotional roller coaster that has the highest of peaks and the lowest of valleys. It's exhausting, and I'm sick of riding it. Moments of absolute euphoria, like when we found the first spring, have continuously been wiped away by other, soul-crushing events, like Macy's snakebite. I long to finally get off this sick carnival ride, for this whole ordeal to end—one way or the other.

But there's nothing I can do to change any of it.

I'll make it or I won't—those are the only two possible outcomes.

I've come to terms with what might await me. I'm not afraid of dying. Not anymore.

But I want Macy to live.

So I'll keep going as long as I can, until my broken body becomes incapable of moving another inch. At least then I can die in peace, knowing that I did everything I possibly could to save us.

If I quit now, while I still have breath in my body, I will have failed.

35

I'm not really walking any longer—I'm stumbling.

I grasp the nearest tree or sapling to hold myself up and then drag my feet forward until I can reach the next one. Without the added support, I'm sure my legs would collapse after every step under the strain of holding both Macy's and my weight.

My tongue feels as if it's three sizes too big for my mouth. I need more water, and soon. But there is none.

My hands are constantly seized with shooting pains from gripping the trees and lifting Macy by the back of her knees. She's so weak now that she's all deadweight, and when she tilts backward, the length of shoelace between her hands digs violently into the raw skin on the front of my neck.

Every step isn't just a struggle now—it's agonizing.

Although I've had to pull my way up a few small rises in the road, sometimes crawling on my hands and knees, the terrain has maintained a general downward trajectory for the last several hours.

I wonder what time it is. Judging by the sun's position, it appears to be well past noon. I attempt to estimate how long I've been awake, but my mind is too slow and foggy to make even the simplest calculation.

I know I've been going for a long, long time.

36

I don't know why I'm walking through the middle of the woods. It seems strange for me to be here. And why does it feel as if I'm wearing a heavy backpack?

Nothing makes sense.

Is this a dream . . . or real?

I have no idea.

For some reason I have an intense need to keep taking steps forward, even though I can't feel my legs. But they continue moving of their own accord, as if someone else is controlling them.

I'm on an old road that's covered with dead leaves, and I have to keep going. I must.

Why?

I don't know.

There's a small bend in the road up ahead, and I stagger toward it. The road curves to my left, and, as I round the corner, I see Kelsey standing there, staring at me. She's dressed in a flowing white gown that falls to her ankles.

Thank goodness. Maybe she can tell me why I'm out here. She's always been good at explaining things to me.

But she seems a long way off. She's waving her hand at me and smiling. I try to wave back, but my arm won't move. I stumble and fall to my knees. That's funny. I never fall. I giggle and get back to my feet, although it seems much harder to do than it should.

I keep walking toward her, step after step, but never seem to get any closer. She's still the same distance away as when I first saw her. It's frustrating.

But I keep moving forward.

The sunlight is almost gone. I can barely see the tops of the trees through the dusky dark.

I can still see Kelsey, though. She's vibrant, almost shimmering. She's still smiling at me, which makes me feel warm inside.

She motions with her arm for me to follow her. I take another step forward, but she runs off and disappears around the next bend in the road. "Kelsey? Come back," I whisper. "Don't leave me here . . . please!"

I stare at the corner waiting for her to return, but she doesn't. I fall to my knees again. This time it's even harder to get back up, but somehow, I manage. I have to catch up with her before she leaves me.

I have to keep going.

As I reach the bend in the old roadbed and round the corner, I expect to find Kelsey waiting on me, but she isn't.

She's vanished.

Where could she have gone?

"Kelsey!" I cry out. I stumble forward and fall down again. I get back on my feet, though I'm not sure how. I stagger forward, searching for her. Maybe she's hiding from me, playing a game. I giggle again. Turning my head to the left and then the right, I try to catch a glimpse of her.

But I can't find her. She's nowhere to be seen.

"Kelsey, please come back," I mumble so softly I can barely hear my own words.

As I turn my eyes forward again, I notice a group of men standing in front of a green truck farther down the road. They're all wearing backpacks.

Why are *they* here?

I don't understand their presence at all, and I don't recognize any of them.

One of them points at me.

I wonder what he wants.

My vision blurs just as I see three of the men begin to run toward me.

The legs that have seemingly been carrying me of their own accord, suddenly give way without warning and collapse beneath me. I land hard on my knees and pitch forward in one uninterrupted motion.

I'm falling, but my arms refuse to move. I can't stop myself.

The enormous weight on my back pushes me face-first into the ground.

Everything is black.

EPILOGUE

It's been three years since I staggered out of the mountains and into the waiting arms of a search party.

The men standing in front of the green truck were part of a U.S. Forest Service crew that had been assembled to find Macy and me. I imagine they were shocked to see one of the subjects of their search stumble out of the wilderness, mumbling incoherently, and carrying the other missing survivor on her back.

I barely remember that part, though.

The crash site had finally been located by another search team just hours before, and to say they were surprised when they found only three bodies inside the wreckage when there were supposed to be five, is a gross understatement.

Everyone, including all the media covering the story of my disappearance, had already written us off as dead.

They were only looking for bodies, not survivors.

But I'm a survivor.

The plane had gone down in a remote area of the Nantahala National Forest in Western North Carolina. Investigators later determined that the emergency beacon inside the plane, which should've quickly led rescuers to our location, had not operated correctly after the crash, just as I'd assumed.

It was discovered that, during a routine replacement of the transmitter's battery pack, the mechanic had failed to properly re-install the new battery. That mistake had occurred just four days before the crash. It was an event that neither Macy nor I had any control over, but one that drastically altered the course of our lives.

I've thought about my time in the wilderness every single day since I've been back. An experience like that sticks with you. It changes you forever.

I often question if I made the right decision by choosing to leave the crash site in an attempt to hike out and find help. The searchers did eventually locate the wreckage, so I can't help wondering if we'd stayed put could we have survived there and spared ourselves all the agony that we endured after I made the decision to leave? Who knows?

Did I search hard enough for a water source near the crash site, which would've allowed us to stay? Probably not.

And because of that, I feel guilty for what happened to Macy.

When I finally woke up in the hospital, I'd been out of it for almost twenty-four hours; at least that's what the doctors told me. I really had no idea one way or the other.

The first thing I recall seeing when I opened my eyes, was my mother and father standing next to my bed. It was awkward at first, since it had been years since I'd seen either of them, and I didn't know what to say. Without speaking, my mother wrapped her arms around me and kissed my forehead. I didn't say anything.

I just cried.

They stayed with me for two days, but then had to return to Oklahoma for work. Even though their visit was short, I was happy they came.

I still remember watching the IV fluid drip from the bag next to my bed, before traveling down the plastic tubing and into my arm, where it transferred its life-giving nutrients into my ravaged body. Behind the IV bag, the mountains of Western North

Carolina rose in the background, and I glared at them through the large glass window in my hospital room.

They were so beautiful from a distance, green and vibrant and full of life.

But I knew what they really were. What they were like when you were deep inside them, fighting for your life, struggling to find that next drink of water, fighting to cover just one more mile.

They were brutal, harsh, and unforgiving.

In addition to pumping me full of fluids, the doctors and nurses poked and prodded me to test for various parasites and infections. Fortunately, all my blood work came back clean.

They also gave me plenty to eat, but slowly, so as not to shock my system. Even though it was typical, bland hospital food, I gladly devoured it. On the third day of my stay, one of the nurses brought me a huge cheeseburger, fries, and a Coke. I loved her for it.

After four full days in the hospital, I was given a clean bill of health and released.

Macy didn't fare as well.

Because of her young age and the delay in medical treatment, her body had a hard time fighting off the effects of the copperhead bite. She was placed in ICU and given antivenom. She had also developed a secondary infection in the wound, so they performed surgery to clean the injury and remove the areas of damaged flesh. For a while, the doctors were unsure if she was going to be able to keep her lower right leg at all.

They told me that if she had stayed out in the wilderness another full day, she probably wouldn't have survived.

I went to see her during my third day in the hospital, once I was able to leave my bed. One of the nurses rolled me to her room in a wheelchair and allowed me to sit and talk with her for an hour. I took her flowers and a balloon with Dora the Explorer on it that I found in the hospital's gift shop. I remembered that her pink suitcase I pulled from the plane wreckage was emblazoned with Dora's face, so I assumed she would enjoy the balloon as well.

She did.

Macy wasn't back to her normal, bubbly self when I first saw her, but once I talked with her for a while, I knew she was going to make it through her hospital stay just fine.

She was released three days after me, with her right leg intact.

Because she's a survivor too.

Mr. Pebbles wasn't in great shape either. He'd been evacuated by the rescuers, along with Macy, aboard one of the helicopters. Amazingly, she'd been able to hold on to him for our entire journey out of the mountains. But his white-and-purple fur was filthy and still a little damp when one of the nurses brought him to me while Macy was in the ICU. When I was discharged, I took Mr. Pebbles for a complete makeover at a nearby fabric store, where they cleaned him and replaced all his old, nasty stuffing with new. Macy was so excited when I reunited the two of them as she was being released from the hospital.

After our medical treatment, there were sad goodbyes to be said. I went with Macy to the funeral of her parents, and she went with me to bid farewell to Kelsey. No one else who attended the funerals knew what the two of us were feeling. There was no way they could've, because they hadn't lived through what we had. The experience made us even closer than we already were as we drew on each other's strength during those difficult days.

Although my last several hours in the wilderness are a blur, I very clearly remember seeing Kelsey out there, and I'll forever be grateful for the encouragement she gave me, urging me forward toward our rescuers during those final minutes.

I miss her.

For all the mistakes I made out in the wilderness, I was certainly right about one thing: The news media salivated over our survival story. There were special programs on several cable news channels for the first few nights after we were found. Interviews were conducted with acquaintances of mine from Nashville, teachers from Macy's school, and members of the search party.

Reporters were also sent to Asheville, North Carolina, and stationed outside the hospital where we were being treated. I could see the satellite trucks camped out from the window in my room. There were several requests for me to provide interviews, but I declined. I just didn't want to talk about it, especially to reporters who wouldn't have understood the magnitude of what we'd been through. How could they?

Unless someone has survived a similar experience themselves, fighting with everything you have just to live another minute, another hour, there's no way they can accurately relate. The only other person in the entire world who knows exactly what I went through is Macy. And that bond between us—the bond formed under the pressures and rigors of surviving—cannot be severed by anyone or anything. It's always going to be there. Something only the two of us share.

I'd also been right about one other thing. After our story got out to the world, there were a line of people wanting desperately to adopt Macy.

But they never got the chance.

I didn't let them.

Macy needed me, and I needed her. And not for just a few days or weeks, but for the rest of our lives. I realized this as soon as I spoke to her in the hospital.

Before I was even discharged, I contacted my attorneys and started the process to adopt her. I was granted temporary custody of her a few days later. Our story of surviving together in the wilderness had been splashed all over various news shows so that virtually everyone had heard it by that time. It had caught the nation's attention, and I knew no judge would want to throw a cold towel on such a heartwarming ending by denying my request to permanently adopt Macy. Besides that, one advantage of being rich is that I can afford to hire the very best attorneys, and mine did a spectacular job of moving the process through the courts.

Still, it took almost two years for the formal adoption to go through. Macy lived with me at my home in Brentwood, Tennessee, while we waited for the adoption process to work its way to completion. I enrolled her in school and shuttled her back and forth myself.

In the months following our rescue, I found that I wasn't quite ready to go back to the rat race and constant personal demands of my old life. I just wasn't the same person who had boarded that small plane in Georgia, desperate to get back to Nashville for work.

I canceled my tour and slowed work on the new album so I could focus on myself and on helping Macy get back to a somewhat normal existence after the loss of her parents. It was a good decision on my part; the downtime helped both of us.

I think often about the day the adoption was finalized. We were in a small courtroom in downtown Nashville. All my attorneys were there, as was Pam, the social worker who represented Macy's interests. She'd become a close friend to both Macy and me during the process. When the judge made her ruling and certified the adoption, I think Pam was just as happy about it as Macy and I were. We all hugged and then went out to Macy's favorite restaurant for pizza and soda to celebrate.

Once I had the official paperwork that granted me full and permanent custody of Macy, I began to seriously consider whether or not I wanted to stay in Nashville any longer. I decided that I didn't. By that time, the new album had been released, and there really wasn't anything tying me down to Nashville any longer.

And being forced to leave Macy with other people every time I had to go out of town for a concert or other commitment was not something I wanted for our future. I knew taking her on the road with me would not be best for her either. She needed to have a normal life, to be able to enjoy the stability and anonymity that comes from living outside the public eye.

It's been a year since I sold my house in Brentwood and walked away from my successful career in country music.

And I don't regret it one bit.

I'm sitting in the wooden swing that hangs from the large oak tree in our front yard, gently rocking myself back and forth with my bare feet against a lush patch of green grass. The new house I had built for us is just a few yards away and overlooks the farm. But the weather-beaten swing came with the property and, at first, it wasn't much to look at. I suppose a lot of people would've just thrown it away. But I saw something in it worth saving.

After we moved in, Macy and I spent an entire day scraping off all the cracked and peeling brown paint and covered the wood with a fresh coat of white. The process was symbolic and, at the same time, therapeutic for both of us. It felt as if we were scraping off our old lives and replacing them with something new and fresh.

Now we often spend our evenings resting in the old, refurbished swing, sipping sweet tea and discussing our day as the sun disappears over the distant horizon and paints the sky crimson and orange.

Today, the sky is deep blue, with not a cloud in sight. A warm summer breeze is blowing across the Oklahoma hayfields and whipping my blonde hair against my face.

It feels so good to be here.

It feels like home.

I purchased an old farm outside the small town I grew up in—the very town I couldn't wait to escape as a teenager—and I've found that I actually love being back here. It's quiet and peaceful. And I can be myself. There are no more media appearances, no more concerts, no more fancy dinners to attend. I still get invitations for all the country music awards shows, and Macy likes to get dressed up and go to those, so I take her. It's nice to catch up with the people I used to work with in Nashville, but it's just not the same for me anymore. The money and fame don't draw me like they used to.

I'd rather be here on this old farm.

Maybe someday I'll return to the music industry—I still love to sing—but for right now, I think it's best for Macy and me to stay right here. Of course, people here know who I am, know what I've accomplished in my life . . . they just don't care. To them, I'm not Lauren Miller, the country music superstar; I'm just Lauren, the once-rebellious girl they knew growing up.

And that's nice.

My parents still live in the same house I ran away from, and we've begun to repair our relationship, but it's taking time, and that's okay. Until recently, I never understood the enormous pain I caused them when I just left without even saying goodbye.

My brother's house is only two miles farther down the same dirt road that runs in front of my property. He and his wife have three kids now, and they come over and visit quite regularly.

Macy's thriving in her new school and has made several good friends. She's growing up so fast. It's hard for me to believe she's ten years old already. Her birthday was just two weeks ago. We had pony rides and a big bounce house set up at our farm and invited all her friends over for the occasion.

She's not here with me right now. It's Saturday, and she spent last night at a friend's house. She was so excited, and a little nervous too, I think, about her first sleepover. She should be back soon, and I'm anxious to hear how it went.

The odds of winning the Powerball lottery jackpot are one in 292 million. Yet, people still play every week, because someone eventually wins.

The odds of being struck by lightning in the United States last year were roughly one in one million. Even so, an estimated three hundred people in the country came up on the wrong side of those numbers.

I know these statistics because I looked them up.

I had to—just to assure myself that sometimes things with astronomical odds of happening do, in fact, occur.

Because I feel as if I've been struck by lightning, while at the same time, holding the winning Powerball jackpot ticket in my hand.

My attention turns to the two envelopes that are lying on the wooden swing next to me. I pick one of them up and remove the folded piece of paper inside. It's a letter from Pam, the social worker who helped me adopt Macy. I received it two months after we moved into our new home. The edges of the paper are worn from the grip of my fingers because I've read it so many times that I've lost count.

Dear Lauren,

I just wanted to send you a quick note to say congratulations to you and Macy on your new home. I know you will be happy in it, and I look forward to hearing updates from you as Macy continues to grow into a vibrant young woman.

I see so many sad stories in my job, kids that are abused or have no one to love them, and this has hardened me over the years to the point that sometimes I wonder if there's any good left in the world.

But your case was different. You restored my belief that good people like you do still exist, and that the job I do is important. Thank you for that.

I was overjoyed when you were willing to take care of Macy after the loss of her parents. She needed you, and I suspect after everything you went through together, you needed her a little bit too. It has been a great privilege for me to play a small part in the amazing story you two share.

I probably shouldn't tell you this, but I feel like I should. It brought me a sense of happiness, so I hope it does the same for you. I was ecstatic when I learned that you had decided to leave the Nashville area and move back to Oklahoma. When I heard the news, I couldn't help but think that it was meant to be.

278 · J. MICHAEL STEWART

You already know that Macy was not the biological child of Adam and Juliette and that she was adopted as an infant. However, the one fact that I didn't disclose previously to you (due to the confidentiality of the adoption records) was that Macy was born in Oklahoma. She was found abandoned in front of a fire station not too far from where your new home is. So you can see why I was so excited when I heard you were from the same area and were taking her back there to raise her.

You're going to be a wonderful mother to her, and I wish you all the best in the future. If I can ever be of any help to you or Macy, or if you just have further questions, please don't hesitate to contact me.

Your friend,
Pam

When I first received the letter, I couldn't believe what I was reading. I had the sudden urge to pick up the phone and ask Pam to go back and recheck the adoption records a second time because what she was telling me just couldn't be true. I didn't know what to do, how to process this seemingly unbelievable piece of news.

It couldn't be.

After I took some time to digest what I'd been told, I decided not to call Pam back and have her double-check the adoption records again.

Because, for whatever reason, I knew the truth in my heart.

Macy is the right age, and she looks a lot like me, a fact I remember commenting on when I first met her right before we boarded the plane in Georgia, although at the time, I thought nothing of it. Who would?

That seems a lifetime ago now.

I fold Pam's letter, place it back inside the envelope, and set it down beside me. I don't bother picking up the second envelope that bears the return address of the DNA lab. I already know what's inside it. I tore it open the moment it arrived at the house seven months ago.

Our house sits on a hill that overlooks the rest of the farm, and I raise my head and stare out across the pasture. At the bottom of our property sits an old wooden barn. It's gray and weather-beaten. A rusty patina covers its tin roof, the result of years of exposure to Northeast Oklahoma's cool, rainy winters and blistering summers. It's old and rugged. Strong and tested. And just as the wooden swing was at first, it's not much to look at, but it holds a special place in my heart.

It's the place where, ten years ago, a terrified young girl gave birth to a baby.

It's where Macy was born.

I now know that my time in the mountains wasn't a punishment at all—it was a blessing. One that I'll forever be grateful for.

Why this happened, why the two of us were brought back together in the most unlikely of ways, I can't fully explain. Maybe I never will be able to. But that's okay. I don't have to understand everything. All I need to do is be thankful and embrace whole-heartedly the second chance I've been given to care for her.

I don't ever want to replace Adam and Juliette. That's not my intention at all. They were, and will always be, her parents. A large picture of them and Macy, together and happy, hangs inside her bedroom. She still loves and misses them, as she should. I'll make sure she never forgets them, because they gave her love and a family when I couldn't.

Someday, when she's older, I'll tell Macy the whole story.

Our unbelievable story.

I'll be honest with her too. I'll tell her about the mistakes I made and why I did what I did. When the time comes, I'll even help her find her biological father if she wants that. But for now, I just want her to be a happy child and enjoy growing up in a place where she can be free to spread her wings and be her own person, away from my fame.

A car turns off the gravel road and travels up our bumpy, rocky driveway. I stuff the two envelopes into my back pocket and stand from the wooden swing. Amanda is driving, and her daughter, Kimberly, and Macy are sitting in the back seat laughing and giggling. I walk over to greet them as the car pulls to a stop.

Amanda was a classmate of mine, and she was one of the few people in school who didn't think I was a complete weirdo, so I'm glad that Macy and Kimberly are friends now. Amanda steps out and gives me a hug. "Thanks for letting Macy spend the night. The girls had the best time," she says.

"Oh, thanks for inviting her. It was all she talked about this past week."

Macy opens the door and comes around to stand beside me.

"Did you have a good time?" I ask her, although I can already tell from the look on her face that she's had a ball.

"Yeah! It was awesome! We had *so* much fun!"

I chuckle and give her a kiss on the forehead. "I'm glad. I can't wait to hear all about it."

I thank Amanda again, and we make plans for Kimberly to come over to our house in two weeks for another sleepover. I laugh inside as we're discussing this, thinking how much I've changed over the past three years. Planning sleepovers for preteen girls wouldn't have been on my list of exciting life events prior to the plane crash.

We all say our goodbyes, and Macy and I wave at them as they drive away. I put my arm around her, and we walk side by side across the front yard.

"What did you do while I was gone, Lauren?" she asks.

"I just enjoyed some quiet time and watched a few movies," I reply. She still doesn't call me *Mom*, and that's okay. I understand. I'm confident that someday she will. At least she's dropped the *Miss* and just calls me by my first name now.

"I missed you," she says.

"I missed you too." We walk over to the edge of the knoll and stare down at the old barn below.

I turn to look at her glowing face. I see myself in her. "I love you, Macy. I'm glad you're home."

"I love you too, Lauren."

I pull her close and kiss her again on the forehead. "I'm glad we're both home."

When I started this incredible journey that summer night in Georgia three years ago, I didn't want the responsibility of a family at all. All I cared about was myself. But now, I can't imagine my life without Macy in it. She's become as much a part of it as breathing. She's made me what I want to be. What I'm *meant* to be.

A mother.

AUTHOR'S NOTE

I normally use this portion of the book to explain how I got the idea for the story and how it developed over the course of the writing process. But for this particular novel, I really don't know what to say, other than it is the story that came to me and the one I felt I was supposed to write at this time.

It's different from most of the books and short stories I've written. There's no murder, no bad guy, no mystery to solve, but I still enjoyed writing it very much.

I dedicated this book to my two grandmothers, Faye and Nina. They both taught me a lot about life and how to be a better man, and I am forever grateful to them for that.

Going through life is hard. Bad things happen to all of us, and at times, we all feel as if we've simply reached the end of our rope. We're exhausted, frightened, and worn out, just like Lauren was when she found herself lost in the mountains. So if you're going through a difficult time right now, my advice is to follow her example and just keep going—because you never know what's around the next bend on the road of life.

But, above all, I hope Lauren and Macy's story allowed you to escape your own troubles and worries, if only for a little while.

Writing a novel is a lot of hard work, and I have to first thank my wife, Janice, and daughter, Grace, for giving me the extra time to follow my dream. I love you both very much.

I want to say a special thank you to my two editors, Sharon Jeffers and Melissa Gray. Their input and corrections have proven invaluable.

Thank you to my parents, Mike and Jeannie, who have helped me spread the word about my writing and encouraged me to keep at it.

Thanks to Travis at probookcovers.com for the awesome covers he creates for me. To my book designer, Rob Siders at 52 Novels, thanks for all your help and the great work you do!

I also want to tell everyone who has offered me words of encouragement, whether written or spoken, just how much I truly appreciate it. You all know who you are, and I thank each of you so much.

Finally, thanks to you, the reader, for taking the time to read my work. I hope you enjoyed it.

J. Michael Stewart

ABOUT THE AUTHOR

J. Michael Stewart is the author of four novels. An avid fisherman, he spends his free time on a lake or river whenever possible. He lives in Northern Arkansas near the White River and Bull Shoals Lake with his wife and daughter.

To contact him, or for more information about J. Michael Stewart, please visit www.authorjmichaelstewart.com.

ALSO BY J. MICHAEL STEWART

SMOKE ON THE MOUNTAIN:
A Story of Survival

(Ranger Jackson Hart Book 1)

Cody McAlister, a 32-year-old Atlanta attorney, had everything: his dream job, a healthy bank account, and a beautiful wife. But two years after a bitter divorce and a bout of heavy drinking, Cody is still struggling to put the pieces of his once-idyllic life back together. In an effort to regain his sanity, he embarks on a five-day backcountry fly fishing trip to revitalize and reassess his life. When the unthinkable happens, Cody finds himself in a fight for his life. It's a battle that no courtroom drama can match—a test that will challenge his own basic beliefs about success, happiness, and what it means to truly live. With the help of a widowed fly shop owner and U.S. Park Ranger Jackson Hart, Cody must dig deep within himself to survive.

FIRE ON THE WATER

(Ranger Jackson Hart Book 2)

Sometimes to live for the future, you have to defeat the past . . .

For ten years, Tiffany Colson has struggled to reclaim her life, but it finally seems to be on track for a bright future. She has moved to a small cabin tucked deep in the heart of the Great Smoky Mountains. She's surrounded by wilderness and solitude, and her job at a small resort as an outdoor guide has been the best therapy she could have asked for.

And she's in love with the man who may just be the one—U.S. Park Ranger Jackson Hart.

But there is a part of Tiffany's past that still haunts her. It's a story only a handful of people know. A story she keeps hidden away deep inside her soul.

Ten years ago, Tiffany Colson killed a man.

At least . . . she thought she did.

Now, all her hopes for the future are jeopardized by the ghost of a man she thought was dead and buried. As the tenth anniversary of his death approaches, frightening things are happening. Things that threaten Tiffany's own sanity.

Soon, she will find that ghosts from her past are not just fleeting shadows moving through the halls of her mind.

They're real . . .

WHITE RIVER:
A Novel

Sometimes the smallest of towns hold the biggest secrets . . .

The clear, cold waters of the White River carve a twisting path through the heart of the Ozark Mountains, passing farms and limestone bluff walls, country roads and large tracts of dense forest on its journey. But for everything this life-giving body brings to the area, its secrets are even more powerful.

During the autumn of 1990, the residents of Fairhope, Arkansas, were more focused on the undefeated high school football team than on deer hunting or trout fishing or any of the other bucolic pastimes that make up daily life in the small Ozark town. But on the night the Fairhope Tigers secured their spot in the state championship playoffs, sixteen-year-old outcast Emma Drake disappeared after telling her mother she was going to the local library for her usual study session. There were rumors that she had left town to escape her poverty-stricken home life or the near constant bullying she received at the hands of the school's most popular girls. She almost became a forgotten name, one of the countless runaways who are lost forever.

But two days later, her nude body was found along the banks of the White River, stripping the community of its innocence and shattering its sense of security.

The Tigers went on to win the state football championship, Christmas came and went, and Emma Drake's murder gradually faded from the minds of Fairhope's citizens—the local authorities ruling her death the act of a passing vagrant who was never identified.

Twenty-five years later, Claire Matthews is struggling to pull her life back together. She was once a shining star in the newsroom of the *Arkansas Telegraph*, climbing her way to the position she was born for: Chief Political Reporter. But lately, her entire life seems to be on a downward trajectory. After a bitter breakup with the man she had hoped to spend her future with, she is surprised when her editor demotes her, forcing her to work on a series of articles about cold cases, rather than covering the political scene she so loves. But when she comes across the story of Emma Drake in the *Telegraph's* archives, Claire sees a chance to salvage her floundering career—perhaps, her only chance.

She travels to Fairhope and begins to dig into the secrets of what happened to Emma Drake that cold November night, but soon after her arrival it's clear someone is desperate to keep the truth hidden. Another murder rocks the tiny community, and Claire must race to uncover the killer's identity before she becomes the next victim.

And when the truth is finally revealed, it will shake the very foundations of this sleepy Ozark town.

SHORT STORIES AND NOVELLAS

A WINNING TICKET

Twin brothers Benjamin and Harrison Zimmerman are struggling just to keep their heads above water. Low crop prices and a recent drought have driven them to the brink of bankruptcy. The family farm is on the verge of foreclosure, and the mounting debt seems overwhelming. In the midst of a Nebraska blizzard, their luck suddenly changes when they hit it big by winning the lottery. In an instant they become multimillionaires. Now richer than they ever dreamed possible, all their problems seem to be solved. But before the night is over, the brothers' true feelings about the farm and each other will be revealed and their relationship changed forever.

DOSE OF VENGEANCE

Everyone has secrets . . .

When the rich and powerful in Big Creek, Montana, are in danger of having their most private and embarrassing secrets exposed, they call Sean Foster. He gets paid to make other people's problems go away. And he's good at it—very good.

But when a simple morning jog goes horribly wrong, Sean is the one who needs a fixer. In the struggle to survive and return to his wife, he forgets the most important lesson he has learned in his business.

Everyone has secrets.

And sometimes, they will kill to keep them hidden . . .